BOOTY-FUL DREAMERS

When *Penthouse* readers aren't having the world's most amazing sex, they're thinking about it—and how their imaginations fly! In these erotic pages, you'll drop in on their decadent daydreams and most daring deeds. Join in the fun as waitresses service rockers, pirates dirty dance with ballerinas, screen sirens get wet with sailors, and farmers' daughters ride bikers very, very hard. These hot, lusty fantasies are the ultimate wet dreams...

OTHER BOOKS IN THE SERIES

LETTERS TO
PENTHOUSE
XXXXVI

Dirty Dares &
Red-Hot Hookups

THE EDITORS OF
PENTHOUSE MAGAZINE

GRAND CENTRAL
PUBLISHING

NEW YORK   BOSTON

Grand Central Publishing
Hachette Book Group
237 Park Avenue
New York, NY 10017
www.HachetteBookGroup.com

Grand Central Publishing is a division of Hachette Book Group, Inc. The Grand Central Publishing name and logo is a trademark of Hachette Book Group, Inc.

The Hachette Speakers Bureau provides a wide range of authors for speaking events. To find out more, go to www.hachettespeakersbureau .com or call (866) 376-6591.

The publisher is not responsible for websites (or their content) that are not owned by the publisher.

Printed in the United States of America

First Edition: June 2013

10 9 8 7 6 5 4 3 2 1

Introduction

Imagine a world with no limits, one in which your wildest fantasies can—and do—come true. That's exactly what the readers of *Penthouse* have done in this collection of pulse-quickening letters.

From sensual daydreams about hot coworkers to lusty fantasies of swashbuckling lotharios to couples' racy role-playing, *Penthouse* readers prove that there is no end to their erotic imagination. When they put pen to paper, they hold nothing back as they replay their favorite sex fantasies for you in breathtaking detail. Some of these tales—like the kinky three-way with a favorite neighbor—set the stage for their later real-life dalliances, while others push the limits of reality with amorous aliens and comic book heroines and create fantastic, lust-laden scenarios.

High-class hookers, booty-hunting buccaneers, saucy secretaries—it doesn't matter who stars in the show, because it's sure to be a sexy good time.

Barbara Pizio
Executive Editor
Penthouse Variations

LETTERS TO
PENTHOUSE
XXXXVI

Hollywood Magic—Femme Fatale Seduced by Tough Private Eye

I am a big movie fan, especially when it comes to those classic Hollywood oldies but goodies. Curled up in front of the TV with a big bowl of popcorn is probably my favorite way to spend an evening. In fact, it has always been my fantasy to be the leading lady in one of those grainy black-and-white film noirs, seduced by the gruff, hard-boiled detective. That's why I jumped at the chance when my boyfriend was sent on a business trip to Los Angeles and invited me to come along.

While Nick spent his days pent up in a stuffy office attending boring business meetings, I used the time to roam the landmarks of Hollywood. The first place I hit was Mann's Chinese Theatre, where I tried to fit my average-size feet into Elizabeth Taylor's tiny foot-prints. After that I had a quick lunch at Roscoe's; then it was off to the movie studios, where I planned to take a tour of the back lots before meeting Nick at Spago for a romantic dinner.

As the tram rode through sets designed to look like the streets of London, Texas, and ancient Rome, I imagined what it would be like to star in a classic Hollywood film. When we reached scenery depicting the seedy streets of New York City, my imagination kicked into full gear. I pictured myself as a femme fatale not unlike Joan Crawford or Barbara Stanwyck, my long brown hair set in rag curls and lips painted so dark that even filmed in black-and-white, you can tell that I am wearing bloodred lipstick. I am walking along a dimly lit street, my high heels clicking on the cement, stopping to light a cigarette. Then, from out of nowhere, an arm in a tan trench coat appears with a lit match, ready to do the honors.

My thinly penciled eyebrows arch slightly as I look at him, taking in his large, masculine form and the mysterious eyes partially shaded by the brim of his fedora. "I've been looking for you, doll," the Robert Mitchum look-alike grunts as he firmly grasps me by the elbow and guides me to a waiting taxi.

I follow without saying a word, not frightened so much as curious about this attractive stranger who appears to know me. He gives an address to the cabbie, and we're off, the gray, bleak buildings flying by as we race along the city streets. When we reach our destination—a brownstone that is functioning as a rooming house—he leads me up three flights of stairs to a room that is sparsely furnished with a single bed, a chair, and a solitary lightbulb hanging from the ceiling. I sit on the edge of the bed, still unsure of what is happening, as my captor pulls the chair over and sits facing me. He runs his hand up my silk-covered leg, and I draw away slightly, reaching for my purse.

He grabs it before I do, pulling out the small pearl-handled gun I always carry with me. "That's not going to help you this time," he says, emptying it of its bullets and tossing it on the desk. "I know all about you, the way you use men in all your little devious schemes, then thrown them out like yesterday's newspaper. Well, this time it isn't going to be so easy." He gets up and throws his coat on the bed, then grabs my hands.

He pulls me toward him in a tight embrace, his hardness pressing against my thigh as our lips meet for the first time. Like everything he does, his kiss is hard and rough, just the way I like it. As the stubble from his five-o'clock shadow scrapes along my jaw, I quickly give in, submitting to his embrace. He reaches up and undoes the pearl buttons of my blouse, exposing my large breasts to his coarse hands. I am dressed only in my tight, straight skirt, and my exposed nipples harden in the cool air. I gasp slightly as he makes his way to those sensitive spots, but he is surprisingly tender, his gruff actions belying his delicate touch.

I, too, have a secret. I look him squarely in the eyes, the tough expression on my face not betraying the moistness I feel dampening my panties. Trying not to let him know that I am melting under his fingertips, I attempt to take control of the situation, sliding his suspenders over his muscular shoulders and reaching down for the button fastening his pants. He doesn't stop me, and soon his trousers are around his ankles, his impressive cock protruding from his undershorts.

His hands slide from my breasts to my shoulders, and he guides me downward to my knees. Aroused as much by his massive member as his kisses, I crouch eagerly at his feet and take him into my mouth. At first

I wrap my lips around only the tip of his cock, teasing him, letting him know that he can't conquer me completely. I grasp his balls in my hand, squeezing them and raking them slightly with my crimson talons. He starts to moan as I slowly swallow his long shaft, feeling the veins that protrude through the skin as they run along my tongue. I suck hungrily, still fondling his balls as I squeeze his ass with my other hand and he starts to writhe. Moving his hips slightly, he begins fucking my mouth, and the tingling between my legs starts to tell me that it is my other lips I want wrapped around his thrusting cock.

Seconds from his imminent orgasm, I pull away from him. Standing up, I draw him toward me for a kiss, and as our tongues intertwine he steers me onto the bed, breaking our embrace momentarily to rid himself of the rest of his clothes. When he is completely naked, he pushes up my skirt and yanks down my panties, my wet pussy glistening faintly in the light streaming through the venetian blinds.

I arch my hips, longing to feel his thick cock filling my tight passage, but he teases me instead, running his fingers over my damp mound and playing them over my thighs. Losing patience as he kneels before me, I begin to touch myself, eager for that sweet release. He grabs hold of my wrist and pulls that hand away as he reaches for the other, pinning them both over my head with his much larger, stronger hands. When he is sure that I will no longer resist, he lets go and runs his hands down my body, stopping at my hips to press them firmly to the bed.

Pinned in this position, I draw my legs up and spread them wide, knowing I won't have to wait much longer. He leans over and, at the first touch of his tongue on my cunt, I begin to shiver, trying desperately to hold back the orgasm that is threatening to overtake my body. Sensing this, he slows down his actions, lapping at my pussy with the flat of his tongue with long, slow strokes that are almost painful to endure but pleasurable just the same. My breath is coming quickly now, my body beginning to buck under his powerful grip. I am desperate to climax, practically willing to beg him to make me come, when he drives his fingers into my wet hole. Instantly I cry out, overcome by waves of pleasure, and it is only his grasp that keeps me solidly on the bed.

Struggling to catch my breath, I slowly regain control of my senses. Running one finger lazily around my nipple, he lies on his side next to me, propping his head up with his free hand. I can feel his hard cock prodding me as he shifts his body into a more comfortable position. It is as though he is reminding me of his presence, and I am quick to take the hint.

I reach down to grasp his cock, running my fist from its swollen head all the way down to the root nestled in its nest of wiry black hair. Slowly, I begin to pump his sturdy shaft, feeling his soft skin move up and down as a result of my ministrations. I reach down between my legs, dipping my fingers into my damp pussy for some moisture to use as a lubricant. As I move my fist over his now-slick cock, he really begins to grind, fucking my hand as though it were my tight cunt. Before he can come, I yank slightly on his thrusting member, urging him to move between my open legs.

He complies immediately, kneeling between my thighs as he lifts my legs to rest on his broad shoulders. With amazing control, he prods my clit with the tip of his cock, causing me to twist beneath him. As I shudder and shake, he inserts only the bulb-shaped head of his cock inside me. I thrust up my hips to meet him as he slowly slides his entire length into my hungry pussy, drawing out the pleasure as I am filled with each delightful inch. Soon he is completely inside me, my pussy snug around his large cock as he slowly pulls back out until once again only the head is inside my hole. We continue like this for a few moments, enjoying each frustratingly slow stroke, trying to see how long we can make this moment last.

It doesn't last much longer, as he increases his tempo and speed and is soon thrusting in and out with a fervor that surprises me. Our bodies meet again and again as he drives his cock into me, his balls slapping against my ass. My fingers play at my nipples, pinching and fondling them as my pussy clenches around his pounding organ. I scream as I am once again overcome by an orgasm, the intensity of my reaction sending him over the edge and triggering his climax. Exploding inside me, he fills me with jets of hot come that I feel trickling down my thighs when he pulls out of me at last.

We lay panting in each other's arms, sharing soft kisses that seem unusual between two strangers, my eyes closed so I can imagine that I am anyplace other than this seedy hotel room. It occurs to me that I don't know his name or how he knows me, and I am about to ask when I am silenced by his firm grip on my upper arm. I open my eyes to meet his, and I am surprised by the energetic smile of a friendly tour guide.

"Excuse me, ma'am," he is saying as I look about, and I realize I am in a tram at a Hollywood movie studio. "The tour's over. You must be really jet-lagged to have fallen asleep on the tram! You missed a really great ride."

I smile to myself, knowing that I just had the ride of my life.

—*Ms. L.T., Henniker, New Hampshire*　O┼■

Rush-Hour Delays Prove Delightful for Horny Commuter

My alarm clock hadn't gone off when it was supposed to, so I was running late for work. I rushed to the subway, and after pushing through the turnstile, I realized that my train was at the station. I ran onto it as the doors were closing, but then it just stood there.

As the conductor announced that the train was being held in the station and would be leaving momentarily, I placed my briefcase on the floor. I looked down and noticed a pair of red high heels, and then my eyes slowly traced a pair of shapely legs upward until they met the woman's gaze. She was beautiful, with big blue eyes, full lips, and a long mane of dark brown hair. She smiled at me before turning away, and I checked out her body as I inhaled her perfume. She wore a sexy short red dress that barely covered her ass and showed quite a bit of cleavage.

The train continued to stand there, and the conductor's voice came over the loudspeaker once again, announcing that it would be another ten minutes or so. I began to get worried that I would be late for work, so to calm myself, I closed my eyes and let my mind begin to wander. I imagined that the train was moving, rocking from side to side, my body swaying with its rhythm. It was so crowded that I was pressed up against the woman in the red dress, my cock bumping against her sexy ass. I knew she could feel my hard-on, but she didn't say anything, so I don't think she minded. In fact, I think she liked it, because instead of moving away, she leaned in to me, rubbing her firm buttocks against my crotch. I was soon getting so horny that each time the train shook us, I pressed harder against her ass. My cock swelled even more and pulsated with the beat of my heart. I wanted to fuck her right then and there, on the crowded subway train.

Suddenly, the lights went out in our car, and a second later I felt fingers on my hard cock. When the lights came back on, the hand disappeared. I looked at the woman, but she kept her eyes on an ad, though I thought I saw a small smile playing on her lips. Then the light went out again, and this time I was ready. When the hand began stroking my cock, I took hold of it so that she couldn't pull it away again. The lights came back on and I smiled at her, and she smiled back as she caressed me with her fingertips.

I could tell that she was as turned-on as I was, so I squeezed her hand around my shaft, encouraging her to continue rubbing it. Instead, she pulled down my zipper and took my cock out. Moaning, she turned slightly and whispered in my ear, "I dare you to fuck me right here."

Reaching down with her other hand, she pulled her dress higher in invitation. Excited by the prospect of fucking a beautiful stranger on a crowded subway train, I pulled her panties down just enough to rub my finger over her clitoris and insert my cock in her pussy. I rubbed the head between her labia, and her cunt seemed to suck me right in. As she lifted her leg a bit, I looked around to see if anyone had noticed what was going on between us. Everyone seemed wrapped up in their newspapers or conversations, so I thrust my dick deep inside her pussy and began pumping it in and out. The woman moaned and groaned, and then started breathing more heavily.

The train, on the express line, sped through each station, rumbling down the tracks as I moved my hips to slide my dick in and out of her pussy. I fucked her hard, smacking my body against her ass. We tried not to attract any attention from the other passengers, but deep inside I knew that someone had to be watching us. The thrill of knowing that we might get caught excited me even more, and I fucked her harder, my thrusts into her cunt in perfect time with the rocking motion of the train.

The woman in the red dress started moaning even louder and moving uncontrollably against me. The aroma of sex was in the air of the crowded car as we fucked, and I sensed that someone was looking at us from a few feet away. I didn't care, though, and kept going, figuring that someone would have to notice a couple fucking on the train, especially during rush hour. Then the woman turned her head and we started to kiss, our tongues tangling together as I kept pumping my cock into her hot, tight pussy. She lifted her leg a little higher and my cock slid deeper into her. We began fucking faster and faster, racing to reach our orgasms before the train pulled into its first stop.

Now we didn't care who saw us—we were two wild and crazy horny people fucking each other on the express train. That was when I turned the woman around so that her back was against the door that led to the next car. I reached behind her to open it, and we made our way to the platform that connected the two train cars. I never removed my cock from her cunt as we moved, and then I closed the door behind us. More people were looking at us now, but we ignored them and continued fucking our asses off. The thrill of it all excited me beyond belief, and I could tell that she felt the same way.

I pulled out of her and turned her around to fuck her doggie-style, my cock swelling in her cunt as I held her by the hips, my thumbs pressed into her fleshy ass cheeks. She trembled as I jammed into her, and I knew she was enjoying it as much as I was because she began to whimper excitedly. I continued shoving my cock in and out of her pussy, and she reached between her legs to squeeze my balls in her hand. Meanwhile, her cunt sucked my cock in deeper and deeper with each and every one of my thrusts.

The woman quivered slightly, and then her body started shivering uncontrollably as each stroke of my cock sent her arousal higher and higher. Her pussy dripped with pleasure, and I felt her muscles hugging my shaft. She started yelling, "I'm coming! Fuck me—fuck me hard!" We knew that no one could hear us over the thundering noise of the train now that we were outside. I pounded into her even harder, and she yelled again as I groaned loudly, both of us reaching climax at the same time as the train entered the station. I filled her with my come, and then I pulled my cock from her clasping cunt and put it back in my pants. She pulled up her panties and fixed her hair, then turned to give me a long, hard kiss. We said good-bye and then exited through different doors into different cars of the train. I knew that I would probably never see her again.

Suddenly, I realized that I was still on the train, which was still waiting in the station, motionless. The woman in the red dress had moved when someone had offered her a seat, and I was now standing behind a handsome guy wearing a gray flannel business suit. *Damn,* I thought to myself as I realized that not only had I imagined the whole experience, but it looked like I was going to be late for work, after all. Some mornings it just doesn't pay to get out of bed!

—*Mr. G.D., Via Email*

G.I. Stationed in Germany Says "Yes, Ma'am!" to Sexy Sergeant

I am a soldier stationed in Germany, where I am assigned to a tank unit. My battalion spends a great deal of time in a training area, where we practice our skills at tank gunnery. It's hard work, and I usually go to bed exhausted and don't get to spend a lot of time—if any—with members of the opposite sex. Luckily, I've got my fantasies to keep me going.

In this one fantasy, it was a hot day in mid-August. We had been on the range all day doing battle runs, firing until almost nine o'clock at night. I was the last to run the range, and after that, it would be time to head back to dinner and my bed. Of course, that's when I broke an oil cooler line to my engine.

Since we were only one vehicle down, our commander decided to send the rest of the company back to the motor pool. Our maintenance section didn't have the replacement part on hand, so Larry—a new-recruit mechanic in battalion maintenance—and I stayed with the tank while the rest of our crew left with the company to return to the motor pool. As soon as they got there, they would send back the part that we needed.

Larry and I sat on the front slope of the tank and watched the company disappear down the trail. As the last tank passed out of sight, we leaned back to enjoy the warm evening. It wasn't long before we drifted off to sleep.

When I awoke, it was about midnight, and the lights

of a Jeep could be seen coming up the trail in the distance. It slowed down as it reached the entrance to the range, and I realized that it was someone returning with the repair part that we needed. I also realized then that Larry and I hadn't started to remove the old line yet. I knew that whoever was in the Jeep would be pretty pissed off, so I prepared myself for one hell of an ass-chewing.

What I wasn't prepared for was the staff sergeant who got out of the Jeep. She stood about five-feet-six-inches tall and had blue eyes and blonde hair tucked up under her cap. I later discovered that her hair flowed all the way down to the middle of her back. Larry and I instantly sprang to attention—and so did my cock.

It was an unusually hot day for Germany, and the night had come without relief. I think that the heat and the fact that she'd had to drive out to the range at such a late hour really set the sergeant off. She began yelling at us for not removing the old line before she got there. I should have felt embarrassed or ashamed, but she was so gorgeous that it really aroused me to have this sexy staff sergeant yell at me like that.

Larry proceeded to immediately get to work removing the old line, but I couldn't move. I was frozen by the fact that I had a tremendous hard-on. Then I realized that the sergeant had also noticed the bulge in the front of my fatigues. She called me to attention and told me that I had a problem with my gig line and that I should correct it immediately. For all you civilians out there, a gig line is the line from the bottom of your shirt down to the fly of your pants, and it always needs to be straight, especially in the company of a ranking officer. I didn't know what to do next, but I knew I had to do something.

I tried to think somber thoughts, but I was still unable to disguise my bulge after several seconds of attempting. She said, "If you can't wear the uniform properly, then maybe I need to show you how." I looked down at my gig line again and then back at her. There was a kind of sparkle in her eyes and an appealing smile across her face that raised the erection in my fatigues another ten degrees. I replied, "Yes, ma'am!" and she told me to call her Maureen.

Maureen ran her tongue across her lips and motioned for me to follow her to a grassy meadow a short distance from the tank. We had been in the field now for twenty-eight days, and the thought of pussy was running wild in my mind. When we reached the meadow she stopped and removed her cap, allowing her lovely blonde hair to fall free across her back. At that instant, I knew my uniform class had been completely forgotten.

I almost came in my fatigues as she knelt in front of me and released my hard cock from its confinement. Her touch was soft, but her lips attacked my shaft in a manner that suggested she wouldn't be retreating anytime soon. My balls were aching, and the sensation of her mouth as it engulfed my swollen member instantly had me on the verge of an orgasm.

Maureen bobbed her head over the length of my dick, squeezing her lips tight around my shaft. Sometimes I felt her teeth scrape along my skin, and the entire time I felt her soft, plush tongue moving over my erection. After so many months with only the company of my hand, this felt amazing. I couldn't hold back any longer, and my cock exploded, shooting out round after round of hot semen into her waiting throat. Maureen tried to swallow it all, but I guess it came too fast for her. Some of my come oozed out of the corners of her mouth, dripping my liquid onto her fatigues.

I pulled Maureen to her feet and began to remove her uniform. I released her beautiful breasts from her bra, which strained to contain them. Her tits were soft but firm, and her nipples stood erect. I took her in my arms and laid her down in the soft grass. I began to caress one breast, then the other. We kissed each other passionately, and then I began kissing my way down the rest of her body. I stopped at her breasts and sucked each nipple, then carried on over her stomach. Finally, I came to rest at her down-covered pussy.

The sweat of my body and the aroma of her sex brought my cock back to life. Maureen begged me to bury my rigid dick in her hungry cunt. I was ready and willing to do just that, but first I wanted to taste her pussy. I began lapping at it, licking and sucking up all her sweet juices. Maureen moaned and once again began begging for my cock. "Fuck me! Oh, fuck me! Oh God, yes!" she cried as her body trembled. My cock throbbed in response. Now it was time to fuck her.

I mounted Maureen and quickly impaled her with my swollen member. I started with long, slow strokes in and out of her tight pussy, and the slow-motion fuck drove her to the brink of insanity. I quickened my pace and began hammering into her slippery hole. She threw her legs up in the air and kept screaming out for more. She was so loud that I was afraid the new recruit would hear her, but luckily he was too far away.

Maureen's hands clawed at my back as I pistoned into her cunt. My balls were slapping against her firm ass, and then I felt them tighten. Her pussy began to pulsate around my cock as she raced closer and closer to orgasm. I was almost ready to come, but I needed something else to push me over the edge. I lowered my head and took one of her nipples between my teeth and bit it hard. She cried out in pleasure, and her cunt clamped around me as together we experienced the orgasm of a lifetime.

We lay in each other's arms for a moment, until we both realized at once that we had to get back to the tank. I looked at my watch and it was two a.m. We quickly got dressed, and when I was finished, I looked at Maureen and said, "Is my gig line straight?" She just smiled, and we hurried off to the tank.

Larry had finally finished working on the oil line as we rounded the end of the tank. Seeing Maureen, he immediately sprang to attention. Maureen barked at him to crank up the tank, and he ran to the driver's compartment. He had been working all that time and never even realized that I'd gotten more than an ass-chewing from the beautiful sergeant.

As Maureen turned to go to her Jeep, she smiled

broadly and said, "I guess it's true—tankers do have bigger guns!"

—*Name and address withheld*   O⊢▪

Girl in Yoga Class Meditates on Blissful Encounter with Hot New Instructor

As a hardworking, fun-loving girl in my late twenties, I like to keep myself in optimum shape. This means a healthy diet, plenty of exercise, and lots of sex with Chris—my steady boyfriend—and Janet—my steady girlfriend. Yes, I'm bi, enjoying the best of both worlds. I recently added yoga classes to my regimen, since yoga's not only a great way to keep the body strong and limber, but the mind as well. I particularly enjoy the meditation portion of the class because there I can release all my tension, clear my head, and center my soul.

I've been at it for a few weeks now, and the classes have been great, but the class I had yesterday was so erotically charged I had to share with you the wild fantasy that it inspired.

I arrived to discover that our regular instructor was on vacation and that a woman named Dani would be filling in for two weeks. Drop-dead gorgeous, she was sitting on the floor with her feet together, bent completely over at the waist with her forehead resting on the floor. When she lifted her head, I saw mesmerizing gray eyes, full lips, and coffee-brown hair framing a heart-shaped face. Immediately my pussy ached with desire.

I spread my mat close to hers so I could have a good view of her technique. The class began with some New Age music and a chant to the universe. She told us to start thinking about prana, the term for breath, and see if we could tune out everything else. I wondered how I was going to manage to pay attention to my breathing when her slender curves were taking my breath away!

Still, I tried to focus on my body and keep my mind off hers—her long legs and firm, perky breasts wrapped tightly in black Lycra, her tan and taut stomach slightly exposed. As we moved from the downward-facing dog pose to the plank pose, I tried to keep my eyes down and my focus inside. But when she demonstrated the cat's pose, with her back arched so that her round ass was upturned right in front of me—so close that I could see the outline of her puffy pussy lips through the stretched material—my knees almost gave way and I struggled mightily to keep my balance.

I managed to keep myself together as we reached the meditation portion of class. I was flat on my back, desperately trying to relax and keep my eyes closed, when I felt the vibrations of Dani's footsteps as she walked around the room. When she knelt beside me and gently moved my neck to help my alignment, I trembled with anticipation upon smelling her sweet aroma of incense. I ached for her to touch me more, lower, all over.

Dani stood and told us in a soothing voice to picture a softly flowing river. Covertly opening my eyes, I was instead watching her stretch her limbs, and it sent me spiraling into a very special meditation of my own.

My mind wandered to a place where I was lying on my back and she was pressing her hands on my collarbone to help me release more tension. Her fingers rubbed circles on my upper chest, gradually increasing in diameter until her fingertips grazed the tops of my breasts peeking out from my sports bra. I craned my neck to give her fuller access to my body, and her warm metered breath brushed against my cheeks.

"Hmmm," Dani hummed as her paced exhalations covered my face, growing in fullness, as were my hardening nipples. She softly caressed my pointed tips under my bra as her circles widened, covering my breasts, stomach, and hips. She kissed me softly on the neck and temples. Every drop of tension poured out of me, but I was far from relaxed. I was too hot for her, too eager to feel her hands rubbing my swelling mound as my clitoris throbbed, beckoning her touch.

Dani eased herself over me so that she was on all fours, and I opened my eyes to the sight of her pelvis hovering right above my face. I stripped off her leggings and revealed her lovely pussy, with its slim patch of dark hair and dewy wet lips. She pulled off my shorts and panties at the same time, and my hot cunt twitched at the sudden exposure. She tossed her silky mane across my labia, tickling me and teasing me, making my juices flow wildly. She blew a kiss gently over my pussy, still not touching me. I almost hurt with need for direct contact. She giggled, knowing what she was putting me through, so I grabbed her firm ass cheeks and thrust my tongue into her pussy, sucking in her lips and drinking her dripping liquid.

I pushed up her top and reached for her breasts, squeezing them and rubbing her nipples between my fingers while I kept licking her cunt. I found her hard nubbin of flesh and lapped at it heartily, then went all up and down her slit. Her hips bucked as her humming got louder, and she threw her head fast into my crotch and sucked on my syrupy cunt.

I let out a scream as she gave me the pressure I needed, and I kept eating her for all I was worth, pressing the tip of my nose against her clit, smelling her musky scent, taking all of her in. I thrust two fingers inside her and fucked her hard and fast with them while still making love to her clit.

Dani was on the verge of orgasm as her pussy got wetter and hotter, and I held my tongue straight out, pointed and rigid, so that she could rub herself against it. She slid her hips back and forth, moaning and grinding against my face. I pulled her down to my mouth and licked all the way back to her puckered rosebud, still pushing two fingers deep inside her cunt. Then I pulled out my fingers, coated thick with her juice, and pushed them into her ass. She cried out as I pressed my thumb on her quivering clit. She shook all over, spasming above me, then collapsed on my face, arms outstretched, sitting back on her heels, resting there to catch her breath.

When she could, she said, "Yoga is all about balance." And with that she turned around to face me and came up to kiss me long and passionately, her tongue massaging mine. I could taste the salty drops of sweat that had beaded up above her lip.

Dani kissed her way down my chin, neck, chest, and belly, until she reached my thighs. She spread them farther apart and rubbed her face in my muff, gently blowing on my sex, sending tingles through my body. I shivered with need for her, and she pressed her lips to my labia, grasping them in her teeth, flicking her tongue against my clitoris. I was ready to explode, and when her fingers found their way inside me, my cunt clamped down against them and I grabbed my breasts, squeezing them hard.

I cried out as my orgasm engulfed me, and Dani kept fucking me with her fingers, bringing on one explosion of pleasure after another. She took my clit wholly in her mouth, rolling her tongue over it, back and forth, nearly causing me to black out. My final orgasm caused my legs to shake out of control, and my juices flooded her mouth as I screamed out my pleasure. We held each other close as we brought our focus back to our breathing.

Soon after I heard her voice instructing us to bring our minds back to center and feel our bodies on the floor. I opened my eyes and realized that I'd gone deeper into meditation than ever before, and my body felt ravished from the experience.

We slowly sat up in the lotus position as Dani checked on everyone in the class, gently adjusting each of our necks. When she touched me, though, I could have sworn she knew what had just gone through my mind, and when she whispered in my ear that she taught private classes, I nearly came right there!

After class I told her to sign me up as soon as possible, and we made a date for the following evening. I went home and took a long hot bath, positioning my clitoris directly under the faucet. I came again and again from the flow of the water, letting my breathing take over and my mind totally relax, imagining that the pressure was from Dani's lips and hoping that the next day it would be.

—*Ms. C.H., San Jose, California*   ⊙━▪

It's Good vs. Evil as Beautiful Voluptua Battles Her Arch Foe, the Penetrator

Comic books are a major part of my life. The joy they bring me is priceless, pulling me into the pages of a fantasy world filled with action, adventure, and sexy women that I idolize. Think back to how hot Wonder Woman was in those little spandex shorts, or the sleek and dangerous Catwoman from Batman. When my boyfriend, John, and I have one of our heated bondage sessions, I sometimes pretend that I am one of these superhuman beings.

John is a night watchman at a warehouse that stores costumes. Recently he stumbled upon racks of tights and latex and spandex bodysuits that have been used to dress mortals like superheroes and heroines. He called to tell me about them. I was in my glory, listening to the descriptions, trying to remember what superhero each costume belonged to. When he told me about a pale blue Lycra bodysuit with a red belt, wristbands, boots, and the letter V across the chest, I was stumped. Which superhero wore that costume?

John teased me, saying it would complement my figure perfectly and that my name could be Voluptua. I laughed and joked back that he would be the evil villain, the Penetrator. When we got off the phone, however, I pictured myself in the outfit and fantasized about what it would feel like to be a superheroine in pursuit of a wicked villain.

The abandoned warehouse is his lair, and he sits in front of the security cameras dressed all in black, knowing that I will soon come looking for him, because he has uncovered my true identity and threatens to tell the world if I do not agree to his demands. But Voluptua makes no agreements, choosing to fight to keep her secret.

Through the haze outside his lair, I try to sneak through a second-story barred window, unaware that the motion detector has picked up movement. With my superhuman strength, I bend the bars and easily slide through and jump to the floor, landing on both feet without making a sound. I look around cautiously as I crouch down low, my hands ready for battle, aware that the latex red and blue mask surrounding my eyes is pointless to a man who knows who I really am.

Suddenly, I find myself in a bright spotlight that is switched on with a whirling sound. I am stunned like a deer caught in headlights. Before I can act, a net is dropped from above and entangles me in its rope. Clawing at it, I try to find a way out, but it is useless. I have been captured.

My heart races as the Penetrator grabs me from behind and takes me off to the basement. I struggle the whole way, feigning anger yet secretly curious and excited about what might be in store for me. He laughs deep and loud as he throws two long strips of rope over our heads. I look up and see them wrapping around a thick pipe. Still holding on to my hands, he takes the hanging pieces, tugs on them, then ties them to my wrists, leaving me bound and unable to move. I long to be touched—to be fucked right there. After all, every superhero has a weakness.

Staring into his dark eyes, I try to hypnotize him. I can get out of these ropes if he would only fall under my spell. But he is more powerful than I believed him to be and he shakes off my first attempt to control him. Leaning in close to me, he places his face in the crook of my neck. I can feel his stubble as he runs his soft lips up to my ear. "You like this, don't you?" he asks. "You'll never escape." I am about to kick him hard when he gently lays his hand on my hip and traces the shape of my waist all the way up to my breast.

He is wearing black leather gloves, and the material catches on my spandex. My nipples harden and become obvious in my tight suit; my chest heaves as the pipe above me drips water slowly onto my tits. Each time a drop of water hits a nipple, I flinch with pleasure. Knowing he likes seeing me so turned-on and bound, I use it to my advantage, pointing my chest straight out and growling with desire.

The Penetrator leans in, holding on to the ropes above my wrists, and kisses me hard on the mouth. I push into him, letting him know I'm not afraid of his touch. Suddenly I suck his bottom lip into my mouth and then bite down on it, showing him that even though I am tied up, I am not powerless. He groans when I release his lip and throw my head back, laughing as if possessed. His cock is hard against my stomach, and I know that I will soon have it in me.

With my legs still free, I pull myself up and wrap my limbs around him. He struggles for a moment but knows he cannot get out of my grip. I pull him even closer to me with my powerful thighs, and he kisses me again. His leather-covered hands wrap around my ass to help hold me up, and I grind my pussy against the bulge in his pants. Looking down at him, I tell him what I want him to do.

The Penetrator then drops to his knees. "That's a good boy," I say as he begins to lick my thighs at the edge of my bodysuit. His tongue is rough against my skin. Pulling the fabric to one side, he licks at my pussy like a hungry kitten. I drape my legs over his shoulders, my stomach muscles tightening as I hold myself up. Swirling his tongue around my clit and nibbling on my entire sex, he works hard trying to please me. I look down as my energy builds. I am getting stronger as he gets weaker.

I thrust my pussy down on his tongue as my orgasm begins to erupt. My blood pumps hard throughout my body, and my superhuman strength takes over when I come. My pussy quivers, and I pull my hands down hard, breaking free from my bonds and towering over the villain who's on his knees. Shocked by my escape, the Penetrator falls back onto the cement floor.

Keeping my pussy above him, I smear my juices all over his face. He smiles wickedly as I tell him that it is his turn to be bound. I pull him off the floor, holding his arms tightly behind his back, and walk him over to a table. I order him onto his back and then tie his arms and legs down securely with the leather straps attached to the table.

I pull my dagger from my ankle strap and slit his shirt right down the middle, exposing his strong chest. He gasps with excitement when I do the same to his black tights. His hard cock springs free. It is the biggest dick I have ever seen. I now know how he got his name. The veins in his shaft pulse, and his cockhead is so plump and hard that I wonder if I can fit it in my mouth.

I lick around the mushroom-shaped head, noting how soft the skin is. I love the feel of it so much that I rub the cockhead along my cheek and then take it between my lips. The Penetrator pulls at his bonds. I know he wants to fuck me hard, and my slow tactics are driving him crazy. My pink tongue licks up and down the shaft slowly, stopping at the tip as I look him in the eye. He thrusts his hips up, trying to force his cock down my throat. I growl, taking everything he offers easily, savoring the feast before me.

Feeling the need to be filled, I find a button on the

side of the table and lower him down. I climb on top of him, my rubber boots dangling slightly above the floor, and gently play with his balls as I pump his shaft. He drifts off into a delirious state of pleasure as I work my magic on him, explaining how the memory of my true identity shall be replaced by the feel of the orgasm about to overwhelm him. My captive moans deeply as I bend to kiss him, our tongues melting against each other.

Lifting myself over his cock, I rub it along my slit and then begin working his girth into my wet pussy. His large size stretches my inner walls to the max, and I have to rock back and forth gently to take him in slowly. When I finally have him balls-deep, I feel fuller than ever before. Sitting there for a few moments, I get used to his thickness, loving the way his cock feels deep inside me.

Riding him slowly, I twist his nipples between my gloved fingers. He turns his head into his extended arm and groans. His cries of pleasure echo off the bare walls of the warehouse. Sweat gathers in my cleavage, and my hair sticks to my forehead. I increase my pace, using one of my hands to manipulate my clit as I ride my dark enemy. I love the way my latex glove feels against my sex and the danger of making love to a man so mysterious.

His cock feels as if it is getting bigger inside me, and my thighs are slapping against his body. I know he, too, enjoys making love to a woman who can easily destroy him. Then I feel his cock explode within me. His orgasm is so powerful that I have to hold on tight to him. Riding his cock for a little longer, I am amazed that the Penetrator has not softened one bit. As I come I feel him watching me, as if looking for the weakness within.

He never finds it, of course, and I climb off my enemy and adjust my suit so that I'm once again presentable. Leaning over his body, I kiss him gently on the head. "I am sorry I have to leave you all tied up like this," I say to him, "but I am sure you will get out somehow, eventually."

I leave my archenemy there, tied to the table, his cock still sticking straight up, as hard as it was before he came. I do hope that the Penetrator and I will cross paths again soon. I look forward to the challenge.

—*Ms. L.A., Thousand Oaks, California*   O┼▮

City Girl Dreams of Life on a Ranch and the Horseplay that Goes Along with It

I'm sitting in my Boston apartment in front of the fire on a cold night, a glass of wine at my side and a pen in my hand. But my mind is far away from the city; it's in Texas, with a ranch hand named Jake.

I saw him as soon as I entered the stables. He was tall and broad, with sandy hair hanging a bit too long over his neck. His chest was bare, and his muscles strained each time he pitched a new fork of hay into the empty stall. I knew I probably shouldn't have been standing there in a pair of daisy dukes and a revealing tank top, ogling the foreman of the ranch, but I couldn't help myself. Jake was so damn sexy.

It was a few minutes before he sensed my presence, and when he turned, his dark eyes shot like lasers right through me. Despite the wicked summer heat, I shivered under his gaze. Jake gave me a slow, sexy smile, as if he knew exactly where my thoughts were headed, but he only greeted me by offering a lazy, "Ma'am." Oh, that deep, smooth voice was perfect with those eyes and that body.

I gave a smile that I hoped appeared worldly but that I suspected showed my nervousness. However, he didn't seem to notice as his gaze swept over my perky breasts and long bare legs. He leaned on his pitchfork and cocked an eyebrow. "This heat'll get to you, even wearing that," he drawled.

Yeah, the heat was getting to me, all right, and I shifted as I felt the flow of moisture between my legs. It seemed as if my pussy had been pulsing ever since I'd first seen Jake a few days before. All I'd been able to think about was his tongue wiggling around on my wet cunt, probing, licking, tasting, and teasing.

No, that wasn't entirely true. I'd also thought about taking his hard cock—which was surely as big and imposing as the rest of him—into my mouth and sucking him deep down my throat. Truth be told, I'd also thought about straddling him, riding him like he was one of those wild horses he'd been hired to break.

He started walking toward me, and I shivered again. This time, he saw my movement. "Don't tell me you're cold." I shrugged, and he stopped right in front of me. I could smell the scent of fresh hay clinging to his damp skin.

"I could warm you up," he suggested in that sexy drawl. That's what I'd wanted to hear for the past three days, and now I was actually going to fuck this sexy ranch hand. I moaned just watching Jake dip his head toward mine. "Baby, you ain't seen nothing yet," he assured me.

He brought his mouth down hard on mine, though his lips and tongue were surprisingly gentle. Without lifting his face away, he moved me to the back of the stables, into a shadowy corner and down on a pile of soft hay. Our tongues danced together, and my hands played over his strong chest and the corded muscles of his arms. He held my face in his big hands while he explored my mouth with his probing tongue. Then his fingers inched slowly down my neck to the bare skin just above my shirt. He played there for a few seconds before his hand moved lower, cupping my breast.

A moan escaped my lips as he drew circles around the hardened tip of my nipple, and I pressed my body against him in an effort to get closer. I felt the rumble of his chuckle in my mouth. I knew he was probably amused by my obvious need. Still, he mercifully tore his mouth away from mine, lifted my shirt over my head, and took my nipple into his mouth. He sucked once, twice, three times. Then he scraped the sensitized tip lightly with his teeth.

I wriggled against him, found the denim-covered bulge at the juncture of his thighs and gave it a good, hard rub. As my hand worked against his cock, I felt it stiffen, and he groaned deep in his throat. I got a heady feeling, knowing that I was able to give this handsome, sexy man so much pleasure.

Managing to get both my hands between our bodies, I worked at the fly of his jeans. After some maneuvering, I pushed his Levi's—along with his underwear—down his thighs, and his massive cock sprang free. I wrapped my hand around the thick shaft and ran the pad of my thumb over the bulbous head. Jake clenched his teeth as his eyes went dark with passion.

Tentatively, I moved away from his probing tongue and worked my way down his body so that I could take his prick into my mouth. It was so big—bigger than any I'd ever seen—but I managed to swallow down the entire thing.

Jake swore under his breath as my lips slid over his length. Taking that as a sign of encouragement, I began pumping my mouth slowly up and down the velvety shaft. I'd lick the crown when I reached the top and then I'd plunge back down, only to rise up and do it all over again. His cockhead hit the back of my throat each time, which seemed to please Jake because he threaded his fingers into my hair and the taut muscles of his ass were like steel in my hands. His breathing was coming in shallow pants, his entire body like one tight coil ready to spring at any moment. The intermittent grunts he let escape from his throat were the sweetest sounds I'd ever heard.

I sucked eagerly, moaning to myself. The smell of hay and musky male invaded my senses and encouraged me to speed up my movements. I wanted to take him completely into me, give him as much pleasure as possible.

I felt his body tense as he pushed my head down onto his shaft one last time. Then, with a tortured groan, he emptied into my mouth, shooting come all the way down my throat. I swallowed the huge load and then slid my lips slowly upward, licking up the excess come as I went.

"Where did you learn to do that, little girl?" he asked as I stretched out beside him. But he didn't wait for an answer before he was at my naked breasts again, sucking, licking, and biting. I didn't have the energy to do anything but moan and buck my hips against him.

Somehow, he rid me of my shorts and panties without me really noticing his actions. But I sure took note when he moved down and nudged open my legs. Then he was at my cunt, lapping in long, slow strokes up from my dripping hole to just below my pulsing clit. It was sweet, sweet torture. I tried to press my cunt more tightly against his face, but he held my hips firmly in his big hands. It was clear that he now had control, and I gave myself up to him easily enough.

When I'd had almost more than I could take of the long, slow licks, he touched my clit with the tip of his tongue. Immediately, I began to tremble and thrash from side to side against the soft hay. The movement of his tongue was small but steady and firm, and he applied just the right amount of exquisite pressure.

Desperate for something to grasp, I grabbed fistfuls of his hair and held his head against my cunt. I teetered on the cusp of an explosive orgasm for what seemed like an eternity, and though my eyes were open, I could not focus. My mouth was dry, and I could make only small, breathless sounds. Then time stopped, and the world went still for a moment before everything shattered and I went tumbling over the edge of ecstasy.

As I came, Jake kept me tight against his mouth, sucking up all of my juices and holding me until the wild contractions faded and I was weary but satisfied. But when he rose above me and I saw his passion-filled eyes and his mouth still wet with my juices, I realized that I wasn't satisfied at all. I wanted all of this man, and I wanted him now.

He seemed to be thinking along the same lines. At this point, there was no teasing, no slow build, no preparation. Jake entered me in one swift stroke, filling my body with his thick, meaty cock, nearly stretching my cunt beyond its limits. I'd never felt so complete, and I welcomed him to the hilt.

He stopped for a moment when he reached bottom, groaning as he looked into my eyes. Then he began moving inside me. He looked into my eyes the entire time, drawing out his entire length and then plunging back in again. I arched toward him, attempting to take him as deeply as possible into my cunt.

We were moving so fast, so frantically, that I had to wrap my legs tightly around his snapping hips to hold on. Jake's arms were clasped tightly around my waist, pulling me hard against him. My breathy moans and his grunts filled the dark space around us.

I could see it in his eyes when he was about to come, and my body responded immediately. I felt my orgasm building in time with his, and when he closed his eyes and threw back his head, I arched toward him. My cunt squeezed his hard cock as he exploded inside me. I felt the blast of his cream, and I cried out while he swore over and over again.

We remained joined together for a long time after that. I listened to the sounds of his breathing and the frantic thumping of his heart. Eventually, our bodies both returned to normal, and we kissed before we pulled on our clothes again. I knew that this had been the start of a beautiful affair.

Although Jake is just a fantasy, I've taken the first step to making it come true by planning a vacation to a real working ranch this summer. Needless to say, I'm hoping I meet a real-life Jake, and I'm confident that when I do, he'll be as amazing as the man I've been dreaming about.

—*Ms. M.D., Boston, Massachusetts*   O┼▓

Office Worker Invents Uplifting Experience on Crowded Elevator with Ravishing Blonde

It was an ordinary Tuesday at work. I got to my desk around nine, turned on the computer, checked my messages, and got a cup of coffee. I spent the morning returning calls, and after a couple hours realized it was time for a smoke. I went downstairs, enjoyed a cigarette, and then headed back inside.

It seemed that I wasn't the only person who needed a break. By the time I got to the elevator, there were about a dozen others waiting. When it arrived, I was the first to walk inside and immediately rested my weary body against the elevator's back wall. I closed my eyes as bodies crammed in. Suddenly, the scent of perfume invaded my senses. When I opened my eyes, I couldn't believe the vision before me.

She was exquisite. I couldn't see her face, but the silk summer dress she had on revealed a body to die for. Her proximity alone was enough to start my heart pumping, the firm cheeks of her ass only mere inches from my waist. She ran her fingers through her hair and, as it brushed against my face, I breathed in her intoxicating scent. I was done for. My heart raced as my Dockers began to bulge, and I fought off an erection with all my might.

We stopped at the next floor and one more person squeezed in. This disruption brought the woman's midsection even closer to my crotch, which didn't help matters any. Just then, a man turned in front of her, knocking her off balance. As she stumbled backward, her body pressed against mine, and my half erection was momentarily encompassed by her ass cheeks. The whole incident took only a couple of seconds, but I knew there was no way she couldn't have felt my bulge pressing against her ass. Then, just when I thought she might turn and slap me, she took a step backward.

Only inches away, she took one more baby step closer to my groin, swaying her hips back and forth. Each time she moved, her ass brushed against my penis, and I could fight it no longer. My hard-on sprang up like a diving board on recoil, and there was no way I could hide it. The way she fidgeted was casual and luckily drew no attention. I looked at the glowing number overhead. We had eight floors to go.

She turned her hips and my cockhead glided across her silk-covered ass. She took a shallow breath, which aroused me even more. Suddenly, she shifted her weight toward me. I spread my legs slightly, which lowered my body a few more inches, as I pressed harder against her. Looking down, I noticed her dress had become wedged between her cheeks. She rose to her toes, then thrust her hips back once again, humping against my cock. I heard a low, almost silent moan as she exhaled.

I had become almost oblivious to the other people in the elevator. If one of them were to turn their head to talk to either of us, we would have been busted. Luckily, the bodies immediately around us were nestled shoulder to shoulder, which made turning practically impossible. When a couple of people exited at the next floor and one more got on, I reached deep into my pocket, grasping my throbbing cock and pulling it away to the side. The sudden change in the woman's breathing pattern showed her disappointment. Sensing this, I couldn't resist.

I redirected my erection, anchoring the base between my thumb and fingers, then leaned forward and whispered, "What's your name?" Before she could respond, I thrust my hips for what I figured would be the last time. My right hand directed my cockhead deeper between her legs than seemed possible fully clothed, and if not for the fabric between us, I would have been immediately inside her. Then I pulled my cock back and pressed it firmly against my thigh, which did just enough to hide my obvious bulge.

As I watched her pull the fabric from the crevasse between her legs, I thought of what could have been if only we were alone or had more time. I looked up, waiting for my floor light to blink, when everything suddenly went black and the elevator mechanism hummed down to complete silence. Pandemonium broke out, and I briefly forgot the woman standing before me. That is, until I heard a whisper within an inch from my ear.

"Diana," is all I heard before a man's voice bellowed from above: "The power's out. The generators should kick in about ten minutes from now. So hang loose, and we'll have you out of there shortly." With that announcement, everyone relaxed and began to chatter and joke with one another—that is, everyone except Diana and me.

I leaned forward and whispered back into her ear, "I'm Josh." She turned and brushed her lips against my cheek, saying, "Nice to meet you, Josh," followed by a shaky breath. When she turned her head back again, our lips met, accidentally at first, but I clasped her chin and guided her face back to mine. We pecked at each other's lips a few times, letting our arousal overcome the awkwardness of the situation. Before I knew it, my tongue was dancing with hers.

Our lips still locked, I wrapped my arm around her waist and pulled her body flush with mine. Her ass once again hugged my erection, and she reached back and grasped it firmly, nearly tearing my Dockers from my waist. I responded by letting my hand slide up her smooth silk dress, from her abdomen to the bottom of her breast. It was not too large, and topped with a nipple that protruded between my fingers. I gave it a little squeeze, and she responded by maneuvering the head of my cock between her ass cheeks. She then began to slide it up and down as though we were fucking.

The crowd of voices seemed distant as my right hand glided over her hips and under her dress, between her legs. Heat emanated from her crotch, and her panties were damp. Before I knew it, my zipper was down and she was freeing my cock from the confines on my pants. I nibbled on her ear as I rubbed her clit, then forced my panty-covered finger deep inside her. This brought her to her toes, and she squeezed my throbbing shaft. Diana whimpered when I freed my finger from her cunt.

"Diana, are you all right?" a man questioned into the blackness in her direction, expressing real concern.

"Yes, I'm fine," she responded with an unsteady voice. It felt as if ten minutes had already gone by, but I knew it couldn't have been more than a couple. Then time slowed as Diana stroked my cock with a hand glossed with her own saliva. I spread my legs, bending my knees slightly. Still massaging Diana's clit with my right hand, I pulled the bottom of her dress just over her cheeks. A familiar voice echoed from above, "Just about five minutes more, people."

Not wanting to waste any more time, I stuck my tongue in her ear and she gripped my shaft even harder. I kept rubbing her clit until the moisture soaked through her panties and Diana had to cover her passionate whining with quick breaths. Just as I thought I might come in her hand, she released my cock. Rising to the tips of her toes, she parted her legs slightly and I quickly whipped her underwear down to her thighs. My fingers met her slick clit, and I caressed it as she gripped my cock and guided the head to her lips. She then turned to me and commanded into my ear, "Fuck me now." We had less than three minutes left.

I thrust into her with such force that she was compelled to part her legs even wider. I let the silk dress float down over my cock, then grabbed her hips. I couldn't believe it. On an ordinary Tuesday morning, in an elevator full of people, I was fucking a beautiful stranger. Pulling out of her cunt, I let my cockhead kiss the base of her clit, then thrust forward even harder than before. The whole length of my stiff member penetrated her this time, and she let out a muffled squeak as her body quivered slightly.

Knowing we were short on time, I thrust into her very quickly. I steadied and directed her hips as I pounded away like a jackhammer. As my movements accelerated, it became clear that she couldn't muffle her cries of rapture. I had no choice but to reach around with my left hand and cover her mouth. At this point I no longer had any concept of passing time.

When our knees began to weaken, I knew we were both near orgasm. Perspiration dripped from my brow. I pulled her close to acquire a better angle of penetration, and as I did she bit my index finger to stifle a scream. I kept plunging into her again and again until the lights came on.

I pulled all but the head of my cock out of her in sheer reflex as people began to crowd toward the front of the elevator. Two seconds later the doors opened. Everyone rushed out, happy to be in open space once again, even if it wasn't their floor. Diana and I were left alone, hoping that no one looked back at us. Her dress was draped over my cock and her ass, so what we were doing was not immediately obvious. Luckily, nobody looked.

Finally, the doors closed. Before the elevator even began to ascend, I spun Diana so that she was facing the wall without letting my cock slip out from inside her. She braced herself against the wall as once again I began to thrust in and out of her tight pussy. We were both ready to burst. I heaved forward with what little energy I had left, and she gave out a little cry as her vaginal walls contracted around my shaft. Gripping her arms, I thrust into her one last time, releasing a flood of semen deep into her.

Just then, the elevator reached my floor. Opening my eyes, I looked around at the other passengers and nodded to a man at my left. The woman in front of me stepped through the doors and walked away, and I strolled back to my desk. Who knows, maybe someday I'll figure out who she is, and we'll get to act out my wild elevator fantasy ride for real.

—Mr. J.N., Via Email

Of Zoot Suits, Seamed Stockings, and a Swinging Couple in a '41 Packard Sedan

Dancing is a hobby of mine, and over the years I have taken many different types of dance classes. Recently, having decided to really test myself, I signed up for swing classes at the local Y. It was a fourteen-week course with classes meeting once a week. The registration fee included a big swing-out dance at the end.

The first few classes were spent getting down some basic steps and learning the history of the different styles of swing. After that, we began pairing off to dance and I was immediately hooked on swing. The fast-paced dance makes me feel the same high I do during an extremely passionate lovemaking session. I spin around, kicking and jumping, until I am breathless, sweaty and dizzy, adrenaline pumping through my body until I collapse, exhausted, to catch my breath and rejuvenate so that I can do it all over again. It also doesn't hurt that my partner, Jack, is absolutely gorgeous.

Lately, I have been secretly fantasizing about the big dance that will signify my "graduation" from the course. In my fantasy it is 1941, and Jack and I meet for the first time at the hippest swing club in town.

I walk into the old ballroom, my hair neatly done up in pin curls and the seams of my black stockings perfectly straight up the back of my legs. My dress is just long enough to cover the tops of my garters, but there is no telling what will show once I start dancing. The dance floor is crowded, but not to the extent that people will knock into one another.

The big band wails throughout the room, and the floor shakes from the jumping dancers. A gentleman offers me a seat at the bar, where I order a whiskey sour and scan the crowd for a familiar face. I pull a cigarette out of my case and am startled by the flash of light offered to me as the filter touches my red lips. Looking up to thank the handsome stranger, I try to hide the butterflies in my stomach.

Jack, on the other hand, is cool and smooth, wearing a blue pinstripe zoot suit with suspenders and a broad-rimmed hat. He exhales from the corner of his mouth, leaving a cloud of smoke hovering to the right of us. We introduce ourselves and make small talk while I wait for him to ask me to dance. But Jack never asks for anything; instead he just takes what he wants.

When he finishes his smoke, he takes my cigarette from between my fingers and drops it on the floor next to his, while placing my drink down on the bar. His shoe covers the burning cigarettes, and he grinds them out while reaching for me. I accept his hand and he leads me through the crowd, snaking between and around people until we are in the center of the floor.

Of course, Jack takes the lead, and a few times I consider "hijacking it" just to see what he would do, but I am having too much fun feeling his large hands cover my rib cage to lift me into the air. I melt as he pulls me between his legs, and then we break away, staring at each other while we dance apart. It doesn't last for long because he likes having his hands on me. He swings me around, and I giggle as we break into the jitterbug, feeling delirious and out of control. My skirt fans out around me and Jack grins and licks his lips, getting a peek at my garters.

As Jack lifts me again, my legs go around his hips and our dance abruptly ends as if someone had stopped time. My heart is beating so fast that I can feel it in my throat, and we both pant as I lock my legs around his back and he leans in to kiss me. "Want to go for a ride?" he breathes into the curve of my shoulder and lowers me back to the floor.

I nod and he leads me through the crowd and out the doors to his brand-new, blue and white two-toned Packard sedan. I can tell it's new because the white-wall tires are spotless and the chrome gleams in the moonlight as if it just came out of the showroom. I run my fingers along the shiny surface, thinking that I would go anywhere with this man.

Jack opens the door for me, and I sink into the cushioned seat, nonchalantly glancing at the backseat, which is definitely big enough for what I have in mind. He removes his hat, gets behind the wheel, and drives away, his arm around my shoulder. Boldly, I place my hand on his thigh, which has an immediate effect on him, made obvious by the way his double-pleated pants suddenly look tighter than before. He steps on the gas and takes us up an abandoned dirt road to the top of a hill.

Shutting off the headlights, he wastes no time pulling me close to him. I immediately follow his lead by straddling his lap and grabbing his head. I cup his face in my hands and kiss him hard, our tongues meeting for a dance. I can taste on his breath the cigarette he just put out as his hands slowly make their way up my thighs. He holds on to my garters as we kiss, and I loosen his tie.

I slide his suspenders off his shoulders, remove his shirt and sweaty white T-shirt underneath. He removes the sweater I have on over my dress. Duke Ellington plays on the car radio as Jack opens the buckles on my shoes and removes them. He rubs my stocking-covered feet and calves, and then pulls my dress over my head. I jump into the backseat wearing just my bra, panties, stockings and garters, anxious to get him undressed.

Jack gets out of the car and returns via the back door. He slides on top of me wearing only his pants, which I quickly remove to find his white skivvies. I pull the cotton over his hard cock and slide them down and off his legs. His cock is beautiful, throbbing in my hand as I debate whether I should take him in my mouth or position that cockhead at my pussy so he can fuck me immediately. Before I can decide, Jack has pulled my bra down and is sucking furiously on my nipples. He grabs my breasts and pushes them together, licking them one after the other until I am begging him to fuck me.

Kissing my neck and touching me all over, he never loses his cool, even after I push him off me and take his cock in my mouth down to his balls. A subdued moan escapes his mouth as he entwines his fingers in my hair and grinds his hips in small circles. I suck on his cock, drenching his flesh with my saliva, the car hot and steamy from our heavy breathing. I pull him to the edge of his seat and crouch to lick him from his balls to his ass, still pumping his cock with my hand. Jack thrusts his hips up to quicken the pace as he rests his head on the seat and clutches the upholstery.

Finally, he pulls me off him and rolls our clothes into one giant pillow for me to rest my head on. He then removes my damp panties and lifts my legs up over his shoulders. I almost scream with delight when his breath nears my pussy, and I come about a second after his tongue makes contact with my clit.

"Fuck me," I beg Jack.

He pushes my legs up even farther, so that my knees are almost touching my ears, and jams his cock deep inside my sopping-wet pussy. The tips of my toes brush against the roof of his car as he thrusts into me while on his knees. I look down to watch Jack sliding into my body while holding on to my hips. I can see the veins throbbing on the surface of his cock as he pulls out of me, and then it disappears again inside my pussy.

Closing his eyes, Jack bites his lower lip and begins to grunt. He uses his thumb to stimulate my clitoris as he continues to pound into me. I scream for him to fuck me harder and he does. My cries of passion begin to drown out Ella Fitzgerald's voice as ecstasy takes over my entire being. It isn't long before I announce that I am about to come. Before I can get the words all out, Jack's come spurts deep inside my contracting walls and my clitoris twitches with pleasure.

Jack and I rest in an exhausted heap in the backseat of his car, his head on my heaving bosom and my arms draped around his back as he squeezes my waist affectionately. Our legs are entwined and I run my still-stockinged foot up his calf as we pant, enjoying our blissful delirium, knowing that we will be all over each other again in moments.

—*Ms. A.C., Valparaiso, Indiana*   O┼▄

Businessman Dreams of Disciplining His Saucy Secretary

I very much enjoy your magazine, especially your readers' fantasies. I would like to pass on a fantasy of mine that I find particularly arousing.

On a Saturday morning, I come into the office to do some work on a proposal, but instead of working in my own private office, I go to the centralized automated systems room to use one of the terminals. At about one o'clock I hear the main door, which I had locked upon entering, being opened. It's not often anyone comes in on a Saturday, so I get up to look. It is my secretary,

Pamela, and her boyfriend, Sid, whom I had met at our company picnic in July. I hear her say, "See, I told you no one would be here." They then move off toward the partners' offices. Actually, I share Pamela with two other partners, and her desk is conveniently located in front of our three offices.

Curious as to what is going on, I quietly walk out of the ASR and down the short hall to the common reception area. Pamela is showing her boyfriend my office and saying, "Now you go in and get comfortable and pretend you are Mr. McCormick." *That's me*, I say to myself, totally confused.

Pamela goes to her desk and turns on her word processor and starts "working." Pretty soon I hear her boyfriend's voice call out, "Pamela, come in here, please." She gets up and goes into my office. I step quietly over to the coatrack, from where I can look into my office and not be seen. I see Pamela standing in front of the desk. Sid, pretending to be me, is saying that now that she has been working here nearly a year, he wants to have a serious talk with her. He asks her if she likes her job, and she replies that she is very happy with it. He goes on to say that he finds her very attractive and is interested in having a "closer relationship."

Pamela acts surprised and offended, at which point Sid gets mad and says that if she really likes her job and wants to keep it, she should do her best to please him. Pamela says she isn't that kind of girl, and besides, he is a married man with grown children. Sid says, most firmly, that that is bullshit and that she has been teasing him for months with short skirts, peek-aboo blouses, and knowing looks. Pamela says she hadn't meant any harm.

Her boyfriend then asks her if she isn't more than a little interested in him, and in a soft voice she admits that she is. He says she has been driving him crazy and that he wants to fuck her right here and now in the office. First, though, he is going to punish her for teasing him.

Standing up and moving around the desk, Sid orders Pamela to bend over the desk and pull her panties down. He picks up the metal ruler that is part of a set in a leather case on my desk. Pamela protests, and he reminds her that if she wants to remain in her cushy job, she'd better do as she's told. She says, "What if someone comes into the office?" Her boyfriend answers, telling her that it's after working hours and the cleaning crew doesn't come in until very late.

I watch in fascination as my secretary slips her skirt up and begins tugging down her bikini panties. She is incredibly petite, five-two and less than one hundred pounds. As she slips her pink panties down and bends over, exposing the cutest little ass I think I've ever seen, I get an instant, throbbing hard-on.

Her boyfriend steps behind her with the ruler and says he's going to punish her for being a prick tease. She pleads, "No, Mr. McCormick. Please don't." He gives her a moderate slap across the ass, causing her to yelp. He then begins massaging her ass cheeks, asking if that makes her feel better. I can tell from her squirming that she likes it. Sid then proceeds to whack her and massage her a little more forcefully, another four times.

Pamela's boyfriend informs her that now he is going to fuck her, and she moans, "Yes, Mr. McCormick, fuck me. Please fuck me!" He unzips his walking shorts and produces a fair-sized but not extraordinary cock and proceeds to rub the head over her wet pussy lips. Pamela cries out that she wants his cock in her pussy now!

I watch transfixed as this young man pretending to be me fucks my secretary as she lays sprawled face-down across my desk. I can't restrain myself from stroking my own cock vigorously. Sid and Pamela come together with shrieks and exclamations of delight.

Sid then tells Pamela to get her clothes on and get back to her desk, but that anytime he asks her to bring in the "Bennett file," she is to get into his office on the double and take her pants down, because he is going to fuck her. She responds with a "Yes, sir!" I retreat to the ASR, and Sid and Pamela leave shortly thereafter.

I am sitting in my office writing this and looking at my metal ruler in its leather sheath, and thinking when, when shall I start calling for the Bennett file?

—Name and address withheld

A Buccaneer Queen, Rapier at the Ready, Arouses Savage Lust in a Chained Cabin Boy

My fiancée, Faye, was wonderfully responsive in bed, but elsewhere she was demure, even shy, about sex. That being so, I was surprised when she called me at work and told me not to come home till eight o'clock— "without underwear."

Intrigued, I arrived at the appointed hour. Dressed casually, she kissed me passionately. Candles sparkled, and an ice bucket with a bottle of wine gleamed invitingly. No, she said, it wasn't a dinner by candlelight. It was celebration of a new chapter in our relationship.

She held me close and her tongue tickled my throat. I started to respond in kind, but Faye drew back, smiling slyly. She said she'd been reading my old *Penthouse Variations*, and she'd gotten a couple of good ideas from it. She let the thought trail away, but I knew what she meant. "Kinky sex games, hmm?" I asked.

Sounding very serious, she looked me straight in the eye and said she never played games. With my hands cupped around her denim-clad buttocks, I said I'd play any role she wanted. We headed straight for the bedroom.

What a surprise! The room was totally different from when I last saw it. The bed looked like part of a gypsy caravan or a pasha's tent. Blazing red and deep blue and purple covers clashed madly, tossed on the bed at random. Cushions peeked out, and everything was silk or velvet except for one small pillow with a lacy white pillowcase edged with golden fringe. Candles gave the room a surreal luminescence.

She'd apparently spent the day turning the room into a love nest, removing all traces of the twentieth century. And now she pulled out what had to be a recent purchase: leg irons and handcuffs whose chains were linked by yet another chain, making one instrument of bondage. My jaw must have dropped, and Faye hastened to reassure me that they had quick-release catches. I stripped obediently, slid on the long-tailed old-fashioned shirt she held out and let her clasp the things around my ankles and wrists. They were heavier than I'd expected.

She pushed me backward onto the bed, and I pulled her down on top of me. She eluded my hampered grasp and smiled down at me, saying I was to lie still until she got into character. Leaning down, she licked my lips with her tongue before she slid away from me. She blew out a couple of candles and transferred the other one to an ancient-looking lantern. A hidden tape player produced sounds of waves and seabirds, and I lay there for what seemed an eternity of anticipation, my cock swelling rapidly in the unfamiliar dark. I could move a little, but I didn't stroke my cock, wanting to save it all for Faye.

What wild costume would she wear? A dominatrix in high boots and gloves, whip in hand? A black leather bikini? The variations drove me wild with desire as the images raced through my mind. I wasn't even close.

My demure girl had turned sexual savage. The

woman who strode toward me was built just like Faye, but I swear I'd never laid eyes on her before. Her hair fell loose and tangled to her waist, vaguely restrained by a bandanna around her head. A jagged design circled one eye and branched off down her cheek like a bizarre tattoo. Her roughly cropped sleeveless T-shirt was skintight and revealed a skull and crossbones on one biceps as well as her tautly defined stomach. Red and gold cloth tucked into thong panties formed a barbaric loincloth. Completing the amazing outfit was a pair of black velvet cavalier gauntlets, jangling ankle bracelets, and a single gold hoop earring.

A dagger was strapped to one hip and a rapier was in her other hand. Move over, Warrior Princess! I started to speak, but she held the rapier across my throat as she rasped out an order to speak only when spoken to and to call her "Captain." The sword was blunt-edged, but I was in no position to argue. I twisted in my chains, but whatever the secret to releasing them was, I couldn't find it. I was locked into Faye's fantasy, and I surrendered completely to the rush of excitement spiced with just a touch of anxiety.

She pushed me back down and drew the dagger. Unlike her sword, it appeared to have a sharp edge. "Obviously, from your lack of discipline, you have never been a cabin boy." She nicked the hem of my shirt and ripped it open with the dagger's edge. My hot, thick erection sprang up, pulsing despite, or perhaps because of, my astonishment. She traced lazy circles on my chest and stomach with the blade while she delineated the first rule of a cabin boy. Holding the rapier blade across my throat again, she forced me to look her in the eye. Her handsome face looked savage, sinister, and utterly erotic as she whispered gratingly: "Stay alive." I shivered as she told me how. "Stay obedient, silent, and"—the dagger blade's blunt edge ran carefully up the underside of my cock—"stay hard."

My heart was racing, and she hadn't even gotten warmed up! Slapping the insides of my legs with the rapier, which was as supple as a birch rod, she made me spread my legs as wide as the chains would allow. My arms would be still, she ordered sternly, hands folded across my stomach. She straddled me, the red and gold of her loincloth teasing my manhood.

She put down her weapons and unclipped her heavy hoop earring. With a click, she closed it around the base of my cock, "To help you stay hard." I groaned at the deliciously tight sensation, and Faye picked up her dagger. "You have a bad habit of talking while you fuck," she growled, driving the blade into the headboard to emphasize her order to keep silent.

She slid off her panties and loincloth and lowered herself onto me, her knees wedged against my thighs. Her hands searched my face and chest and hair, her mouth nipped and sucked, her tongue stroked me, and all the while I was bound and helpless, embedded in her tight pussy. I got some kisses in, but mostly all I could do was lie there and enjoy it.

With the barely lit darkness, the silk sheets, and Faye's abrupt personality change and barbaric costume, with the sounds of the sea in my ears, it was easy to imagine the once-familiar bedroom as the captain's cabin of a pirate vessel crewed by bare-breasted Amazons. Faye had become a menacing, lustful buccaneer queen, and I was her sex toy. She was right. This was no game. It was temporary reality.

My cock ached, pulsing with the blood trapped by the cockring. She was moving now, sliding up and down my thick and distended pole, pleasure and ache blurring into one amazing sensation. A growl warned me not to come before she did. Faye closed her legs, locking my penis in a fleshly vise and making me wince. The cockring had my manhood almost unbearably swollen. My protests died as she planted her hands on my chest in a partial push-up that did amazing things to my cock.

She rode me up and down like that until she was impaling herself violently at each stroke. Waves of pleasure coursed through me, and only the constriction of the cockring held back my climax. My cock was achingly hard, and every move she made was sweet agony.

Suddenly her fist clenched, her back arched and, throwing her head back with a guttural cry, she came, driving my shaft even deeper and rocking back and forth to savor the moment. "Now you," she said, moving more rapidly on my bursting dick. When a third stroke brought no climax, she reached for the rapier and once again held it to my throat, counting to three. Blunt or not, it was the edge that I was waiting to fall from. I exploded inside her so forcefully that she rode the wave to another orgasm of her own. Rolling off me, she unhooked the cockring, creating a wild sensation as my cock was allowed at last to shrink. Still chained, I fell asleep in Faye's arms.

She has never looked back. Fantasies of drill instructors and sinister interrogators are now staples of our lovemaking, and our sex life is hotter than ever.

—*Mr. H.A., Howell, New Jersey* O┼▪

In the Arms of Her Best Friend and an Exotic Stranger

It was summer, and my best friend and I had rented a cottage on a lake. It was our third evening there, and Martha and I spent the night drinking wine coolers. By three a.m., she was asleep on the double bed, but I'd just opened another bottle and wasn't tired yet. I went outside on the porch, where it was dark and quiet, and let my mind wander...

I'm sitting on the beach when a man with long dark hair held back in a ponytail approaches me. Sitting down, he offers me an inviting smile. I've seen him around, mostly on his boat, shirtless, displaying a perfectly lean body. He's extremely attractive, with high cheekbones and dark eyes that look almost black.

Suddenly, I feel a firm hand between my legs, and immediately, a jolt runs through my body. But instead of pulling away from the stranger's touch, I stay put, waiting for his next move. I can smell the remnants of beer and cinnamon gum on his breath as he leans in and gently kisses my lips and then invades my mouth with his tongue.

Breaking away, he stands and starts walking to a boathouse. Without a word, I follow him. We enter the shack, and soon my eyes adjust to the darkness. I follow him to his boat as though I'm captured by a spell.

He steps onto the boat and extends his hand for me to join him. I take it without hesitation. We are now standing close; in fact, my tits are pressing against his chest. He brings his lips to mine, and I feel my pussy moisten. He is awakening sensations in me I have never felt before, and I have never wanted a man the way I want this stranger. The boat is rocking gently, making this all the more exciting.

He lowers my pants, sits me on the seat of the boat, and kneels before me. My heart is racing. Though it's dark in the boathouse, I can see the desire blazing in his eyes. I feel his hands on my knees. He slowly spreads them apart and then presses his mouth against my pussy. I can feel his hot breath through my satin panties. He pulls the fabric aside and kisses my nether lips, softly at first, and then he invades them with his tongue. A moan escapes my throat as I untie his long hair and run my fingers through it. He gently bites my clit and caresses my pussy with his magical tongue. Then, at the exact perfect moment, he sucks hard on my sensitive button. I moan softly, my body trembling as a small but wonderful orgasm washes over me.

I lie down in the boat and pull him on top of me. Arching my back, I offer him my breasts, my hard nipples poking through my top and demanding his attention. One of his hands slides underneath my shirt and seizes a breast while the other slides into my panties. When he pinches my nipple, I feel another orgasm building. I slide my hand to his hard cock, which I can feel through his jeans. I really want him inside me, but first I have to taste him. I lower his zipper and slide my hands inside, urged on by his groans.

He leans against the steering wheel as I lower his jeans and briefs. A gorgeous cock is displayed before me, and I stroke it gently at first, matching my strides with his breathing. Then I wrap my moistened lips around his knob, kissing and licking it while I stroke him. He grunts when I take all of his cock into my mouth, and I feel his hands on the back of my head, tugging at my hair.

His noises are exciting me, so I cup his balls in my hand, gently squeezing them. Burying my nose in his pubic hair, I smell his masculinity. Suddenly, he pushes me away and lifts me to my feet. His eyes burn with passion as he invades my mouth with his tongue. Turning me around, he places my hands on the windshield. His hands slide down my back to lower my panties. He leans in, and when I feel the warmth of his cock against my bare ass, I spread my legs farther apart to welcome him in. First, though, I feel his fingers slide over my moist pussy, and one slithers inside. I beg him to take me.

He guides his cock inside me and begins sliding in and out. I am really wet by now, and I can hear my juices as he thrusts. His grip tightens on my hips and his pumping becomes more powerful. I let out a soft scream, not caring if anyone hears.

He grabs my tits and pinches my nipples. His thrusting grows faster, harder. He kisses the back of my neck, works his way around to my ear and nibbles my lobe. Grabbing my hips, he gives me full-blown thrusts. I beg him to slow down a bit because it's making me so dizzy. Then I hear the door to the boathouse open. I look, and Martha is standing there, watching. I don't say anything, just smile.

She gets into the boat and slips off her nightgown. I notice that she isn't wearing panties, and this excites me. Martha slides her hand between my legs. I have known her for many years, and she has never come on to me. I like it. She kneels before me and massages my hungry clit with her fingers and then settles her face up against my desperate pussy.

The stranger grunts as he fucks me from behind. He slides his hands to my pussy, where Martha is displaying her extreme talent, and spreads my lips so that she can lick every inch of my cunt. I hear her moaning and look down to see her fingers disappear into her sex. Her mouth is on my clit, sucking it, licking it with the tip of her tongue. The stranger is fucking me harder, making my pussy bang against Martha's face. She loves it. Her sucking becomes more powerful, and I come, grinding against her mouth, moaning as she licks up my juices.

The man then slides his cock out and lays me on the bottom of the boat. While he sits and strokes his hard cock, I feel a hand on my pussy. I lift my head and see

Martha. She slides one finger inside and then another. Rotating them, she feels for my G-spot as she continues to force her fingers in and out. I play with my tits, pulling and pinching my tiny nipples.

The stranger kneels beside me, stroking his thick cock, and places the knob at my mouth. I eagerly lick it as he pumps his shaft. Meanwhile, Martha pulls her fingers from my pussy and slides in something else. It feels cool, but wonderful. She guides it in and out and plays with my clit with her other hand. When she speeds up the rhythm, I moan.

The stranger is jerking off faster, and I open my mouth for him to enter. He continues to pump his shaft while I suck on his knob. Then I grab his balls and squeeze, and he grunts his approval. By now I am bucking against whatever Martha is ramming into me, and I momentarily slip his cock out of my mouth so I can beg her to eat my pussy. Immediately, I feel her hot breath against my clit. I can't believe how horny I am.

Martha removes the object and thrusts her fingers into my cunt, licking my pussy while the stranger jerks off in my mouth. Then he pulls his dick from my lips, and Martha moves up. She pinches my nipple, and I let out a moan as I feel the man's hands spreading my legs. I wrap them around his hips as he slides his cock inside me, filling me with pleasure.

Martha reaches down and grabs the dildo she had been using to fuck me and slides it inside her pussy. I wonder where she got it from and then decide that it doesn't matter. All I care about is the pleasure I'm receiving. She masturbates while the stranger fucks my wet pussy.

She pulls the dildo from her cunt and rubs it on my tits. Her warm juices on my skin excite me even more. She takes one of my erect nipples into her mouth and teases it with the tip of her tongue. The stranger slides out his cock and sits me up.

Martha lies down, and I straddle her, my pussy in her face. She eagerly licks it while I spread her legs and slide a finger inside her cunt. I'm surprised by the tightness, how hot and wet she is. I spread her labia and take a little taste. She tastes wonderful, so I begin feasting. I hear her moan against my pussy, her hips moving, fucking my face.

I can hear the stranger jerking off, the slapping sounds getting faster. When Martha sticks her finger in me, I reach for the dildo and slide it in her. She squeals, so I fuck her with the toy as she devours my pussy. I feel the stranger's cock rubbing against my ass and then sliding into my pussy. He bucks against me as Martha takes my clit into her mouth, biting lightly. As I slide the vibrator into her pussy, she sucks my clit vigorously. I push my cunt into her face. The stranger moans and pushes his cock as far as it will go, grinding. It feels so fucking wonderful.

I take the dildo out of Martha's cunt and roll her clit between my thumb and forefinger. She moans against my pussy, and her eager noises urge me on, so I spread her lips and stick my tongue into her hole. She lets out a scream as the stranger thrusts in and out of me. His speed increases while my pussy rubs hard against

Martha's face. Finally, he slides out of me and jerks off onto my ass, his warm come coating my skin. Martha comes then, too, crying out her release, and I soon follow.

That night we all slept in the double bed, and when I awoke the stranger was gone. Then I remembered that it was all just a fantasy. Still, when I saw the man later that day, working on his boat, I gave him a wink and a smile.

—*Ms. J.H., Wayne, New Jersey*

Up in the Highlands, a Rebellious Captive Gets a Good Spanking from a Great Scot

All right, I'll admit it. I read historical romance novels one right after the other, keeping them in my purse, on my nightstand, for whenever I can grab time to get in another chapter. I enjoy stories of larger-than-life men sweeping innocent heroines off their feet and carrying them away for night after night of orgasmic bliss.

My husband, James, except for the occasional snoring problem and the famous position-of-the-toilet-seat issue, is my romantic hero. A native of Scotland, he speaks with a cute Scottish brogue and has long black hair and seductive brown eyes. He is physically active, so his body is as hot as that of any romance novel cover model, and with a seven-and-a-half-inch cock, he is even more satisfying in the bedroom.

I met him at a Scottish festival, and the first time I saw him he was in his family's plaid kilt. He took my virginity a couple of weeks later, and it was more romantic than anything I'd ever read. He was gone when I awoke that morning, but he left behind on the pillow where he'd been sleeping a single rose and a short note saying how much I meant to him.

Often I fantasize about what it would have been like if we had met two or three hundred years ago. What would the first time we had sex have been like back then?

Up in the Highlands of Scotland, where my husband claims his heritage, the chieftains were fierce and clan wars were nothing out of the ordinary. Midnight raids where fields were burned, livestock stolen, and rival clansmen either murdered or kidnapped were expected occurrences.

In my fantasy, James and I belong to rival clans. My father has just arranged a marriage for me with a man old enough to be my grandfather, and rather than face the old coot in the marriage bed, I pack a change of clothes in a knapsack and make my escape in the dark of night. I have almost made it to the borders of my father's land when I am discovered by one of my gazillion cousins. He loves me dearly, but plans to return me to my father at first light, when his guard duties are over. He claims it's for my own good.

James's clan (we'll make him a laird; I know he'll love that) performs a daring early-morning raid, when the guards are getting sleepy and the rest of the clan is still foggy from its night's rest. I see him for the first time on horseback, leading a group of men toward me and my cousin. His eyes are fierce and his long hair blows in the wind as his horse advances with amazing speed. We try to run, but on foot we don't have a chance and are quickly captured.

James lifts his heavy sword and prepares to take my cousin's last breath with a single stroke. I cry out, begging for his life. He looks me up and down, and I can see desire in his eyes as he focuses on my long blonde hair, large breasts, slender waistline, and the swell of my curvy bottom. He agrees to let my cousin live if I will go with him as his captive.

I nod my consent, and he scoops me up onto his horse with very little gentleness and rides off toward his ancestral home, leaving me to wonder what will happen to me. He promises that as long as I comply with our agreement he will call off the raid, but gives me no proof that he has kept his word.

I am locked up in what appears to be his bedroom, the laird's lair. Two guards are placed at the door to keep me from escaping. For hours, I wait and pace and wait some more, wondering what my fate will be. Then a little maid appears with a tray of food. I adamantly refuse and she says, "Milord said to eat. You'll need your energy."

I am so angry that I throw the tray at the door, splattering the walls and my guards with its contents. The maid runs away in tears.

Night falls, and I can hear heavy footsteps coming closer, crunching the rushes on the floor outside. He busts through the door and yells back to the guards, "Do not open this door, no matter how loud she screams. I will not be disturbed!"

He slams the door before they can finish saying, "Yes, milord."

James yells at me for being so rude to his servants, reminding me that in his household they have higher rank. I scream back at him, telling him that leaving me locked up in this room for hours with no idea what has happened to my family is not a way to treat a lady. I will not be lower than a servant.

I rant at him. "If you are going to rape or beat me, be done with it. I refuse to just sit here and wait. Enough!"

Never once in all of the novels I've read had the hero ever lifted the skirts of his lady and given her a sound spanking, and I've read about quite a few heroines who needed it. In my fantasy, I am one of these women.

"No," he replies. "I am not going to rape you. When I take your body, you are going to be begging for it, but a sound spanking might not be such a bad idea."

I run, but don't get very far in the locked room. James captures me, drags me to the bed, and with little effort, he sits down and throws me across his knee. Tossing my petticoats over my head, he delivers the first slap, which lands on my bottom with a loud smacking sound. I gasp from the bite of its sting. He continues to pop my tight little ass until I'm sure my tender cheeks must be bright red and tears form in my eyes.

He begins to caress my bottom between spanks and, every once in a while, probes my pussy with his index finger, making contact with my clitoris. He massages it until I can't tell if I'm moaning from pleasure or pain.

Once he is satisfied, James pulls me into his arms, sitting me down in his lap. The fabric of his kilt rubs softly against my raw bottom.

After gently caressing my cheek, he presses his lips against my full, soft ones and drinks from my sweetness. As his tongue penetrates my mouth, I find myself breathless in the erotic bondage of my tight corset, and I surrender to the pleasure and allow him whatever liberties he desires. James slowly unlaces my stays and watches as my bosom is released into rough hands as he undresses me. Before I realize what he has done, he commands that I disrobe him.

I try, but my inexperienced fumblings don't get the job done fast enough. He loses patience with me and merely lifts his kilt. I am amazed at the size of his cock and how quickly it grows erect. It makes me excited and aroused at the same time.

Climbing on top of me, James plants kisses on both cheeks, then works his way down my neck and shoulders. He grinds his hard body against mine, and I feel the roughness of his kilt rubbing against my stomach.

After massaging my nipples with his fingers, he leans down and sucks one into his mouth. The apex between my thighs becomes wet with desire. I begin to squirm underneath him as the pleasure takes over my body, and he grunts out loud, taking my response as encouragement to suck harder.

He explores every inch of my body, leaving nothing untouched by his hand and mouth. My need for orgasmic release is so great I think I'm going to explode with desire. I cry out, but he says he won't take me unless I beg for it.

"Oh, please, milord," I cry. "Push your big cock inside me. Fuck me hard. I'm begging you."

James parts my thighs and shoves his cock into my pussy all the way to the hilt. He fucks me with slow strokes at first, and then gains speed until the only thing I can think about or feel is the pounding of his sword into my sheath.

I feel myself preparing to come, but before I achieve that bliss, he pulls out and flips me over, taking my pussy from behind. With each stroke, his groin slams into my sore, reddened bottom and the pain intensifies the pleasure. He drives in and out of my pussy forcefully until I come. It is an orgasm like no other because I receive it at the hands and the cock of my noble captor.

I am awakened several times during the night to tend to James's pleasure and learn not only to take him in my pussy, but also in my mouth and up my virgin ass. I love waking up with all of my orifices filled with his come.

Days later, after fucking me to exhaustion, he says, "I can give you everything you desire, if you will only submit to my will."

I give myself to him, heart, body, and soul, and he negotiates a deal with my father. He will cease pillaging the countryside if my father allows him to marry me instead. He agrees, and our marriage brings peace between the clans. We live a long life together, but I find myself needing a sound spanking quite often. It's a good thing James is more than happy to oblige.

My husband is asleep right now, but I know he will get a kick out of this story when he reads it in the morning. I only hope his response will be, "Come here, my pet; you have been a naughty girl," as he rolls up his sleeves and pats his lap, telling me to take my place on it.

—Name and address withheld   O┼▪

On a Dark and Stormy Night, a Lonely Wife Summons Her Lover

With my husband away on engineering jobs all over the world, it doesn't take much to have my busy mind at work, summoning my tall, dark, and handsome fantasy lover. I suppose he's a bit of a cliché, but that makes it all the more exciting, like beginning a gothic tale with "It was a dark and stormy night..."

Rain beat down on the roof as I looked at the clock for the hundredth time. Darkness still shrouded the sky and the room was cold and dark. The only light came from the clock by the bed, reminding me of a sleepless night. The stairs creaked and I jumped, startled as the door swung open to reveal his sleek, wet figure standing in the dim light from the passageway.

I ran to him and brushed his wet hair back from his face, kissing him passionately before turning to pull a towel from the back of the door. I took but a single step and then felt his firm grasp on my arm. He whirled me around and kissed me deeply, passionately. "Don't bother," he whispered. "Just help me get out of these wet clothes."

My hand obligingly moved to the placket of his soaked shirt and skillfully unfastened each of the buttons, kissing each freshly exposed inch of his chest as I worked my way downward. The shirt came off his muscular shoulders and fell to the floor. I placed a kiss on his abdomen and then looked up at him. His eyes sparkled in the low light. I had completely forgotten my solitary vigil, kneeling before him as he sat on the edge of the bed to take off his boots. Even after all this time, I was in awe of his strong body.

Lightning flashed outside, and thunder boomed. I flinched, shaken by the violence of the storm. He stood up and wrapped his arms snugly around me. "It's all right. I'm here now."

Feeling his warmth give me more than courage, my response was to pull off my T-shirt and toss it to the floor next to his. He gasped slightly at my nakedness, and I reached to unbutton his jeans. The bulge in the denim was not an illusion created by the poor lighting. He threw his pants over a chair in the corner, his freed member rock hard and standing at a forty-five-degree angle from his body. It was I who gasped this time.

We stood naked in the middle of the room, arms wrapped around each other until he turned me to the bed and we lay down. Our lips and tongues began to explore each other, and his kisses covered my face. I was only vaguely aware of the pouring rain as it continued to beat down outside and exceedingly aware of the lips that were kissing their way down to my collarbone. That sweet mouth was all over my shoulders, then kissing and sucking my hard nipples.

I moaned with sexual excitement as his kisses moved farther down my quivering body, and I began to writhe with anticipation and pleasure. He spread my legs and tenderly kissed my thighs, then moved to my mound and ran his tongue gently along the folds of flesh. He kissed and tongued and sucked until my body shuddered under his mouth and hands. I let out one last, lingering moan, realizing how weak my orgasm had left me.

I ran my fingers through his hair and made an effort to pull him up to join me. He kissed his way back up my body, pausing a moment to tease each of my still-erect nipples and caress the roundness of my breasts. Then a trail of kisses ended with him nibbling at my earlobe. I was delirious with passion.

I wanted a million things at once—to kiss him all over, to run my hands across his body, to explore. I wanted to consume his big, long cock, taking it deep into my throat. I wanted to suck him dry, but I also wanted to make long, luxurious love with him inside me—everything at once. No, I would bide my time, so I unwound my arms and positioned myself slightly above his body.

I let my hands rove his sensual body, and he muffled a groan when one of them found his erection. I massaged it for a few moments while we kissed passionately. Soon I was kissing my way down his body, trailing my tongue along his stomach, making him squirm and run his fingers through my hair to urge my hungry mouth closer to his engorged penis.

I refused to hurry an experience that I wanted to ferment in his memory like a fine wine in a dark cellar. I kissed his hips, his thighs, ran my tongue over his abs, up and back down through the tuft of hair that trailed to his genitals. I kissed and licked his balls, taking each one into my mouth and driving him insane with every flick of my tongue.

The rain kept beating down. Thunder roared and lightning lit the room like a strobe. His hands were braced on my shoulders as he gasped and moaned. I teased him for a long time, then mercifully swept my tongue up the length of his shaft and sank my warm mouth down on him. He shuddered with delight and surprise as my lips encircled his penis and slid to its base. He moaned and started thrusting to meet my starved mouth. Occasionally, when I felt him close to coming, I would distract him by halting my rhythmic motion to kiss his thighs or his balls, then casually resume sucking him.

Time after time I brought him to the brink of ecstasy, stopping only to start all over again. My lips moved up and down and his hips rose to my rhythm. His hands tensed on my shoulders, his legs stiffened. A second later he erupted, filling my mouth with his come. When the spasms subsided, he opened his eyes to watch me swallow every last drop, and I licked his cock all over to make sure I missed nothing.

For a minute or two he just looked at me, his fingers playing in my hair as he gazed deeply into my eyes.

We were lost in each other, oblivious to the storm. I moved quietly into his arms and we lay there, our naked bodies pressed together, listening to the rhythm of the rain on the roof.

We kissed with increasing intensity. His fingers crept down my body, creating sensations I didn't know could come from hands alone. Soon I was overwhelmed, my eyes clenched shut as another earth-shattering orgasm arched my back, bringing my breast to his mouth. His dick was stiffening against my leg, and I told him I desperately wanted his hardness inside me. He answered my plea with a slow, passionate kiss. His lean body towered over me, and I lay there, helpless against him, wanting and waiting.

He entered me with a thrust that sent chills up my spine. We rocked together, our bodies arching to meet with equal fervor. I shuddered uncontrollably each time he drove into me, wrapping my legs around his waist, one arm around his neck, the other hand roaming his back. I kissed his neck, loud groans emerging from him as my kisses spread across his jaw and his whole face. His tongue caught and probed my mouth as he filled my climaxing body with his load. We held each other tightly, his cock still inside me until my trembling body quieted.

We calmly rested in each other's arms as the rain beat steadily down. His subtle and distinctive aroma filled my nostrils. I was missing him already.

Shaking my head, I leaned back against the cool tile of the wall and turned off the shower. The clock radio had come on, announcing further water restrictions in our parched county. On wobbly legs I stumbled to the kitchen to fix coffee before the drive to work. A glance at the calendar told me it would be only a week until my tall, dark, and handsome husband would return from Pakistan to relieve the drought in my heart. Over the rim of my coffee mug, I smiled at the memory of my ever-faithful fantasy lover.

—*Ms. N.P., Waco, Texas* ⦶▪

My Hero, Hank Rearden, Leaps Off the Page and into My Heart

It was probably the third time I had read Ayn Rand's *Atlas Shrugged*, but I knew it would certainly not be the last. Fictional character or not, I was simply in love with Henry Rearden. I thought nothing could be as enjoyable as getting lost inside his world for a few hours (okay, a few days; no one can read 1,100 or so pages that fast), pretending to be Dagny Taggart or his wife, Lillian—or any other female lucky enough to touch him...hold him...fuck him.

Every time I read about his undeniable self-confidence, it is as if I can feel his presence next to me. He leaps off the page, a passionate, honorable, and austere man, one whom I can admire. One who makes me feel safe.

On that third read, Hank Rearden was more alive to me than ever. I was familiar with him now. I knew how he would speak, what he would say. After reading about his lovemaking with Dagny, I was sure I knew how good he would be in bed. I had invented a strong, deep voice for him and imagined him suddenly materializing in the doorway of my living room, telling me to put the book down in a sexy, bedroom baritone.

I blushed at his command and then obeyed, meeting the stare of his steel-blue eyes. They seemed to burn right through to my soul, so I had to look away. He sat down then and moved into my personal space, so close that I could feel his hot breath on my face. I kept my head down, avoiding his stare, and eyed his strong hands instead. The hands of a workingman. I imagined him working in his steel factory, flattening and bending the lustering metal with those sexy hands. And when he sat down on the couch beside me and then reached out to touch me, a sensation of warmth overcame me like never before.

"Security" was the word that came to mind as he pulled me into his strong arms and locked his lips on mine. He kissed me with an animal passion, making my every hair stand on end while my nipples hardened into points and my pussy tingled with anticipation.

In my daydream, Henry was already undressed, pressing his steel-like organ into my groin and rubbing up and down against my pubic hair as he hungrily tasted me with his tongue. He kissed my lips so hard that I was sure I bruised them, and then he bit and sucked his way down my neck.

Rearden yanked open my blouse, and I could hear a button hit the floor as he snapped off my bra and freed my breasts. In seconds his manly hands were exploring my body, kneading my nipples until they were sore little points. Although I was relishing his manual attentions, I halted his advances to offer him some oral pleasure.

First, I grasped Hank's cock and started to slowly massage it, kneading and squeezing his balls with my free hand. When his cock was so hard it felt like petrified stone, I quickly ducked my head down in his lap and began to ardently lick the top of the mushroom-shaped shaft. I ran my tongue up and down his hard, unflinching member before filling my mouth with it. A guttural moan escaped Rearden's lips as I began to pump all the cock my mouth could fit in and out. My hand worked the neglected flesh at the base of his cock until I thought he was going to come.

I stopped dead in my tracks then, unwilling to sacrifice the chance to have his durable cock inside me. Once again, Rearden took me in his arms with an air of absolute authority, and as he kissed me, a rush of endorphins had me reeling.

Hank's lips darted from my mouth to my neck and then back up to my ears, as if he couldn't get enough of me. When he touched me, it was like a thousand tiny fingers strumming my every nerve ending, awakening desire from my deepest recesses. Hank's hands moved along, as if responding to my silent desires, and he clutched at my breasts and ass cheeks before finding his way down to my cunt. At first he diddled with my vulva and then delved into my hole with two of his thick digits.

Plunging into my pussy, Hank began finger-fucking me at a dizzying speed, all the while cupping one of my alabaster breasts, tweaking the nipple with his fingertips. Feeling my need growing more urgent, Hank worked his hand faster across my clit, lashing my pussy until I was on fire.

I arched my body up to allow him further access inside me, and in seconds of him plunging in and out, I had a small orgasm—as if saving the real eruption for what was yet to come—my body quivering slightly.

I could feel my juices dripping out of me, and without missing a beat, Hank finally thrust his cock home. He filled me up so wonderfully, and I wanted us to stay entwined like that forever. But the passion was too intense to sit still, and in seconds we started to thrash around wildly on the floor—one moment he was on top, another it was me who was riding his cock, sliding it slowly in and out of my wet hole. At one point I think we even stood and he pummeled my cunt while slamming my ass into the wall. The feel of his cock sliding in and out of my velvety tunnel again and again was a galvanic pleasure. And when I felt Hank steeling himself for orgasm, I couldn't help but join him, allowing myself to convulse with my most uninhibited orgasm to date.

Perhaps it was the book dropping to the floor that woke me from my reverie. It startled me back into the stark reality that I was alone and that Hank Rearden had never existed—at least not beyond the pages of *Atlas Shrugged*.

I was still feeling horny though, so I brought one hand down to my sopping pussy and with the other I picked up my book and continued to read about the brilliant and irresistible Hank Rearden. I had to agree with the words of Ayn Rand: Henry Rearden could "outlast any hunk of metal in existence."

—*Ms. S.T., Sumter, South Carolina*   O┼▪

Salesgirl Models Her Naughtiest Lingerie for Handsome Customer

After searching in vain for *Penthouse Variations* in my neighborhood, I finally decided to subscribe. Now that I'm an "insider" with the secrets of what turns people on, I've decided to share with you what gets me hot.

Recently, I opened my own lingerie store. While it is a dream come true, getting the business started has been very time-consuming. With so little time for a social life, my erotic fantasies have become extremely vivid. After all, people are in my shop all day purchasing erotic attire for their exciting evenings. Some of them get pretty graphic and tell me exactly what they've planned, giving this pleasure-hungry girl even more of an appetite.

I chose to open a lingerie shop because I love to wear pretty things myself. Lingerie makes me feel incredibly sexy, and I love the response I get from men when I am dressed up. Most of my customers are men buying bedroom attire for their wives and girlfriends. This means I spend my days around good-looking, unavailable men. I would never think of coming on to any of them, but I sure do have a few regulars who enter my fantasy world.

My favorite fantasy involves a customer, Thomas, who comes in every month. He always takes my advice, telling me how much he enjoyed his last purchase. He asks a million questions: "What should I buy this time? Do you think this is sexy? How do I take this off her quickly?" I answer these questions professionally while secretly taking in his alluring smile and eyes and burning his mannerisms into my memory for when I am alone.

Thomas was my last customer this evening, looking incredible in his dark blue dress shirt and tie. After he left, I locked the door and began to put out the new line of matching bras and panties that had arrived in the morning. As I leaned against the counter, I drifted off into my little fantasy world . . .

Thomas walks through the door. Friendly as usual, he asks me what he should purchase tonight. I hold up a black lace bodysuit. "I like it," he says, "but I can't picture what it will look like on someone."

I pick up another set, this one in a pale blue, and explain to him how it is innocent and sexy at the same time. "That's nice, too," he agrees. This goes on for some time, but I am patient with his indecisiveness because I enjoy his company so much. I wonder if it is my imagination or if he is really flirting with me. The eye contact between us is intense, and the pauses between our words are building up a deep erotic tension.

"I can't decide," he says, throwing his hands up in the air. I pull the stretchy lace teddy from his fingers and it snaps against my wrist. "Does this help?" I ask, holding it up to my chest to help him picture it on his girlfriend. Thomas leans on the counter, pushing his glasses down slightly so that nothing is between our gaze, and brazenly asks, "Can you try it on? Please? It will help me to decide." When I agree to try some things on, he takes off his coat and settles into the sofa in front of the dressing room door.

I decide to put on a great show for him. First, I slip into a long silk nightgown. It is a tease, covering the flesh while clinging to every curve of my body. His face turns serious as I come into view. Thomas straightens up in his seat and clears his throat. Beckoning me toward him, he takes the material at my waist between his forefinger and thumb. "Very smooth," he comments, running the palm of his hand from my waist down to my thigh. I shiver as his rough skin pulls at the fabric. He nods his approval but explains that he is looking for something a bit more revealing.

Back in the dressing room, I take the silk nightgown off, basking in the feel of the smooth material sliding over my nipples and ass cheeks. Choosing another outfit, I select an adorable baby-doll nightie made out of the most clingy material on earth. It is peach with light blue flowers and a trim of ruffles that brush against my upper thighs as I return to the floor and stand in front of him. "How's this for revealing?" I ask, smiling.

Thomas moans as I step before him, and I notice that his cock is tenting his pants. I encourage him to set his hard-on free, unbuttoning his pants and pulling out his stiff cock. Thomas brings his hands to my hips and pulls me onto his lap, nuzzling his face in the crook of my neck and inhaling the lavender perfume I had put on earlier. I run my lips along his neck in return, extending my tongue and tasting the salty cologne below his jaw. His cock is between my legs, so I squeeze it between my bare thighs while tickling the plum-shaped head with my manicured fingernail. Thomas pulls at my soaked panties until he tears the dainty fabric. "It's very nice," he confirms, "but how about something that isn't so cute and fragile? Do you have anything really naughty?"

I knew just the thing and wasted no time changing into it. It had arrived at the store the other day and I was dying to put it on. As I pull it out of the box, the smell of leather wafts through the dressing room. It is intoxicating. First I put on the black panties, then the matching bra with tiny holes for the nipples to show. It has no lining, so I can feel the leather stick to my skin and twist my areolas. I slide the thigh-high boots up past my knees and look at myself in the mirror. My wicked reflection excites me even further as I add the final touch, a leather choker.

By the time I get back to Thomas, I am so hot I can barely contain myself. He lets go of his erection as I walk toward him. His face is flustered while mine is confident, as I feel the amazing power of my attire. Towering over him in my spike heels, I raise my eyebrow as if to ask, "Naughty enough for you?" Thomas tries to stand and take control, but I shove him back down and push on his chest until his head is against the sofa's armrest.

I hover over his face so that he can smell the smooth leather mixed with my arousal. Thomas inhales deeply as I pull the material to the side and lower my pussy onto his tongue. I sway my hips back and forth while tweaking my nipples. His groan vibrates my clit and I shudder, bending at the waist to take his eager cock into my mouth. I swirl my tongue around his hard shaft while fondling his heavy balls. We find a good rhythm, sucking each other in time and slowly building to that moment of crisis.

Thomas wraps his arms tightly around my thighs, pulling me so close to him I fear he might suffocate. But his ecstatic moans assure me that he is enjoying himself as much as I am. He has the back of my leather panties bunched up in his fist to hold the material away from my swollen, dripping sex. When Thomas announces he is going to come, I firmly grip the base of his ready-to-explode cock and hold off its eruption.

I take a few steps away from Thomas and ask him to remove my leather panties. He slides them down my thighs and over my boots. As I step out of them, he sits up and leans forward with his lips covering his teeth and bites down on my nipples where they peek out of the bra. I cry out and push him back. Throwing one leg over his torso, I impale myself on his cock with both my feet on the floor. The leather is hot, and I need to let my pendulous breasts free. I unsnap the hook between my cleavage, and my tits comfortably fall into their natural place.

I ride Thomas for all he's worth. He keeps his hands on my boot-covered calves until my orgasm takes me over and I begin to convulse on top of him so fiercely that I lose my rhythm. Thomas pulls me off him and positions me with my head on the armrest, my ass pointing straight up in the air. He stands behind me with his stiff cock poised directly at my entrance. He is teasing me, knowing how much I long to be stuffed with him again.

I beg to be taken and filled with his come. Thomas runs his finger over my choker and down my spine, finding his way between my ass cheeks and then invading my pussy to gather my juices. Moistening my anus with my wetness, he pushes his thumb against the resistance. Once inside my ass, he works his thumb in and out and then slides his cock into my pussy.

A thumb in my asshole and a throbbing cock in my cunt; I am in heaven. He moves the two in and out of me at the same time. I feel so full that I need to brace myself on the sofa. His breathing quickens, and with three more thrusts Thomas is filling me with his semen while still pumping his thumb in my ass. I cry out a second later and we both collapse.

I snapped out of my erotic daydream with the vision of Thomas's head resting on my shoulder. In reality, I was sitting on the sofa, holding the leather bra and panties that had just arrived up to my face, inhaling the strong scent and wondering how Thomas enjoyed this evening's purchase.

—*Ms. C.M., Cleveland, Ohio* ⊶▪

Getting Rear-Ended in a Parking Garage

My fantasy starts when I get to the office. There is a woman I work with named Gina. She has long, curly brown hair and turns me on something fierce. Gina sometimes wears high heels with cotton anklets, which to me is very sexy. When she comes into my office on business, she will often stand so that I can see her ass, and then, with her back straight, she will bend way over. This kind of behavior always makes my cock stiff.

Gina has a delicious teardrop ass, and the way she carries herself makes me feel that she is a very sensuous woman who enjoys sexual experimentation. I have often dreamed about the two of us arriving at the parking garage at the same time. She is horny, and instead of wanting to flirt, she wants to fuck.

Gina starts by opening the car door and putting one leg out. Her skirt hikes itself up to her crotch, and I can see her creamy white thighs. She is wearing a red garter belt with black stockings. No panties. And wow, now I can see that her pussy is framed by curly brown hair.

When I look up at her face, I discover that she

is watching me. "Do you like what you see?" Gina asks.

"Yes," I reply. After a moment I ask, "Would you like me to eat you on the hood of your car?" Gina says yes. She steps out of the car, and I lift her up by the waist and sit her on the hood. We are staring longingly into each other's eyes. I gently lay her on her back. "What if someone should see us?" she wonders aloud. I whisper, "That's half the fun. Just think—we may get caught!"

With that, I lean down and begin to eat her hot pussy. Her moans of pleasure echo through the half-empty garage. I run my tongue from the top of her clitoris to her asshole and back again. Again her moans fill the garage. At this point I wrap my lips around her clit and begin to suck. As Gina moans louder, I suck harder, until she is quivering in orgasm. With her third orgasm, she reaches down and grabs my head, trying to pull me away, but I suck her harder. This causes her to have another climax, this one greater than the others. Now I let go and lean back to look at her. She is breathing hard and sweating.

"I have always wanted to fuck you...in the ass," I say.

"Fuck my ass," Gina says. "Now, please!" Finally, what I always wanted.

She slides down off the car, and I hear her ass rubbing against the hood. I turn her around so that she is facing her car, and she bends over. I lift her skirt slowly to reveal the taut cheeks of her creamy-smooth ass. Quickly, I unzip and pop out my cock. I rub it up and down Gina's wet pussy and then slowly slide into her asshole. Gina grabs the hood ornament with both hands and moans with pleasure.

As I fuck her ass, I can feel my balls bouncing against her pussy. The sensation makes my body tighten. My thumbs are pressed into the center of her lower back. I slowly rise onto my tiptoes as I pump harder and faster. Gina urges me on with dirty talk, and soon I am shooting my hot load deep in her ass. What a thrill!

Tired, I slump over her back and we rest cheek to cheek. We can hear a sound over our heavy breathing. We both open our eyes at the same time. There is a car approaching slowly, and the driver is looking straight at us. He blows us a kiss as he drives by. Gina and I smile at each other and then quickly fix our clothes and go up to our office. What a fantasy!

—*Mr. S.A., Birmingham, Alabama*

Fantasy Lovers Come with a Guarantee to Please

As an unmarried, forty-year-old woman devoted to (some friends and most of my relatives—my mother especially—would say "obsessed with") my career, I have precious little time for sexual pleasure. That's not to say I don't appreciate a good fuck and an orgasm that leaves me weak and breathless. I treasure memories of long weekends, few though they've been, when a male friend and I have gone off to some romantic spot where our total relaxation was interrupted only by our vigorous coupling.

Working twelve hours a day five and often six days a week doesn't exactly stimulate a woman's libido, yet there are times when I get as horny as hell. But I'm in no condition to go out when I finally leave the office, even if I know that drinks with an attractive guy will lead to me getting my erotic itch scratched. Happily, there is an alternative, and as I drag myself home I think of the delicious bubble bath I'll be slipping into and try to decide who among my small but exceedingly talented group of fantasy lovers will satisfy me that night.

Will it be Jacques, my wickedly wonderful Frenchman, charm oozing from every pore as he seduces me? Will I conjure up Brett, my rugged park ranger, with whom I'll make passionate love in a leafy glade? Or will it be Hans, that decidedly devilish bearded industrialist who summons me to his magnificent estate for an evening of kinky pleasure?

More often than not it is Kirk, ever so dashing and desirable in his tuxedo, whom I summon from my court of admirers. Kirk is the most romantic of my imaginary lovers, the most worldly, his joy in pleasing me equal to the skill he brings to the task. We have traveled extensively, he and I, making love in many exotic locales. Kirk has pleasured me on the Orient Express, in a cozy château in Switzerland, in a wildlife preserve in Africa, in New Orleans during Mardi Gras, and under a canopy of stately evergreens in a tropical rain forest.

Usually, though, we can be found in his magnificent Victorian home, dancing cheek to cheek in the ballroom to music that seems to caress my soul. I have been wined and dined in the most elegant of restaurants, gifted with a precious stone, showered with affection, the evening exquisitely orchestrated by my dream lover so as to be foreplay itself, an artful stroking of all my senses leading up to this, the grand finale.

The music stops and my head lifts from Kirk's shoulder, so I can once again bask in the warmth of his smile. He is tall and lean, with rough-hewn features and long, curly brown hair that suggests a rugged outdoorsman. His brown eyes are full of love as he pulls me to him, planting his lips on mine. I all but swoon in his strong embrace, and his kiss, sensuous and demanding, leaves me breathless.

Kirk scoops me into his arms and carries me up the long circular staircase to the master bedroom. Once there, he puts me on my feet and begins removing my white satin gown. Patiently, confidently, he bares my body, removing my shoes, stockings, garter belt, and bra to leave me standing before him in only my flimsy panties. I gasp when he places his hand on my flat stomach and then shudder when he slips that hand down inside my panties to cup my pussy. In a voice thickened by desire, he expresses pleasure at my wetness, one finger slipping between the folds of my sex to stir, as it were, the juices flowing so freely from me.

He finds my clit, taps it gently, and I have to hold tight to him to keep from falling down. "Please," I say softly, "don't tease me. I need you so much." Kirk removes his hand from inside my soaked underpants and then gently lays me down on the queen-size bed. Savoring the feel of the burgundy satin sheets, I watch my fantasy lover undress. I spread my legs and idly stroke my pussy through my panties as I await the sight of his magnificent cock. And there it is, finally, a beautiful pole of pulsating flesh jutting proudly, defiantly from his loins. I whimper in anticipation of its taste and feel.

Kirk moves gracefully onto the bed and between my legs. He teases me anew by munching on my pussy through my panties and then, at my urging, rids me of the annoying obstacle to pleasure. He slips a pillow under my hips as I lift them for him. This elevates my pussy a bit, as if it has been offered up for his pleasure. It is, Kirk says, like placing a fine jewel on a bed of velvet.

In a comfortable sprawl between my spread legs, he commences his feast, his tongue snaking out from between his lips to begin a serpentine crawl up, down, and all around my pussy. I mewl with pleasure as his tongue slips inside me to play among the folds of my aroused sex. A cry of delight bursts from my throat when that tantalizing tongue finds my clit and caresses it lovingly.

I place my hands on my breasts and squeeze as I start squirming on the bed, Kirk's oral expertise driving me ever closer to orgasm. At times he likes to tease me, bringing me to the edge of an orgasm and then backing off, repeating this exquisite torture until I beg him to finish me. But this time he doesn't make me wait. He continues to lick and suck my sex, with frequent detours to my clit, until I go over the edge, my hips arching off the bed and a moan of pure pleasure exploding from my throat as I climax.

Moving up onto his knees, he watches with a smile on his handsome face as I come back down to earth. I smile up at him and then lower my eyes to his cock, so majestic in its erect state, so inviting. I get up on my knees so that I am facing him and then place my lips on his, tasting my juices as we kiss. His hands glide down my back to rest on my buttocks. He squeezes the taut half-moons of flesh and then pulls them apart. Immediately I'm reminded of the night he took me back there and how deliciously stuffed I'd felt with his big cock sawing in and out of my back passage.

Breaking our kiss, I start licking my way down Kirk's chest, pausing to nibble on his nipples and swab them with my tongue before moving on. My tongue trails down his flat stomach, dips into his navel, and then disappears in a nest of curly brown hairs. I am now in a low crouch with my ass sticking up in the air as I inhale the musky aroma of my fantasy lover's crotch. It is an uncomfortable position, and Kirk thoughtfully suggests a different one.

No sooner is he on his back, his cock pointing toward the ceiling, than I swoop down on him. I lick up one side of his cock and down the other, then trail my tongue over the sensitive underside until I am at the bulbous head, which I lave lovingly. I am tempted to tease Kirk, to postpone, for a little while, taking him in my mouth, but my hunger for his cock will not permit me this devilish aside. So I encircle the head with my lips and then slide down the shaft, taking all but an inch or so of tasty cock in my mouth before sliding back up to the head and beginning my journey anew.

As always, the taste of my fantasy lover's cock, the throbbing fullness of it in my mouth, ignites a fire in my pussy. I hear Kirk moan, and I know that the sight of me naked and crouched between his legs, my head bobbing rhythmically up and down, is enhancing the pleasure derived from the feel of my lips sliding up and down his manhood. I bring one hand back between my legs and discover that, not surprisingly, my pussy is soaking wet. I slip two fingers into my hole and then take my arm out from under myself and stretch it toward Kirk, gooey fingers extended. He lifts his head to take the fingers in his mouth as I continue sucking on his cock.

Do I want him to come in my mouth? I consider it, knowing the pleasure it would give him to watch me gulp down his creamy ejaculate and then lick his cock clean. But my pussy is demanding immediate attention, so I finally take Kirk's glistening organ from my mouth and roll into position on my back. Drawing my legs up and splaying my knees, I beg my fantasy lover for his cock.

Seeing the lust in my face, Kirk wastes no time. Smoothly, effortlessly, he mounts me, his pulsing member sliding all the way inside my slick pussy in one delicious stroke. I moan when penetrated, happy that my pussy is filled at last. Kirk quickly establishes a nice, even rhythm, his cock sawing in and out of my pussy as I bring my legs up and rest my heels on his buttocks.

My fantasy lover is fucking me with authority, going as deep as possible with each solid, no-nonsense thrust, his cock a fleshy cudgel as it pounds my pussy.

I am beyond the pale now, oblivious to all save the beauty of this vigorous fucking. I whimper as I feel my orgasm begin, and Kirk, recognizing the sound, drives me over the edge with a final flurry of jarring thrusts, spilling his seed on the last one. With his cock pulsing inside me, semen gushing into my pussy, I come with an animal-like cry of sheer joy, my arms as well as my legs now wrapped fiercely around my fantasy lover's body. I hold him close as together we come down from our high.

—*Ms. C.C., San Francisco, California* ⊙━■

A Farmer's Daughter Dreams of Outrageous Thrills with a Pair of Brawny Bikers

I grew up in rural Iowa, on a small farm that's been in the family for generations. I really enjoyed the life-style for twenty-two years, but then, having earned my degree, I realized the time had come for something new. The big city beckoned me, and so with the best wishes of family and friends, I set off to make my fame and fortune.

Well, here I am at twenty-six and nowhere near famous or rich, but I have a job I love, a cozy apartment in a wonderful neighborhood, and lots of good friends. Blessed with good looks, I don't lack for dates and I enjoy all there is to do in the city. Still, I treasure the memories I have of my carefree time on the farm, one of which continues to provide hours of masturbatory pleasure as I have turned it into an outrageous sexual fantasy.

One late afternoon in the spring I took the pickup into town to purchase supplies at the general store. I was talking to Joe, the grizzled proprietor, when suddenly we heard the roar of two huge Harley-Davidsons as they pulled up outside. I jumped, thinking the worst, but Joe quickly assured me that Hank and his biker buddy, Eddie, were basically good guys who came into town occasionally to buy six-packs. They might look tough, he said, but at heart they were pussycats.

Pussycats? Two burly, leather-clad guys riding monster bikes? It didn't seem likely. Joe's words, however, put me at ease, and once Hank and Eddie were in the store I saw them in a different light. With their rugged good looks and muscular builds, they were decidedly appealing. Threatening? Perhaps a little, but in a sexually exciting way, and as I followed them with my eyes while they gathered the stuff they needed, my heart beat faster and my pussy moistened. And it didn't help when they started talking to me, flirting, really, but in a perfectly acceptable manner. By the time they left, each one smiling and blowing me a kiss, I was hornier than I'd ever been in my life.

All during the drive back home I thought about Hank and Eddie, imagining how it would be to have sex with them. I'd been fucked by farm boys, and sometimes really well, but something told me a roll in the hay with these two biker dudes would be special indeed. Soon after arriving at the farm I went to my room, where I masturbated to an explosive orgasm, creating the fantasy that to this day remains my very favorite. This is how it goes:

I'm back in Joe's general store, clad in a checkered shirt, tight jeans, and sneakers, watching Hank and Eddie as they prepare to leave. Instead of blowing me a kiss good-bye, Hank asks if I'd like a ride on his bike. With my heart racing, I answer yes, and minutes later I'm sitting behind him and holding on tight as the Harley roars out of town. Eddie stays alongside us until he speeds ahead and turns off onto a dirt road. Hank follows, yelling out to see if I'm okay as we bounce along. I'm more than okay as the constant vibrations of the bike against my crotch have me thinking sex, sex, sex.

The seldom-traveled old road takes us to a ramshackle cabin in the woods, which I'm told is their club's headquarters. Once inside, my eyes go immediately to the king-size mattress lying on the floor in the center of the room. As I'm wondering how many girls have been fucked on that mattress, Eddie turns on a beat-up radio to a country-western station. He returns to stand in front of me, and with Hank behind me I'm now sandwiched between their two strong bodies. Slowly, and with obvious pleasure, they remove my clothes, complimenting me on my "beautiful tits" and "fantastic ass," feeling me all over.

When I'm stark naked, Eddie tells me to get on the mattress and masturbate for them while they undress. One hand goes to my tits and the other to my pussy as I begin playing with myself, keeping my eyes on the guys. I guess them to be in their late twenties. Eddie is clean-shaven, his face bronzed by the sun, while Hank sports a beard and mustache. They undress with a certain conceit, obviously proud of their bodies, and rightly so. Tattoos come into view now, the most prominent being the green and yellow serpent that travels up Hank's well-muscled right arm, the "I Love Mom" heart on the bulging biceps of his left arm, and the American flag adorning Eddie's back. Each wears an earring, and each has a big, beautiful cock in full erection. My mouth waters at the sight.

An involuntary moan of desire escapes my lips as the guys get on the mattress. Hank kneels by my head and feeds me his cock as Eddie crouches between my spread legs to eat me. I'm so excited by this time that I suck frantically on Hank's dick, almost swallowing it, and he has to slow me down. Meanwhile, down below, Eddie is feasting on my pussy, slurping up my honey and making me moan around his buddy's shaft every time his tongue lashes my quivering clit.

I come, pulling Hank's shiny cock from my mouth

to let out a cry of pleasure. Eddie, chuckling in satisfaction, gets into position between my legs, and without pause, plants his meaty manhood in my soaking sex. He fucks me at an even, steady pace, hitting bottom with each stroke, as I gobble Hank's cock as if it were the most delicious treat ever, which at that moment it is. In the haze of my arousal I remember that I hardly know these guys. To them I am but a conquest, another girl, this one a pretty blue-eyed blonde, in real need of some biker-style fucking. That thought merely adds more fuel to my fire.

After a while they change places, with Hank getting between my legs and Eddie kneeling by my head. Hank's bushy beard tickles as he sweeps his tongue over my pussy a few times before sinking his cock into it. Eddie, saying, "Open wide, Marilou," stuffs his cock into my eager mouth and starts fucking my face, which I find wildly exciting—so much so that I'm soon coming again.

The minutes go by, and with a big cock in my mouth and another big one in my pussy, I'm lost in lust. All of a sudden, Eddie pulls out of my mouth and walks over to the radio, singing along to the tune that's playing. He turns up the volume a bit and returns to the mattress, where Hank, having flipped me over and pulled me up onto my hands and knees, is now fucking me from behind.

Hank's cock feels even larger this way, and I moan with pleasure. Then Eddie returns to the mattress, kneeling next to his buddy. Looking back, I see Eddie stick a finger in his mouth, and then, while Hank holds still inside me, I feel that finger push into my small rear hole. "Tight," Eddie says. "An anal virgin, I'd bet."

Hank asks me if it feels good, and I answer yes, remembering the naughty pleasure I felt when Tommy, one of the farm boys, did me that way. Sawing his finger in and out of my asshole, Eddie asks if he can fuck my "beautiful butt." I tell him yes, and that he should do it hard. This stuns him, but he recovers quickly, and spurred on by the knowledge that here was a girl who had no qualms about taking a cock up her ass, he pushes Hank aside and takes his place behind me. In no time he's pushing into me, going deeper and deeper, until the full length of his cock is buried in my rear passage. Although it's been a while since I'd had a cock in my back hole, the unique thrill of being ass-fucked returns with a vengeance, rattling me to the core.

Hank stands by, watching his buddy pound into my bottom and stroking his dick, somewhat miffed at being left out of the action. The feel of Eddie's big cock slamming into me again and again has me practically sobbing with joy. I drop my shoulders onto the mattress and reach underneath me to stroke my pussy, which is all it takes to start me coming like crazy. I'm still in a state of euphoria when Eddie withdraws his cock from my behind on orders from Hank, who's come up with what he thinks is a great idea. "We'll DP her," he says excitedly. "How 'bout that, Marilou? A cock in your pussy and one in your ass. Bet you've never done that before."

He's right, but the idea of being stuffed full with

two big cocks is devilishly exciting. "Do it," I say with authority. "Please."

They do, and it's the most amazing, most thrilling experience of my life. There I am, sandwiched between these two burly bikers, Hank flat on his back and punching his cock into my pussy while Eddie, behind me, rams his hard dick into my asshole. Never before have I been so full of cock, and the sheer pleasure of it all engulfs me completely. I come twice before the guys do, and I'm still trembling when Hank shoots his semen up into my pussy and Eddie drenches my rear passage with his mighty orgasm.

Thoroughly sated, we relax with the three cans of beer Hank's taken from the small refrigerator. The guys then help me into my clothes, and Hank gives me a ride back into town. Once in the pickup, heading for the farm, I think about Hank and Eddie and all the pleasure they gave me, and I almost come yet again.

It's the whole outlaw thing, I guess. You know, girls wanting to be with renegade types whose demeanor and lifestyle suggest danger and sinful delights. I haven't met anyone like that in the city, but I'll be ready if and when he comes along. In the meantime, there's Hank and Eddie, my favorite biker buddies, who never fail to make me happy when I welcome them into my imagination.

—*Ms. M.T., Via Email* O—◼

Beautiful Secretary Wants to Get It On

I'm a twenty-five-year-old secretary at a rather prestigious brokerage house on Wall Street. And every day, usually while I eat my lunch in my cubicle, I fantasize about fucking the company's chairman of the board. He's a seventy-year-old man with a halo of white hair surrounding his bald head, a crinkled-up bulbous nose, and a genteel manner. I think he'd be a wonderful bed partner.

Most of the men in the office where I work think I'm one of the sexiest women they've ever met. They're always coming on to me, telling me how beautiful I am. The compliments are nice, but I'm not some naive kid. I know what these young guys really want. They just want a one-night roll on the feathers, a suck, a fuck, and a smoke. What do I get out of it but maybe a dinner and cab fare home? This I don't need.

Wendell, on the other hand, is special. I can tell. At Christmas he always makes a point of stopping by and wishing me a good holiday, he always sends me flowers on my birthday, and he makes a point of opening doors. He treats a lady really well. He's a true gentleman and a pleasure to behold. I realize that the age difference would make some people tilt their heads in wonder, but Wendell turns me on. He makes me feel pretty and important. I like that.

I realize, too, that Wendell is married and that the chances of us ever getting together for real are slim. But a girl can hope. Meanwhile, I fantasize.

I had this really hot fantasy the other day. I dreamed that I was called to take the minutes for a big executive conference in the boardroom. About twenty men in dark blue business suits are sitting in plush swivel chairs, discussing money matters in this huge room with wood paneling and what seems to be a mile-long oak table. At the head of the table sits Wendell, who listens attentively to all of the other executives before cutting them off.

"I'm tired of hearing all of this bickering," he finally says with authority. "Jessie, come sit on my lap."

Without batting an eyelash, I walk up to the front of the room and slither into Wendell's cozy little lap as the other men look on, their faces donning hopeful looks of lust. But my heart's with Wendell.

The two of us begin making out, and I can feel his practiced hands venturing up my short skirt and quickly finding the wet crotch of my panties. Filled with passion, I hoist my blouse over my head, shimmy out of my panties and skirt, and lie back on the table. As Wendell draws closer to me, I spread my legs apart and lift them high in the air to give him complete access to my sex.

I can hear the other men breathing heavily as Wendell slides his tongue into my wet crease. Shudders of ecstasy race through my body as he teases my rigid clit with the tip of his tongue.

"Let me suck you," I say, and as Wendell opens his trousers and pulls out his cock, I spin around on the table and hang my head over the edge to accept his organ. My pussy is exposed to the rest of the executives and I can sense their passion. They want me. But I am reserved especially for the CEO.

Wendell's cock is surprisingly large and thick. The head is a beautiful mushroom shape, and I twirl my tongue around it while I play with his ample balls and finger myself with my free hand. After several minutes I spin my naked body about once more and invite Wendell to mount me.

He fumbles his way up onto the table with the help of some of the others. I wrap my legs around him as his erection slides gracefully into my sopping pussy. He thrusts and bucks and fills me to my very core, giving me a mind-altering orgasm. My entire body comes alive, my nipples tingle, my thighs quiver, my belly contracts with passionate reverberations, and I am soon lost in a cloud of ecstasy.

I let Wendell take me from the rear. As I bend over the conference table, he pushes his cock into my eager cunt. With each thrust I become more and more consumed by our sexual union. My tits sway in total view of the others, who watch as beads of sweat drip from my brow and expressions of bliss decorate my face.

"Fuck me," I whimper. "Fuck me harder, faster."

Through tears of joy I can see that several other executives—men who have wanted me for years—have taken out their cocks and begun to masturbate to this titillating exhibition.

Suddenly I sense Wendell's impending explosion. His body grows rigid and he grabs my fleshy hips with a sturdy grip.

"Come on my ass!" I cry out. "Shoot it on my ass!"

With that, Wendell withdraws from my pussy and spews a hefty load of semen all over my back and on my nicely rounded bottom. Reaching behind me, I scoop a dollop of come from my backside and feed myself the sweet seed. I savor the salty taste and wish only that I could enjoy this exquisite pleasure every day of my life.

After I clean up and get dressed, the meeting continues—business as usual—but I can tell that all of the executives are looking me over, hoping that I will choose them as my next partner.

I realize that he and I will probably never sleep together, but I have no doubt that Wendell could satisfy my sexual needs just as well, if not better, than most men half his age.

The young men I've known have been too fast, too rough, and not sensitive enough to my needs. Wendell's not like that. Perhaps one day the door he opens for me will be the door to his bedroom. And then, finally, I'll be able to realize my ultimate fantasy.

—*Ms. J.J., Bayside, New York*   ⊙━▪

TV Executive Dreams of Sexy Private Fashion Consultant

As I dress for work each day, I feel pretty good in my pinstriped button-down shirt; I may be seeing electrical contractors or Fortune 500 corporate types.

But there are parts of me that those types never get to see.

Jennifer, or Jenny, is the all-American girl. She is a cheerleader. She is the color pink. She is lace. She is bubble baths. She is a lady.

Christie—she never goes by the name Christine—is every man's desire. She is the head-turner. She is the color red. She is a tease. She is an alluring perfume. She is class.

I am looking forward to the day my fantasy is fulfilled. I would be traveling overnight, enjoying a drink in the hotel lounge. There is some nice jazz in the background as a tall, confident, sexy lady approaches my table.

"My name is Linda," she says. "You seem to be enjoying the music. I like jazz, too. May I join you?"

Linda has green eyes and dark red hair. I notice her well-rounded buns and her perfect breasts as I seat her. Electricity builds between us, a current of desire. We quickly discover that we share a variety of interests. A few times our hands or legs brush, and there are sparks.

Linda suggests that we continue our conversation elsewhere as the lounge begins to fill and get noisy. I agree and offer the obvious. In my deluxe room with the pay-as-you-go bar, we have a glass of wine. I excuse myself to use the bathroom. When I return, I notice that a dresser drawer is open slightly. A pair of pink fishnet stockings is visible; Linda has noticed, too. I feel myself turn red as she says, "It looks like someone special has left something behind."

Linda excuses herself, stepping out into the hallway with her cell, using the pretext of having to check in with her West Coast office. I figure the evening is over and begin to remove my clothes. I gather the fishnets and draw them up my legs. I love the feel of those stockings on my legs. I pull on a pink body shaper with garters that I have sewed onto it. I flip on the radio and head for the bathroom to start applying my makeup. It is only a short business trip, and I have brought only my minimal "necessities." I wish I had brought more of Jennifer and Christie's wardrobes. It will be a long night alone in my room.

Before I reach the bathroom, I hear the door to my hotel suite open. There, with a suitcase, is Linda! I must look flabbergasted. She says, "You shouldn't leave your key in the door. You never know who might use it."

I start to mumble something, but she stops me by placing a finger on her lips. "Honey," she says softly, "I told you I'd be back. I had a pretty good hunch that those fishnets were yours. I thought I might be able to help out." Linda puts her suitcase down and approaches me. "Just try to relax," she says softly. "Now, what shall I call you?"

"Jennifer, but I guess I really prefer Jenny."

"Jenny, I knew we would have a special evening together from the moment I saw you downstairs. I just love to dress up my dolls. Will you be my little dress-up doll tonight?" I nod, and Linda gives me a gentle kiss on the lips. She tells me to start a nice warm bath and to remove my clothes.

A few minutes later, Linda enters the bathroom. She is wearing only lacy red tap pants and a matching bra. She pours bubble-bath crystals into the water and has me get in the tub. She starts gently washing my body. "Don't be scared," she says. "Remember, I'm only here to make you feel pretty."

After the bath, Linda asks me what I like to dress in best. She told me earlier that she sells women's clothing; what she omitted was that it is mainly lingerie. That explains the suitcase filled with delicate treasures. She pulls out an ultra-feminine bodysuit and helps me put it on. It is white with lots of pink lace in the panels. The panty portion is completely pink lace.

Next she pulls out a hot-pink garter belt and places it around my waist. This is followed by black hose. "Now let's go take a look and see if this fits your mood." She has me model in front of the mirror. I adore what I see.

"Listen, Jenny," she says as she places both hands on my shoulders, "I want you to tell me that you'll trust me completely. This has me as excited as it has you." When I nod, she again gently kisses my lips—I feel as if I am in heaven. Bright red lipstick completes the picture. And strappy heels. She tells me I look gorgeous. And I do. She works on my walk until it appears natural.

She has me put on a sleeveless black turtleneck. She puts a scoop-neck red pullover blouse on me. I am taken by surprise when she tells me to stand and spread my legs. From behind me she unfastens the snaps at the crotch of the bodysuit. I feel her soft hands gently pull my cock back between my legs and deftly refasten the snaps. "We don't want any unsightly bulges," she explains. The finishing touches are a tight black leather skirt and a printed scarf that she drapes over my back.

"Jenny, you are far too pretty for me alone. I think we're ready for the lounge again."

"But I've never been out before," I argue.

"Jenny, you are a wonderful companion for the bar. Can't you see how this is really you? We will be together." Linda is right. I have been longing to do this. She takes a blow-dryer out of her suitcase and, in a few short minutes during which she feathers my hair here and there, she accomplishes the one thing I've never been able to do for myself: a really decent Jenny hairdo.

In the elevator, I ask, "What if someone talks to us? How do I respond?" Linda tells me not to worry. If someone approaches us, she will do the talking. She tells me simply to listen to other women. Many have voices not too different from mine.

When we get to the lounge, Linda orders our drinks. It has gotten very noisy. We find a table and talk, as we did hours earlier. Two gorgeous men approach and ask if they may join us. I place my purse on the table, a prearranged signal for "Not quite yet" that Linda and I had agreed upon earlier.

Later two other men make an identical request. Linda watches for the purse. I hear myself say, "We'll be leaving shortly, but you may join us for a while." Linda smiles; she's obviously pleased with me. Forty-five minutes later, I hear myself say, "Excuse me. I must go to the ladies' room." Linda picks up on my cue and joins me. When we enter the restroom, I let out a big giggle. I say, "We did it!" Linda replies, "No, Jen, you did it!" We decide on one more drink before going home.

When we get back to "our" room, Linda hugs me. I feel my breasts against hers. We kiss deeply. Then she removes my outer clothing and removes all of hers. She pulls me to the bed and gently lays me down on it. Linda climbs on top of me and caresses my stockinged legs and runs her fingers over my bodysuit. We kiss more and more passionately. She unfastens the snaps at the crotch of my bodysuit. She moves down my body, and suddenly I feel her soft, warm mouth engulf my erection. After a few minutes, she swivels around until she is straddling me with her lovely pussy hovering over my face.

Without delay I plaster my face against her aromatic bush, my tongue slicing through the warm, slick folds of flesh. I tongue her clit and she moans around my cock, which she has taken all the way down her lovely throat. I can't get enough of her sweet pussy, and I eat it hungrily as her juices gloss my face.

Finally Linda swivels around again and this time squats down over me. Smiling, she takes hold of my aching cock and slips it up inside her wet hole. I watch my cock disappear inside her and then moan as she starts moving up and down on me. I thrill to the fact that she is fucking me—that she is in control. I am a woman being taken!

It isn't very long before we both are coming, Linda driving down hard on my cock and then emitting a cry of pleasure as her orgasm sweeps over her. I moan and squeeze my breasts hard as I erupt, shooting semen up into her convulsing pussy.

When I wake up the next morning, Linda is gone. But I will never forget her.

—*Mr. V.O., New York, New York*   O┼▪

How I Get the Hot Women in My Office to Perform Outrageous Sexual Acts

You know how it is, working late. I spend the whole time fantasizing about the women in the office. I imagine them doing outrageously sexy things. To me. With each other. You know—impossible stuff. Take last night.

I was burned out and needed to take a breather, so I decided to get a cup of coffee. As I walked down the hall, I noticed that the lights were on in Jodie's office, and I started dreaming about her. Jodie is the office dish. She's a tall, full-bodied redhead who makes heads turn every time she walks down the hall. In my fantasy, I opened the door to her office and peeked in.

My eyes grew wide and my erection came to full attention. There was Jodie. Of course she happened to have her skirt hiked to her waist and was lying on her desk moaning as Betty, the secretary I have voted most likely to climb my cock, ate her pussy. When both women noticed me, they froze for a second. Then Betty said, "Look, Jodie, here's some real meat." Jodie eyed me, licking her lips in lust. "Hey, Phil, wanna penetrate a new market?" she asked as she took off her dress. She stood there in a bra, garter belt, stockings, and heels. Betty had stripped down to a red lace teddy. It took me less than a minute to rip off my clothes and join the lusty ladies.

I leaned on Jodie's desk, offering them my dick. They both knelt, and their tongues lapped at my cock. The feeling was fantastic. My hands went to their breasts. Jodie's large tits were barely contained in her bra. I unsnapped it, and her mounds spilled out. Betty had smaller breasts, but her nipples were the size of silver dollars and begging to be sucked.

In the meantime, my cock was getting a royal sucking. Betty decided to take it all, so she stuffed my cock deep in her throat. Jodie stood up and offered her tits to my hungry mouth. I dove in, my face buried in her cleavage, and then began chewing on her nipples. "Oh, Phil, suck my nipples—bite my tits," she said with a moan.

After a while, Jodie said she was hungry and took Betty's place swallowing my cock. I was leaning on the desk enjoying Jodie's oral stimulation. Betty got up on the desk, unfastened her teddy at the crotch, and positioned her pussy right above my face. She lowered herself until my tongue could reach her honey. She was dripping wet, and I greedily licked up her juices. Down below, Jodie was getting her mouth thoroughly fucked.

Jodie released my meat from her lips and told me to lie down on the floor. I did so, and she squatted on my rod. Betty sat on my face so I could continue my feast. I brought Betty to orgasm while Jodie rode me. The ladies swapped places, and now I was eating Jodie while Betty bucked on my erection. I could feel my balls tightening as I grew near orgasm. "Ladies, Mount Phil is about to erupt," I announced. Betty dismounted from my cock and took my balls in her mouth. I came all over her face.

Other times I'm jerking off, and I picture these two delicious babes surprising me with their sex toys. This fantasy always starts with me peeking into Jodie's office and hearing Betty's husky voice. "Oh, look, Jodie, let's give Phil a show. What do you say?" Jodie smiled wickedly, got up and went to her desk. She unlocked a drawer and pulled out the double-headed dildo. I love it when they do this. The ladies sat close together, facing each other. They then lay on their backs, inching their pussies closer to each other. Each woman took hold of her end of the dildo and inserted it in her vagina. Again they inched closer, the length of the dildo slowly disappearing inside them.

They lifted their legs, feet resting on feet, and their hips began to sway back and forth. I sat there, stroking my hard-on, enjoying the show. Betty told Jodie to change to "position number two."

Both ladies got on their hands and knees with their asses touching. Jodie pushed in her end of the dildo from behind, as did Betty. Then they started to rock back and forth, their asses slapping together, the dildo going deep inside them. "Great show, ladies," I said. "You two are going to make me come very soon."

Jodie and Betty squealed in delight and proceeded to move faster. Both were breathing heavily and, like magic, they came in unison. I was pumping my rod in delight. When they had calmed down, they crawled to me and started to lick my shaft. In no time at all, I was shooting a big load.

In my fantasies about Jodie and Betty, I've been treated to stripteases, lingerie-modeling shows and torrid lesbian love scenes, as well as all the delicious things I can dream up that they do to me.

—*Mr. P.B., Chicago, Illinois*

My Handsome Husband, My Beautiful Friend, and Me— A Threesome to Dream About

My husband and I have a very active sex life. I think we're both rather good-looking people. I'm blonde, like David, and tall, with green eyes. I keep myself in shape by working out regularly and get facials and massages. David is also very body conscious.

We are a passionate couple, and I have this great fantasy that I often think of while I am alone. With my mind full of sexy thoughts, I imagine having coffee with a good friend of mine. Mandy, who works out with me at the health club, is very pretty—perfect body, with a long, luscious mane of auburn hair. I often fantasize that she's sitting right across from me in my house and we are chatting about everyday things. As I sip my coffee, my eyes watch her every move over the rim of the cup.

At one point, Mandy leans over for a cookie, and her arm brushes against mine. Sparks fly when our flesh touches. She looks at me and smiles. I reach out to her and touch her cheek. Mandy presses my hand to her flesh. The coffee is forgotten as we hug tightly.

Mandy presses her body closer to mine, and I lower my lips to hers. "I've thought about this for a long time," she says, and her tongue twirls in my mouth. It's hot and wet, and my pussy reacts instantly to her touch.

I lower her body onto the couch and press my full length onto hers. We are still kissing and caressing each other when Mandy whispers, "Please, let's go into the bedroom. I want to see you naked."

I lead her to my king-size bed. She coos and sighs as she removes my clothes. When she has me naked in front of her, she finally removes her own clothes. I watch her do a slow, sexy striptease, and my hand strays to my moist cunt. I thrust one finger into my sex as she removes the last of her garments: a pair of red bikini panties.

Mandy pulls me into her arms and says, "Let me do that for you." I lie back on the bed, and she climbs over my form, kissing and licking my skin, caressing me and whispering about my beauty.

Then she lies directly on top of me. Mandy kisses

me full on the mouth, and I grab her behind and grind my cunt into hers. She moves lower and lower down my body, licking all the time. I know where she is headed, and I murmur about how good this feels.

I reach down and spread my pussy lips for her. Her fingers caress my vulva, and she tells me how pretty my cunt is and how she is going to lick me until I cry out in ecstasy. Her tongue gently licks my outer lips, and then she takes each one in her mouth and sucks and pulls while inserting her finger deep into my hole. I become very slick, and I know that my pussy must be glistening, because Mandy is making slurping sounds. I bring my hands up to my breasts as Mandy sucks on me deep and hard. Her face is buried in my cunt, and I lift my hips off the bed for more.

While I pull my nipples, Mandy tongues my clitoris with feather-light touches. This sends me over the edge, and I start to quiver and shake in orgasm. Then I hear David's voice. "What's going on here!" he says.

I lift my head off the pillow and look toward the bedroom door. Mandy lifts hers from my cunt and gasps, "Oh, my!" Instead of jumping up, I grab Mandy's head and say, "Don't stop!" David looks shocked, but I notice that the bulge in his pants betrays his excitement, and as Mandy resumes her actions on my hot pussy, he moves closer to the bed.

"Beautiful," my husband says. "You two look so beautiful." And he begins to remove his clothes. He gets on the bed and eggs us on. He caresses my thighs, and Mandy continues to slurp at my pussy. "Wider, baby, spread your legs wider so I can see," David says, and I do as directed. I feel so totally open and turned-on.

I want my husband to fuck Mandy from behind while she worships my cunt. I reach out for his cock, which is hot and huge, and I tell him, "Fuck her, David. Let her feel your big cock."

David asks me if I'm sure, and I nod while coming once more. He positions himself behind Mandy, and she raises her buttocks in anticipation. Moving her mouth off my cunt for a moment, she cries out, "Stick it in me. Put that big cock in my pussy, stud!" David rams his cock home, and Mandy moans.

I let him thrust into her for a few minutes, being content with watching them fuck furiously. Then I reach out and pull Mandy's face back between my thighs. With each of my husband's thrusts into her pussy, her face presses against my slit, bringing my pleasure to new heights. I am crying out now, lost in passion. I can hear David sliding in and out of my beautiful friend's wet cunt and her cries that she is going to come. As the first spasms rock her body, she lifts her head off my pussy again, and I slide my finger into its wetness.

I am playing with myself, watching my husband fuck my friend and loving every minute of it. David growls that he is about to climax, and I tell him that I want to see his cream all over my pussy. He thrusts harder into Mandy and pulls out just before the big moment. She scoots over and holds his cock while he strokes it furiously over my pussy. Mandy helps him pump, and suddenly the first ribbon of come shoots out of his dick, all white and creamy.

I massage the come into my vulva, and he keeps ejaculating more. Mandy scoops some off his cock and licks her finger. David finally stops coming and lies down on the bed. My fantasy ends with the three of us cuddling and resting up for another round of wonderful lovemaking.

—*Ms. K.H., Atlanta, Georgia*

High-Society Miss Would Welcome Some Blue-Collar Loving

Writing to a magazine like *Penthouse Variations* is not something I do all the time. In fact, this is my first and probably last letter to you. I didn't even know *Variations* existed until my wild and crazy girlfriend Stephanie showed it to me. She said it was more fun to take to bed than any of the guys we date. After reading it, I agreed.

You see, Steph and I reside in that precious world of the rich and influential. High society, if you will. Our parents are incredibly wealthy, incredibly successful in their respective careers, and incredibly protective. They view our desire for independence as adolescent rebelliousness, even though Steph and I are both twenty-three.

Our dates are culled from a list of well-bred young men deemed suitable suitors. Oh, they're nice, all right, polite and respectful and attentive, but being treated like a porcelain princess all the time does get

to be a bore. Steph and I are always saying how terrific it would be to date a hot guy with a vivid erotic
imagination, someone to whom we could suggest wild
and "dirty" things without hesitation. We also tell each
other about our sexual fantasies, and it was Steph who
talked me into sharing mine with you. It couldn't hurt,
she said.

As it happens, "hurt" plays an important part in
most of my fantasies. The kind of hurt that is very
pleasurable. Of the men I've been dating, the one I like
best is Charles, and he frequently appears in my erotic
dreams—only his name is Chuck, and instead of being
stiff and formal, ever the proper gentleman, he's strong
and assertive, treating me not like a breakable, pretty
doll, but like a flesh-and-blood female he enjoys bringing to orgasm time and again in a dizzying variety of
ways.

Chuck is not a very patient man and is quick to take
control when I act up. (I can be a bit snappish at times.)
In one of my more potent fantasies, Chuck—offended
by something I have done or said—orders me across
his lap for a sound spanking. I protest, although, of
course, a spanking was exactly what I wanted in the
first place. Chuck, seated in a straight-backed chair,
crooks a finger at me, and, head bowed, I walk over to
him and drape myself across his lap.

Slowly he lifts up my skirt and arranges it over my
back. With my panty-covered bottom now revealed to
his hot gaze, I mewl in anticipation and squirm on his
lap. Chuck strokes and squeezes my buttocks through
the silky underpants, teasing me the way he knows I

love to be teased. He runs a finger up and down the cleft of my ass, working the material into it, then begins a steady tapping on my asshole with that same finger. Slowly he pushes it inside me as I moan softly.

Now, after asking me if I am ready for my spanking and hearing my tremulous answer, Chuck inserts his fingers under the waistband of my panties and tugs them down my bottom until they are banded about my quivering thighs. My ass, naked and vulnerable, is now his to turn a blushing pink.

"Do you want it?" Chuck asks.

"Yes, spank me," I fire back, tensing my buttocks for the first blow.

My wonderfully aggressive lover brings his hand down on my right ass cheek, and I cry out. A moment later, he smacks my left ass cheek. With his free hand on the small of my back, he quickly establishes a delicious rhythm, alternating between buttocks, slapping one and then the other as tears fill my eyes.

Of course, I'm loving it all—the searing embarrassment of the spanking itself, the sound of Chuck's hard hand clapping down on my taut bottom, the feel of it, the heat that seems to be radiating from my ass to my pussy. Each smack seems to be nudging me closer to orgasm, and adding to my pleasure is the feel of my aroused lover's cock pressing up against my belly.

Several blows delivered in rapid succession have me teetering on the brink, and over I go when Chuck wedges his thumb into my asshole and slips a finger inside my soaked pussy. And the best part is that

I know there is more to come. The real Chuck, or Charles, would never think of spanking me. Nor would he think of tying me spread-eagled to the bed with silk scarves and eating me to a wicked orgasm, but that's exactly what he does following the spanking—sometimes.

Other times I'll fantasize that he puts me on my knees and orders me to suck his cock, which I do with unbridled joy. He'll tease me, of course, perhaps running the sticky head of his dick all over my face, or placing it on my tongue but then quickly withdrawing it, as I moan in frustration. Or—and this might be my favorite—he'll hold my head in place with his strong hands and gently but firmly fuck my mouth until all that sweet cream comes gushing forth and I'm swallowing greedily so as to not lose a single blessed drop.

Not surprisingly, given the types of men I'm required to date, I've never experienced anal penetration. When I'm really horny, I'll imagine Charles—oops, I mean Chuck—doing me that way. I see myself in a low crouch with my head resting on the bed and my bottom up in the air. As I whimper in anticipation, he greases my little asshole and his big cock with lubricant. My fingers dig into the sheets when I feel him pressing into me back there, the head of his cock suddenly popping inside me and making me groan. Carefully he eases himself into my upturned bottom, his cock stretching my anus, filling me up so beautifully. And then he's doing it, fucking my ass, slowly at first, and then faster and harder, until the feel of his semen spilling into my forbidden orifice sends the ecstasy of my own orgasm spiraling through me.

How terrific it would be if I could wave a magic wand and turn staid, stiff-as-a-board Charles into impulsive, adventurous Chuck, confessing to him my deepest, darkest desires, sure in the knowledge that he will act accordingly. Alas, that is never to be, but as Steph is quick to say when we're bemoaning our lack of imaginative lovers, "Thank God for fantasies!"

—*Ms. O.Y., Worchester, Massachusetts*

My Dream Domme Has Me Completely Under Her Spell

This is my very favorite sex fantasy about my perfect dream domme:

My mistress beckons me to her home. When I arrive, there is a note on the door along with a collar and a leash. The note instructs me to remove all of my clothes right there on the front porch and put on the collar. Moments later, I am standing there naked and terrified that someone will see me!

After what seems like an eternity, the door opens. There stands the most beautiful woman I've ever seen. She is six feet tall with red hair that falls to her ass. She is wearing a black leather corset, elbow-length gloves, black lace stockings, and spike heels. She commands me to kneel, and I find myself staring at a smooth, shaved pussy. How beautiful!

My visual delight is cut short by a sharp jerk on the leash. My dream domme orders me to crawl into the house. Obediently, I do as directed, admiring her beautiful bottom. She turns around suddenly and berates me for staring at her ass without her permission. She says she must punish me for that. To make sure I don't stare at her without permission, she blindfolds me. Before leaving the room, she tells me not to move.

I am kneeling there fantasizing about this gorgeous redhead when suddenly I am brought back to reality by a sharp smack on my bare ass. "This should teach you to admire me only when you are told to!" she barks. She proceeds to give me twenty lashes with her riding crop. When she is finished, she makes me thank her for my punishment. This I do, even though my ass is on fire!

My dream domme pulls me to my feet by the leash and orders me to follow her, which is no easy task as I am still blindfolded. She pulls me into a room and removes my blindfold. There is a long table with shackles at each end, and she orders me onto it. Mistress chains me spread-eagled to the table. She attaches nipple clamps to both my nipples, which really makes me squirm. She climbs up onto the table and straddles my face, ordering me to lick her to orgasm. I bury my face in her beautiful cunt and lick with wild abandon. After what seems like hours and many moaning orgasms, she pulls away from my honey-smeared face and releases me from the table.

"You did well today but not well enough to earn my

pussy yet," she informs me. "Think about that as you drive home." With that, she hands me my car keys and pushes me outside—stark naked!

—*Mr. P.K., Palo Alto, California*

Beautiful Actress Puts All She's Got into Her Role of a Happy Hooker

My girlfriend and I have a great relationship. Helen is an actress, so she brings a lot of inventiveness into the bedroom. One of our favorite things is role-playing, which we do every chance we get. We've played out several fantasies: teacher and student, master and slave, pretending to be shipwrecked on a desert island, etc. But there was one fantasy I hesitated to bring to her attention. I wanted her to play the part of a hooker.

I have long held a fascination for high-class call girls. I guess it started way back with the film *Klute*. I frequently peruse prostitution ads in underground newspapers and get quite a thrill fantasizing about visiting a play-for-pay gal. When the Mayflower Madam business was big news, I was beside myself with excitement. In reality, however, I knew I could never visit a house of prostitution. It just doesn't suit my personality, and I was convinced the actual experience could never match my fantasy.

When my birthday rolled around, Helen asked me if I had any special fantasy that I'd like her to enact. I figured now was my chance to level with her.

"What would you think of trying to play the part of a call girl?" I asked. She looked at me quizzically. "I would be your client. Our scene would be like a make-believe trick. I'll be your john. Just like in the movies."

Helen was quiet for a moment, then said she'd have to think about it. I didn't talk to her for a few days, and I feared I'd blown it. But one night I received a call from her, only it didn't sound like the Helen I knew. She greeted me very formally by calling me mister and ignored my attempts to start a regular conversation.

"I'm sorry, sir, I haven't the time to chat. My agency tells me that you desire an appointment. Would tomorrow be agreeable?"

Finally I was able to figure out what was going on. "Yes, certainly." We agreed to meet at a fashionable restaurant in Tribeca. I took it that I was to play the part of some hotshot Wall Street man. She would be my very expensive date.

The next evening I got out my most conservative pinstripe suit, put on suspenders, and splashed on some cologne. As I rode the subway downtown, I was practically trembling with nervousness. I had been intimate with this woman dozens of times, but tonight it would be like the first time, for we would be playing out a dark part of our sexuality.

I was early and took my seat at our table. When I saw Helen sashaying into the restaurant, my heart skipped a beat. She looked like a different person. Helen is a beautiful woman, a blue-eyed blonde, very petite, but with a country-girl quality that looks out of place in an urban setting. But now she looked like a sophisticated city slicker. Her tawny hair was swept up on top of her head, and her high heels made her almost as tall as me. She usually wears no makeup, but that night she was sporting quite a bit, and she looked smashing with her dark red lipstick and fingernails polished to match.

She was wearing a sleek black dress slit up the sides, revealing a good deal of her slender legs, which were now encased in the finest stockings. The neckline of the dress was cut quite deep, and when she leaned forward it was easy to see her fancy lace bra.

She took my hand warmly but professionally. After I sat down, she took out a cigarette. I quickly whipped out my lighter and lit it for her. Some women look extremely sexy holding a cigarette; Helen is one of these women. We ate an excellent Italian dinner holding a polite conversation. We pretended we had never met before. We talked about art, theater, a little politics, but nothing intimate.

After dinner we took a cab to her apartment. During the ride, her hand surreptitiously crept into my lap and drew soft circles over the fabric on the insides of my thighs. My cock was as stiff as a board and very apparent. She looked in my eyes and licked her lips. "My, my, do I excite you?" Her thigh was exposed due to her dress riding high, so I slipped my hand over to caress it. She caught me and slowly pushed my hand away. "Not now," she whispered.

Once in Helen's apartment, she turned on a lamp

with a soft lightbulb, undid her hair, and shook it out. She then turned to me, her lips moist and pouting, and said, "There is now the matter of the fee."

I pulled out my wallet. "How much do I owe you?"

"Two hundred dollars for an hour, one thousand for the entire evening."

I opened my wallet and pulled out ten one-hundred-dollar bills of Monopoly money. Helen nearly burst out laughing but quickly checked the impulse. Instead she took the money and spirited it away. "Very good, sir. Would you like a drink?"

We had a few snifters of brandy as she continued to tease me. She kicked off her shoes and ran her foot up and down my leg as we sat next to each other on the sofa. My wandering hands were not turned away, and after caressing her thighs a bit, they inched upward to her delicate panties. They were quite wet.

"Perhaps we should retire to the bedroom," she said softly. We rose, and she took me by the hand into her boudoir. Entering it was like seeing it for the first time. She had done a bit of redecorating, and it now looked like the inner sanctum of a premier courtesan. "Please undress," she said, her voice quavering. I quickly removed my clothes, but laid them down carefully on a chair. There was plenty of time. She sat on the bed with a cigarette, watching me. When I finished, she stood and removed her clothing slowly, lingering over each article. I observed, my cock sticking straight out in front of me, a divining rod that had found its treasure.

Helen turned down the covers and stretched out

on the bed, beckoning me. I slipped in beside her and took her in my arms. We kissed, just a peck on the lips at first, then a fiercer, hungrier union of tongues. My hands explored her back and dropped down to her ass, which I squeezed and probed. She stuck her tongue in my ear, something she hadn't done with me before. We drew tighter together, attempting to occupy the same space. She whispered in my ear, "Would you like me to suck your big, hard cock?"

I nodded, and she kissed a trail of lipstick prints down my sternum to my navel and then in a circle around my dick. She took my balls in her mouth and sucked on them; it felt as if she were trying to draw them through a straw. The effect was truly tantalizing. Then she popped my cock into her mouth and sucked me with infinite skill and tenderness. I would be at the brink of orgasm when she would stop and ever so lightly draw her fingernails up the shaft, leaving my whole body quivering like jelly.

Helen used this technique several times until I was mad with lust; I had to fuck her. I pulled myself up and told her so. And since this was a new experience, I was going to fuck her in a way I had never done before. "I want your ass," I said devilishly.

Her eyes lit up with excitement. "Well, that'll cost you extra," she said, her voice hardening.

I grabbed my wallet from the nightstand, pulled out a phony five-hundred-dollar bill and tossed it to her. "Would this be enough?" I asked.

She put the money away, and I laid her down on the bed. She lifted her legs, and I positioned them so they went far over her head, her toes touching the head-board. I sat back on my haunches, soaking in the awe-some erotic sight. Her pussy and asshole were pointing straight up, as if they were being served on a platter. I lowered my face and dined. Her cunt was creaming as it never had before. I rose and slipped my cock into her bubbling pussy. She was so slick that I had my shaft lubricated after only a few strokes. I withdrew from her cunt and moved my cock to the doorway of her dark passage.

"All right, Mister, fuck my ass!" Helen hissed, her fingers busy pulling on her nipples. Slowly, I sank my rigid member into the musky entrance of her upturned bottom. I surged forward patiently, concerned that she might not be able to handle my erection. Her moans of passion told me I needn't have worried. "Yes, God, all the way! Shove your cock all the way up my asshole."

It was done. I was balls-deep in her ass, and the sensations were indescribably phenomenal. I sawed my swollen manhood in and out of her with ever-increasing speed. Helen exhaled on every thrust, emit-ting an animalistic grunt. She had completely lost control. She locked her ankles around my neck and hung on for the ride.

Minutes later, I fired off round after round of semen into her bottom. She tightened her legs around me and came with a scream. We collapsed and lay heavily on the bed, our limbs outstretched, our hearts pounding, breathing heavy like winded decathletes.

When we recovered our strength, we bathed together and began our lovemaking anew. This time I fucked her sweet pussy. Before the evening was over I would come in every one of her orifices. She would have twice as many orgasms as me.

The evening was a triumph. Helen gave a masterful performance, playing a bewitching seductress who comes out only at night. And I realized my most tantalizing fantasy.

—*Mr. R.O., New York, New York*

A Horny Mailman's Special Delivery for a Sexy Redhead

I am a mailman in a small town out West. Around here everybody knows everyone else; privacy is sometimes hard to come by. That's why I have a secret fantasy that I hope might come true one day.

I know just about every woman in town. I'm a twenty-five-year-old bachelor, but in order to have a little fun, I usually have to drive over fifty miles to go dancing at a club in another town. I usually score because I'm a good-looking guy, but what I'd really love is to get it on with someone on my route, so my fantasy goes something like this:

The old Clancy house, one of my last mail drops, has been empty for a year now. I hear that someone has moved in, and I get a notice at the post office to deliver mail there. The name's G. Packard. I can't help but hope that G. Packard turns out to be a lady—preferably a young, sexy one.

It's a hot, sunny day, and I have quite a few magazines and packages for the new occupant. As I walk under a rose arbor to the front door, I hear a dog barking in the yard. I ring the bell, breathless with anticipation.

"Just a minute!" Feminine voice. That's a good sign. The door opens, and this tall, red-haired Amazon stands there, wearing the sexiest white tank dress I've ever seen. She looks about my age, and I notice she has no underwear on under that dress.

"Hi," she says, smiling. "Would you like to come in and dump all that stuff in the hall?" I'm speechless. She has the most amazing brown eyes, sort of chocolate colored. Her dress clings to her every curve, and boy, does she have some nice curves.

"My name's Ginny," she says, extending her hand. I shake it and tell her that my name's Doug, the mailman.

"Okay, Doug the Mailman," she says with a giggle. "Would you like a glass of water or something? You look beat."

I tell her that would be real nice. And, of course, as she walks to her kitchen I admire her tight ass. Ginny returns with some cold water and tells me to sit down. She joins me on the sofa.

"I don't know many people around here. I'm kind of lonely. My grandma was the late Mrs. Clancy. I just inherited all this." When she talks, her eyes light up. "I'm really lonely," she continues. "And horny."

I can't believe it! Am I in a porn movie? When I tell her I can fix that easily enough, Ginny leaps right into my arms. She smells like oranges, and her long wavy hair is all over the place. I can feel her heat through her silky dress as I touch her firm breasts.

I pull her dress top down and massage her beautiful breasts as she moans. Her nipples are cinnamon colored, and I immediately lick them into hard little points. She tastes so good, clean and fresh. Ginny's hips buck up against mine, and my cock springs to life. She moves her hand from her hair and touches my cock through my pants. It twitches with desire for this supremely beautiful woman.

I peel the rest of her dress off her, and then she tells me to take all my clothes off. It's hot, and we're both sweating. I stand, remove my mailman's uniform, and then leap back on top of her. She's soft all over, but taut, and I lick and caress every inch of her. When I get to her ginger-haired cunt, she gasps out loud.

"Put your tongue inside," she whispers, and I dive in. Ginny's very wet, and her soft folds are nearly on fire. She tastes spicy, and I rub her clitoris with my index finger. Meanwhile, my cock is rock hard and aching for her. Ginny trembles. Her orgasm makes her cry out and then, a moment later, she tells me to fuck her. I immediately move into position, plunging my engorged penis inside her wonderfully juicy pussy.

She's so hot—like an inferno! I slide into her buttery tunnel with ease, and she clasps her legs around my ass, pulling me extra close. Ginny's like a firecracker, telling me to fuck her hard and fast. Believe me, I oblige the lady.

What great luck, I think, as I fuck her hard and

then soft, making her beg for my cock. We continue like this for some time until I tell Ginny I feel like I'm going to come.

"Wait," she says. "I want to taste you!" Moaning because I want to stay inside her precious warmth, I remove my cock reluctantly and slide it into her mouth. Ginny sucks it hard, and the sensation of her mouth feels almost as good as her pussy. After a few more of her loving licks, I come. My load is hot, thick, and creamy, and Ginny swallows it all and then continues to suck me until I'm soft. We lay there together for a while. Spent. Sated. What a wonderful woman.

Nice fantasy, right? I always think of my fictitious Ginny, especially when I masturbate. I'm sure that a lot of mailmen have the same fantasy, or one very similar. Maybe one of them got lucky already. Anyway, life goes on, as they say. I keep my fingers crossed and someday, who knows, I just might meet a beautiful red-haired girl with chocolate-colored eyes.

—*Mr. D.F., Via Email*

I'd Love to Watch My Husband Having Sex with Our Neighbor

A while back, in your travel issue, you published a letter from a woman whose greatest thrill is watching her well-hung husband pleasure another female. She related the experience she and her husband had while vacationing in Italy, in which they seduced a pretty

French woman. That letter really got my attention, for while I have never actually watched my husband with another woman, it's been a great fantasy of mine for a long time.

It was ten years ago that I first laid eyes on Mitch. We were at the beach, he with his buddies, me with my girlfriends, and one look at his handsome face and muscular body had me swooning with desire. And I wasn't alone. All the girls were checking him out, admiring his golden tan and noting his great smile, their eyes roving over his magnificent physique to eventually linger, as mine certainly did, on the snug black briefs that so perfectly defined his beautiful butt and hinted strongly at a really big cock. Happily, Mitch picked me out of the crowd, and we started dating. Six months later, we got married.

Today I'm as much in love with my husband as I was on our wedding night—and still deriving immense pleasure from his great looks and big cock. The fact that so many women stare openly at Mitch, hunger in their eyes, has never bothered me. On the contrary, his obvious appeal has spawned deliciously wicked fantasies. I don't remember when it all started—soon after we were married, I guess—but the idea of watching my husband fuck another woman to orgasm after orgasm continues to excite me to no end.

Sometimes a fantasy will spring full-blown into my head with little coaxing on my part. We could be out grocery shopping, for example, and if I notice a shapely female eyeing my husband, right away I'll envision her sucking hungrily on his big cock in the frozen food aisle or bending over in produce to take him from behind. The same thing happens if we're at the park, or at the beach, or even strolling down the street—let me spot a gal checking out my man and, presto, my imagination goes into overdrive.

Lately, however, my fantasies have focused on one particular female, my new next-door neighbor, Delores. She and her husband, Ed, moved in about three months ago, and a few days later, when Mitch and I went over to introduce ourselves and welcome them to the neighborhood, I knew she'd be the next woman Mitch would fuck in my dreams. Over coffee, she couldn't seem to take her eyes off him, and when we left I thought her panties had to be soaked. I was willing to bet she had dragged Ed up to their bedroom as soon as we were gone.

Since then I've had great fun imagining Mitch and Delores going at it hot and heavy. One of my favorite scenarios has Delores—who, by the way, is a very pretty blue-eyed blonde of medium height—sunning herself in her backyard, which she is wont to do most afternoons. I see her stretched out on the chaise longue, her body bare save for a skimpy bikini that barely covers her tits and pussy. Eyes closed, her hand wanders downward, slipping between her legs to gently stroke her covered sex. She's thinking of Mitch, of course, and how nice it would be if he were to suddenly appear at her side.

And he does! At least in my fantasy. Opening her eyes, Delores smiles up at my husband, who sinks to his knees and immediately takes over the stroking of her pussy. Delores sighs and, moments later, sits up so Mitch can remove her bikini top. Settling back in the chaise, she purrs her approval as my husband kneads her beautiful tits with one hand while continuing to fondle her pussy with the other. Now Mitch gets to his feet, and the giant bulge in his shorts evidences his arousal. Delores swings her legs over the side of the chaise so she is sitting erect, facing Mitch, and quickly pulls down his shorts and briefs to reveal his big, beautiful cock.

She comments happily on its size and then takes it in her mouth, sucking hungrily as Mitch places his hands on her blonde head and urges her on. With surprising ease, Delores succeeds in swallowing all but an inch or so of my husband's cock, using her hands on his ass to pull him as deeply as possible into her throat. She pauses a moment to lick Mitch's heavy balls, her tongue swiping at them playfully, and then again she's sucking on his cock, her blonde head bobbing rhythmically.

After a while Mitch steps back and orders Delores to her feet. "Get them off," he says, pointing to her bikini bottoms. Delores is quick to obey, and no sooner is she naked than my husband orders her onto her hands and knees on the grass. "Yes, from behind," my pretty neighbor says excitedly. "I love it that way."

Mitch wastes no time dropping to his knees and burying his well-sucked cock deep inside my neighbor's eager pussy. The forceful penetration wrenches a cry of delight from her throat, and she drops her head to the ground, cradling it between her arms as Mitch continues banging into her from behind. The expression on her flushed face eloquently expresses her fierce arousal, and she claws at the earth as Mitch pounds his cock into her. "Give it to me!" she shouts. "Harder! Faster!"

My husband does just that, slamming his member into the cozy confines of my neighbor's pussy again and again until he finally comes, his orgasm sparking Delores's. She cries out in ecstasy and then slumps to the ground. Mitch covers her body with his, the two of them resting like that as his cock softens in her pussy.

Sometimes in my fantasy I'll have my husband fuck Delores in the ass, which is something I personally enjoy every now and then. Usually I imagine them in her bedroom, but last Saturday night, when we had Delores and Ed over for dinner, I came up with the idea of having Mitch do Delores anally while she bent over the dining room table! Ed, having volunteered to help with the dishes, was in the kitchen with me. My husband and my neighbor were in the living room deciding on the video we'd watch later. But in my mind, they were still in the dining room.

Standing at the sink, my hands in soapy water, I felt my pussy grow damp as I pictured Mitch and Delores sneaking in a quick ass-fuck while they were alone. I had Delores bending over our solid oak table and Mitch quickly throwing her short skirt up over her back and yanking down her panties. Then, scooping up some butter from the dish still on the table, he greased her asshole as she whimpered in happy anticipation.

Whatever it was that Ed was saying to me went in one ear and out the other as in my mind's eye I saw Mitch push his cock balls-deep inside Delores' curvy backside. And then she was grunting and groaning as my husband fucked her, urging him on with gutter talk, telling him, in a voice choked with lust, how much she loved getting it back there. My husband finally spilled his load into my happy neighbor's back passage, provoking a moan of joy from her.

It was on rubbery legs and with a soupy pussy that I went into the living room when the dishes were done. Mitch and Delores were seated on the couch, looking over the movies spread out on the coffee table. I smiled inwardly, thinking that in my fertile imagination they'd had much more fun.

The day will come, I'm sure, when I'll tell my husband all about my secret dreams. Although I can't be a hundred percent certain, I think his response will be favorable and I'll actually get to watch him screwing another woman. For all I know, he may have fantasies about watching me with another man. Now, that would really make things interesting.

—*Ms. A.K., Cleveland, Ohio*

Shoe Salesman Witnesses Feats of Outrageous Pleasure

Let me start by saying that my profession and I are as far removed from the "Al Bundy" image as possible.

Yes, I'm a shoe salesman, but I happen to work in an exclusive women's boutique where shoes cost two hundred dollars and up. My customers are attractive and well groomed, and there are days when my cock remains hard throughout my shift. I've been treated to sights of exquisite lingerie, stocking tops, and even bare pussies.

My experiences to date have engendered some pretty wild fantasies in which I'm treated to more than just a look up an attractive female's skirt. In fact, I routinely lapse into my secret fantasy world after a particularly interesting day at the store. One day recently, ten minutes after I opened the shop, in walked a group of four exceptionally appealing women, triggering a sexy scenario I created that night at home.

The women were selecting styles to try on, and they didn't seem to mind that I was the only salesperson present. I took turns helping them and was treated to a few "glimpses," if you know what I mean. It was at this point that my mind began to wander into fantasyland...

I overheard one woman whisper to another that she wasn't playing fair, that the dare was to see who could flash me in the most subtle way. I went to the back room a few times and could hear them giggling. Their selections made, I started ringing up the bills. One of the women said they had a full day of shopping ahead and asked if it would be possible to have all the shoes delivered. When I informed her that we did not have a delivery service available, she winked and said, "It'll be worth your while." I quickly agreed and was given the room number and address of the hotel where they were staying.

I arrived at the agreed-upon time and found the four ladies seated on a sofa. Each one was wearing a very short skirt with her stocking tops visible. All were shoeless. One by one, each woman stood and introduced herself. Naturally, I gave them names that suggested sensuality. And, of course, each possessed a beauty of a particular kind. Alexandra was of medium height, with long blonde hair and an athletic body. Rachel was about the same height, but buxom with full hips. Maria had classic Latin features, dark skin, and a well-proportioned body. Finally there was Simone, a tall redhead with a pretty pair of pouty lips. And as I am a leg man, all my fantasy women had great legs!

"With all of our shopping, we've forgotten who bought which shoes," said Rachel. "Can you help us try them on?"

"But let's make things a little interesting," Alexandra said. "Can you strip down to your underwear?"

I grinned. "Well, if you really want to make this interesting, you ladies should do the same," I said boldly. Maria stood up and began to unbutton her blouse, and the others soon followed her example. I tore off my clothes, keeping only my briefs on. Within a few minutes, I was treated to the sight of four beautiful women clad in only panties, stockings, and garter belts. They all sat down and crossed their legs.

I knelt in front of Alexandra and took her foot in

my hands. As I gently massaged it, my eyes followed a path from her polished toes all the way up her leg. I surveyed the shoes, trying to remember which style she had purchased. I grabbed a pair of bright red pumps and slipped one on her. It was a perfect fit. "Well," she said, "you have a very good memory. Or was it just a lucky guess?" She placed her other foot on my crotch and gave it a quick rub.

"Can I be next?" Simone asked. The smoky-gray hose she wore created a very erotic contrast with her fair skin and red hair. Looking at the selection of shoes, I picked a pair of blue satin pumps. Unfortunately, they were not her size. Simone frowned. "That's too bad. If you had been right, I was going to give your cock a nice wet kiss."

Maria lifted her leg, pointing her toes suggestively. "Let's see if you're right this time," she said. I studied her foot, trying to estimate her size. She seemed to have the smallest feet among them. Still, I wasn't sure. My heart raced as I chose a pair of white pumps. Another perfect fit. "Good going, young man. Now, will you please pull down your briefs so I can get a better look at your cock?" I lowered my briefs, and my cock sprang out. Slipping her shoes off, Maria wrapped her nylon-encased feet around my cock and started jerking me off.

"You still have two customers left," Rachel reminded me, as she extended a leg toward me. By process of elimination, I fitted Rachel's tootsies with the blue satin pumps. She smiled and told me to stand up. I did as ordered. Sitting on the edge of the sofa,

Rachel brought me closer to her chest. She fitted my cock between her large breasts and asked me to fuck them. I pumped my cock in her cleavage and was close to orgasm when Simone intentionally cleared her throat.

"One more customer to go," Simone said. Without hesitation, I took the last pair of shoes, black patent-leather pumps with towering heels, and put them on Simone's feet. "You know, watching my friends tease you has gotten me real hot. Bring that cock over here." Simone licked me in small circular movements and then, without warning and in a single bob, she swallowed my cock to the root. A few strokes of her lips and I was ready to shoot.

Simone released my cock from the vacuum of her lips and manually stroked it in full view of her friends. I came with such intensity, I almost fell over. The ladies cheered.

Simone gave my wilting cock a kiss and then Alexandra scooped up some of my cream with her fingers and savored it. "Mmm, tasty." She crawled toward me and started to lick my cock clean as I sat on the edge of the sofa. Rachel sat beside me, offering my hungry mouth her tits. As Alexandra licked me, I nibbled on Rachel's nipples.

After a few minutes, Simone said, "You gave us quite a show. Sit back and enjoy this one." Simone had strapped on a dildo and now approached a kneeling Maria, who began licking the latex lover. Alexandra and Rachel watched with me from the sofa.

Simone's "cock" glistened as it slid in and out of

Maria's mouth. "Get on all fours, my pretty one," Simone said. "It's time to get fucked." Maria obediently got into position, and without delay, Simone buried the dildo deep in her friend's pussy.

Rachel leaned over and whispered in my ear, "I want you to fuck me like that." Then she positioned herself so that her ass was up in the air. Alexandra's hand guided my cock to her friend's wet pussy. I glided in effortlessly. "Let's see who can make their partner come first," said Alexandra.

Simone and I were soon fucking our respective partners with total abandon. Midfuck, Alexandra called out for a change in positions. Now Simone and I were on our backs while Maria and Rachel rode us. The four women were absolutely wild! Alexandra kept having us change positions periodically while she sat spread-eagled, masturbating.

"I'm coming," I began to gasp. In unison, all four ladies converged on me. Suddenly, there were four hot tongues licking my shaft and balls, lapping up my come. After they were done licking me clean, they took turns licking the remains of my semen from each other's faces.

Pretty wild, huh? Those four ladies I waited on during the day should only know how much pleasure they gave me that night.

—*Mr. T.T., Scarsdale, New York*

On the Beach at Midnight, Heart Racing, Awaiting a Passionate Lover

Allow me to share with you my favorite erotic fantasy. It goes as follows:

It is midnight and I am walking on the beach. It is misty, and I listen to the sound of the ocean waves rhythmically pounding on the shore. I am waiting for you. I am wearing a long cream-colored silk dress, with nothing on underneath. I sit on the sand. I unbutton my top and touch my breasts; my nipples are hard, longing for the touch of your tongue. My fingers wander to my pussy, which is wet with excitement. I caress the soft mound and find my button. In my mind I feel your lips closing in and trapping me. I cannot move. I slip fingers into my hole and imagine you are there. I am so wet, so hot for your cock.

I flick my clitoris, and it hardens under the pressure and with the anticipation of you. I am on the edge, moving my fingers in and out of my cunt, and then I taste my own juices, which are coating my fingers. I hear a noise and sense that someone is close. My heart is pounding. I open my eyes, and you are standing there, watching me. Your tight jeans give away your desire. I want to touch you, but you say no, you want to watch me. So I continue to touch myself and slip over the edge, sighing to the sound of the waves.

Now you come close to me as I stand up. I reach down to touch the bulge in your jeans, stroking from your balls to the tip of your penis. Oh, I want to taste you, to wrap my tongue around your thick, hard cock and lick you until you explode.

You grab me and hold me tight, smothering me with kisses, exploring my mouth and every inch of my face. As you rip my dress, pulling it out of your way, your tongue slips down to my nipples, making me quiver. I reach down to undo your belt, but you stop me. You pull me down to the sand, continuing to worship my body with your tongue. Your lips find my hard, pulsing clitoris as your fingers reach deep inside my hot pussy. God, I want you to bring me to an explosive orgasm. I scream because it's all so intense, but you don't stop, your lips remaining on my knob until my orgasmic quivering is done.

I reach to unbutton your shirt. Red flannel—I love red. I touch your chest and lick your erect nipples, inching my way down your furry chest. You ask me to lick your balls. They taste so delicately wonderful. I love doing that to you. Carefully, I suck one of your balls into my wet mouth, then the other, eventually working my way from the base of your hot, throbbing cock to the head. You shudder with excitement, and I want you to explode in my mouth and let me swallow your load. But no, you won't let me take you that far.

Pulling me up, you roll me over onto my back. Your hot erection enters my wet pussy, just a little, to tease me. I beg for more, but you hold back. Please, I want to feel you deep and hard. You turn me over, and I feel your hard cock against my ass. Yes, I want it there, but please go gently. Slowly at first, rhythmic like the ocean, building like the waves, I feel you spreading me. I feel like I'm going to rip apart! How can you possibly be so big?

But I want every inch of you. I want you to fuck my ass. Take me completely. You begin moving inside me, pumping your hot cock into my tight ass. We explode together, your hot come filling me. But we still can't seem to get enough. I don't want this moment to end.

—*Ms. A.B., Key West, Florida*

Now Who Will I Find in Our Bed Tonight? Cleopatra? An Apache Princess? Erika the Red?

Last Friday afternoon, my wife, Beatrice, called me at the office to say that Mistress Beatrice was in town and that she planned to stay at our house for the weekend. After five years of an inventive, exciting sex life, this was her way of letting me know she was feeling dominant and had planned a scene for our mutual stimulation.

When my wife wants me to wear the panties in the family, she calls herself "Mistress Beatrice." If she's feeling like a naughty lady in need of a sound spanking, she's "Bea." A session with "Beatrix" may be any kind of wild fantasy she's dreamed up. Sometimes I select the role, and sometimes she tells me what she's in the mood for. It keeps things interesting.

It happened that I had been through a real high-pressure week on the job, and I was in the mood for a laid-back weekend. I wanted to relinquish control, not make a single decision. Mistress Beatrice's visit was exactly what I needed.

It was dark when I arrived home, and Mistress Beatrice was nowhere to be seen. My instructions were attached to the refrigerator door as I entered the kitchen. The strains of soft classical music were drifting down from the bedroom, and the soft glow of scented candles flickered gently as I followed the written directions to proceed to the guest bathroom on the first floor.

I was already excited as I took a quick bubble bath. Then I toweled off and powdered my body. Although I keep my body almost hairless as a sexual turn-on, I ran the shaver over my beard to remove any traces of five-o'clock shadow. My mind was buzzing with visions of what I would find when I entered Mistress Beatrice's bedchamber. I hoped she would be wearing the red satin corset and thigh-high boots I had given her for our recent anniversary.

My own outfit for the evening was laid out on the bed in the guest bedroom. Mistress Beatrice hadn't selected much in the way of wardrobe—just a suede thong. I put it on over a semi-hard-on.

My dream dominatrix was sprawled across our bed, sipping champagne and reading *Penthouse Variations* by candlelight. Her outfit was not the red satin corset and black boots I had hoped to find, but a gold brocade and red chiffon Cleopatra costume that barely contained her breasts and scarcely masked her pouting labia. Her choice was a stunning success. Her mons was shaved clean, and an Egyptian goddess–style black wig concealed her strawberry-blonde tresses. I hardly recognized her in her heavy eye makeup. A bright red stone was shining from her navel, and ersatz gold and diamonds adorned her ears and limbs.

"Peel me a grape," she commanded, as she offered her glass for more wine.

I couldn't take my eyes off her as I fumbled with the bottle. I suddenly had a gigantic hard-on pressing against the tight suede. This Queen of the Nile routine was a whole new variation on her usual domination scenarios, and it was turning me on big-time!

"Be careful you don't spill any, my sweet slave, or you may have to lick it up."

I was so turned-on that I don't know if the stream of champagne that missed the glass and ran down her arm was an accident or a deliberate act. I saw it happen in slow motion, the golden liquid splashing among the bracelets, flowing down her arm to drip from the inside of her elbow, splattering over her magnificent breasts.

Beatrice sprang to her feet and delivered a stinging slap to my face. "Fool," she snarled. "Clean up every drop of the wine, first from my jewels and then from my person."

I dropped to my knees and begged for mercy. Beatrice sat on the edge of the bed and placed her feet between my knees. She removed her rings and bracelets one at a time and offered them to my mouth. I licked and sucked the sticky remnants of the champagne from her jewelry as she twisted and turned the jewels in front of me with her bloodred fingernails. My hard-on was throbbing under the confines of my thong.

Suddenly, I felt Beatrice's toes brush my balls. She raised her knees and began to massage my erection with the sides and soles of her feet. The sight of her brightly painted toenails tracing patterns in my erection-packed pouch was driving me nuts! Beatrice stopped her toe teasing and lay back on the bed. She commanded me to begin removing the sticky wine from her body.

Still kneeling at the bedside with a raging erection, I swirled my tongue over her hand and wrist. I worked my way to the inside of her elegant elbow and tried a little teasing of my own. I licked the silky flesh in a manner calculated to tickle my imperious Queen of the Nile. Beatrice went out of character for a second, squealing like a young bride and trying to squirm away from my swirling tongue. She grabbed my head with both hands and pulled me to her for a long, invasive kiss.

"How can I stay angry with my little slave," she murmured against my lips, "when he knows just what to do to soothe my wrath? Come now, and put that sweet mouth to work and make me come!"

I sprang from the floor and dove for the gold and scarlet lattice that marked the portal of her sweet cunt. I pawed the brocade and chiffon aside and plunged my face into her labia. Then, to my astonishment, Beatrice maneuvered her head toward my hips, groped under my loincloth, and guided my boner to her mouth. As her hot wetness engulfed me and her tongue swirled against the underside of my cock, I went over the edge and shot my load into her throat.

We thrashed around on the bed in a cloud of nylon, chiffon, and satin. One minute I was on top and the next I was pinned beneath her clasping thighs. Not content to bring me to a shuddering climax, the Nile Queen sucked the seed from my balls as I nearly drowned in the sweet swamp of her cunt. I knew she was getting off as much as I was, for the shuddering contractions of her pussy muscles on my tongue signaled multiple orgasms.

Saturday morning we played out a Wild West scenario in which my wife became an Apache princess and I was the last survivor of a wagon train. Later in the day, Beatrice suggested I change characters, so I donned my blonde wig and became Ingrid, a Nordic beauty captured by Beatrice's lesbian Viking, Erika the Red. Saturday evening saw Ingrid and Erika the Red cruising the local lesbian bars. I made quite a picture in my red spandex minidress.

On Sunday I sneaked up on her as she was reading the Arts section to ask her if it wasn't submissive little Bea, hot for dominant sex, who I'd spied masturbating between the sheets when we were sleeping in. Mistress Beatrice immediately produced a paddle and took me across her lap. She peeled down my briefs and spanked me to a glorious climax. Then she said she was too tired to really finish spanking my bottom to her satisfaction, so she told me to report to her after work today and promised to make my buns redder than the cardinal-red rep tie she ordered me to wear to the office.

So I'm sitting here at work now with a killer hard-on under my desk, waiting impatiently for five o'clock. Beatrice just called to ask me if I'm ready for her. Am I ever!

Take it from me, this sexual role-playing stuff is the greatest way I know to get in touch with all the facets of your sexuality.

—*Name and address withheld*   ⊙┼▪

Brawny Army Officer Takes Special Delight in Breaking in Young, Good-Looking Recruits

A fantasy I've had recently has been getting me incredibly hot. It goes like this:

I am a young private stationed at an army base way out in the country. My sergeant is a big, brawny hulk of a man who seems to have a weakness for clean-cut, young recruits. I notice his dark eyes following my movements in my tight khaki uniform and high combat boots. He goes out of his way to clasp my shoulder or tight ass in a comrade-like way. He creates a nickname for me, "Buck," and soon that is all I am called.

Near the end of one hot afternoon, I am summoned to my sergeant's private quarters in the rear of our barracks. Stepping inside, a strange sense of excitement grips me as I hear the pounding of a shower spray and see steam rising from his small bathroom. Straddling a low bench at one end of the room, I soon catch sight of the handsome officer's dark, hairy frame through the bathroom doorway. Water is dripping from his drenched body as he swabs himself vigorously with a thick white towel.

I start to speak, but he shakes his head for silence and gives me a slow salute. I am mesmerized as he approaches the bench and straddles it right behind me. I turn my head back and find myself staring into dark eyes that are gleaming with hunger. My sergeant leans forward to close his mouth over mine, and soon he is thrusting his rough tongue down my throat as his giant hands begin roaming over my hard, uniform-clad frame, sending hot bolts of pleasure through my body.

His mouth leaves mine only to attack my smooth neck with that probing tongue. This muscular brute's heaving frame pushes up against my still-clothed body, and shivers run through me as I feel his huge slice of meat jutting into my clenched ass cheeks. The officer's probing hands now slowly unbutton my tight uniform. Piece by piece my clothes are chucked aside until I am stripped down to my jockey shorts and high white athletic socks.

"Oh, Buck...Oh, Buck..." he groans, as his eyes take in my smooth, nearly naked body and the bulge jutting out through my white cotton shorts. He wants nothing more than to work this hot, young soldier over but good, and in a flash he has me on his huge bed and thrashing against his beefy body as we grope each other. The heated bull of a man can't take much more of this and soon pushes my thighs apart to get at my bulging prick.

I start moaning in pleasure as I feel his wet attack on my hard tool. Over and over, he swabs my shaft and balls through my jockeys as his strong, hairy hands slip under me to grasp my firm buns. The spongy head of my cock slips out over the elastic band of the shorts and immediately his mouth closes over it. The sensation of his tongue on my bare rod causes my young frame to buck uncontrollably.

By this time my hot officer is beside himself with lust and is all set up for the ultimate conquest of his prize buck. With his powerful arms, he flips me over and in one motion has my shorts peeled off and flung aside so he can zero in on my ass. I cry out with lust as his rough finger spears my asshole and pushes in with one long thrust! Soon he is pumping into my tight channel with deep thrusts as my uncontrollable cries of pleasure drive him on.

I yell hoarsely as my handsome officer suddenly replaces his fingers with the fat head of his huge dick. In one heart-stopping plunge, he thrusts his shaft all the way up my hot channel as searing bolts of sensation flash before my eyes. His lust is in power drive by now, and his jutting prong attacks my hole with thrust after long thrust, sending jagged pulses of hot pleasure through me.

Almost as unbelievable is the rush this powerhouse of a guy behind me is getting from the sensations of this slick fantasy fuck. He starts crying out uncontrollably, "Buck, man...oh, my Buck..." as our bodies synchronize into two fucking machines. His hand reaches around to pump my throbbing cock while his other hand hungrily paws my nipples.

When the big hunk's warm mouth unexpectedly closes over the back of my neck and he gently bites into the tender surface, I am sent over the edge. My bucking body gives a long final thrust, sending my tool through his huge jacking fist one last time. Jets and jets of fresh cream spray out of my jumping dick. Over and over my prick spurts, triggering the most delicious squeezes on the monster still plunging in and out of my tender soldier ass.

The horny officer can bear no more, and with a final hoarse cry of pure delight, his big sweaty frame leaps and his giant cock starts pumping thick, white cream up my tight young ass, just as if a fire hose had been shoved between my buns. Again and again our loads spurt out from churning balls until finally our sweaty bodies collapse together in a helpless heap on the bed.

—Mr. F.K., Tulsa, Oklahoma   O┱▪

Forest Ranger Camps in Wild Imagination of Hot Married Woman

I returned with some good slides and a great tan from our last camping vacation, but one of my favorite mementos was a fantasy lover I developed while my husband and I were driving along the Skyline Drive in West Virginia.

We'd never camped this far away from home, and it was rather amazing. The vistas were much grander than anything I'd ever seen before and the folks who ran the place were all military-looking—and hot. Driving into the national forest our first night, we were met by a forest ranger the likes of which I've never seen in Connecticut.

His uniform did not conceal his thick neck and broad chest. His curved, muscular arms swayed from his massive frame as he sauntered up to our car like a bulldog. He was as solid as a rock. He welcomed us and gruffly apprised my husband of the rules and procedures for this particular campsite. As the men talked, my eyes skidded all over his body and I undressed him in my mind, fantasizing about him as the pushy fuck of my dreams. His name tag said "Officer B. Smith." So just for fun, I named him "Brad," after a former boyfriend, as I watched him through the windshield and my mind began to wander...

As "Brad" explained the setup, I couldn't help but admire his great body. I wondered if his neck was any indication of how thick his cock was, so I got out of the car to find out. There was a definite bulge, but I couldn't quite tell how large it was because his pants were baggy. When I turned my attention to his face, I imagined he knew I was checking him out and that he flashed me a dazzling smile.

That night, I went for a stroll and happened upon a secondary lake not far from the one we were camped near. I sat with my back propped up against a sturdy tree, unwinding from the day's drive, listening to the quiet sounds of nature and masturbating. Of course, Brad was right there with me. I heard footsteps behind me and felt his masculine presence. "It's only me," he whispered, teasing me.

We talked for a minute or so, and I was aware of him looking me up and down. "I saw you looking at me today. You were wondering how big it is, weren't you?" I loved his audacity. "Do you want me to show it to you?" A tingle simmered within me, and I nodded. He unzipped his pants, letting them fall down around his ankles, and proudly displayed his cock. My question was impressively answered; it was the biggest cock I had ever seen, and my mouth watered. "You want to touch it, don't you?" he asked. Again I nodded and slowly reached out for it. He grabbed my hand before I made contact and said, "Not so fast. I haven't seen you yet." *So he wants to play a teasing game,* I thought. *Well, I can tease, too.*

I undressed slowly, stripping seductively for my forest ranger until I was completely naked. Then I backed up against the tree I had been sitting near, with my legs spread apart and my arms above my head. My nipples were standing at attention. I felt like a porn star.

Brad liked what he saw and came to me. First he took my erect nipples into his soft, warm mouth. His tongue was velvety-smooth, and I squirmed with each lick and suck.

He grabbed both of my wrists with one hand and held them in place high above my head, digging them into the rough bark. With his other hand, he grabbed my right ass cheek. Having him in control really turned me on, and so did the cool breeze of the night air across my exposed body.

He moved up to my mouth and kissed me fiercely, plunging his thick, stiff cock into my drenched pussy at the same time. The initial intensity of his cock forcing its way up my narrow tunnel took my breath away—God, I loved it!

He fucked me hard, forcing my back and ass to bang up against the tree. The feel of his heavy balls slapping against the underside of my ass cheeks increased my pleasure. He continued to feed me his manhood, in and out, in and out.

The friction caused my vaginal muscles to tighten around his girth, and my entire body tensed in anticipation of orgasm. An incredible sensation grew inside and exploded into a burst of delight. I moaned as I had never moaned before, and Brad increased his pumping speed, which sent him over the edge into orgasm. I felt his semen shooting from his hot, raw cock, filling me splendidly.

We cooled down together, Brad still inside me, pumping much slower now with both hands pulling my ass closer to him.

In the tent that night, I used this scenario of my forest ranger aggressively approaching me in the woods. But the next day, when I was alone, I brought my dream lover right into the sleeping bag with me.

In my fantasy, he was in the flap of our tent, and in a matter of seconds, our clothes were off and we were fondling each other. He had two fingers up my pussy, moving them in and out. Then he removed them and stuck them up my asshole! His wet fingers wiggling around in my asshole sent an exhilarating thrill through me; I begged him to fuck me from behind.

He flipped me over on all fours so that I was facing the front of the tent, slowly slid it into me, little by little, until I had taken his monster cock completely. His thickness was especially overwhelming at first, but I got used to it. Brad moved rhythmically in and out of me, and I closed my eyes while moaning with each thrust.

Wouldn't my husband love to see this? I was thinking, and I began to include him in the scene, peeking in. He never entered the tent, just watched. Having him watch me screw turned me on even more, and I was determined to give him a show. Brad was really ramming me now, my firm, round breasts rocking back and forth with his determined thrusts. I lifted one hand off the ground and began stroking my clit.

My favorite voyeur was still watching, and a rush charged through me, like lightning. I came for what seemed like an eternity, quaking with ecstasy. Brad simultaneously released his hot load while grabbing my sweaty breasts. We collapsed onto the soft padded flannel of the sleeping bag.

Happily, Brad's sexual prowess is not confined to the forest. He continues to entertain me at home, leaping into my imagination when summoned like the dutiful lover he is. He's pleasured me in countless ways since that camping trip, and not long ago I learned that in addition to a mighty fine cock, my fantasy lover has a simply marvelous tongue!

—*Ms. D.Y., Stamford, Connecticut*   O⊶◼

Camille Revealed in All Her Sexy Glory

My neighbor Camille is a real prudish type. She never swears and wouldn't dream of dressing sexy if anyone other than her husband is around. She's always covering herself in baggy clothes to hide her big, beautiful breasts. Her husband and I tease her terribly. She usually gets embarrassed and leaves in a few seconds. She's so shy about herself and thinks we're joking. But now, Camille, if you read this you'll know just how serious I am about wanting to fuck you!

The sexiest thing about Camille, in my opinion, are her eyes. She has the most beautiful eyes I've ever seen. Sometimes when she looks at me I get these horny flashes, followed by a hard-on that could break rocks. And because I'm a leg and ass man, I'd love nothing more than to see Camille in a garter belt and stockings. She isn't skinny, just softly rounded. The way I like 'em.

I've shot many lonely loads fantasizing about Camille—how her pussy would taste, how many times I could make her climax, what it would be like to make her nipples hard with my tongue and to look deep into her eyes as I came inside her. My number-one fantasy goes something like this:

I'm closing up my store one night, getting ready to go home, when Camille stops by, looking thoroughly ravishable. I let her in, and we sit down. I ask what I can do for her. She says she has something for me and hands me a couple of Polaroids of herself—completely naked! She says she picked them out for me. I reply that they're wonderful and that I'll "use" them a lot. I add, though, that nothing could compete with the original. To my surprise, she says, "That's why I'm here."

I lead Camille to the back of the store, out of sight. I put my arms around her and kiss her, finally getting to explore her mouth with my tongue. I then slowly move to her ears and neck, kissing and nibbling as I go. I ask her if I can remove her top and she nods. I do it slowly, so I can watch her gorgeous breasts fall out.

Soon I am urging her back on the bed, kissing, sucking, and biting her nipples, making them stand up and causing her to moan. This sexy lady is lying there, half-naked, just for me. I can't wait to get her pants off so I can feast on her wonderful pussy, and as I pull them off, I notice that Camille is wearing garters and stockings for me.

I start at her legs and slowly lick my way up each one. I can see and smell her pussy, untouched but hot just the same. I turn her over on her tummy and begin to feast on her upturned ass, devouring it before passing my tongue over her tight anus. After a bit, I turn her over and see that her beautiful eyes are glazed with lust. Camille asks me to eat her pussy, adding that she wants to come against my mouth.

I part her wet pussy with my fingers and begin to gently tongue her sweet hole. I work my way to her clitoris, and Camille moans loudly as I make contact with it. I use my lips and tongue on her sensitive love button, and she starts to come almost immediately, grinding her hot cunt against my mouth while pulling roughly on her nipples.

I kiss her, and when I ask her if she can taste her pussy on me, she moans and kisses me harder. My cock is so swollen it hurts as I rub it against her stockinged thigh. Camille kneels between my legs, holding my cock in her hand and rubbing it against her face before slowly pushing her mouth down, down, down over it. She deep-throats me until I make her stop. I want to save my load for our big finish.

Camille settles over my cock, rubbing it thoroughly on her wet pussy before finally taking it all the way inside her in one quick motion. She fucks me slowly as I squeeze her beautiful breasts, and before long she tells me she's ready to come again. She moves faster and faster on me, her ass slapping against my thighs. When she comes on my cock, I can feel her juices dripping over my balls. She smiles down at me with those sexy eyes and tells me to come inside her. Looking up at her, I finally fulfill a long-held desire by shooting a giant load into her clasping pussy.

We lie next to each other for a while, and I ask Camille why she decided to visit me. She answers that her husband suggested it, and she figured that after all these years of teasing, it would be as much of a turn-on for her as for me. Hearing this, I dive back between her thighs and begin to clean up the mess we both made down there.

Camille turns over on her tummy and asks me to lick her "back there." It's a request I fulfill without delay. After a while, I ease my finger into her asshole until it's buried to the knuckle. I slowly fuck her this way for a while before adding a second finger. Her sexy ass is loose and open now, and I coat my cock with the lubricant she happens to have in her pocketbook.

I position myself above her, my cock poised at her little hole, and then slowly sink into her lovely bottom. I begin to fuck Camille's hot ass, grinding my cock into her as she fondles her breasts and cunt. She's so hot and tight, so fucking sexy, that I can't hold back and let go another hot load, spurting my semen into the sexiest ass I know.

Well, that's my fantasy. And, Camille, if by some chance you're reading this, I hope it turns you on. And if it does, you know where I am!

—*Name and address withheld*   ⌖▪

A Hunk for Hire—Imaginative Couple Act Out Her Fantasy of Anonymous Passion

My wife and I have been playing gigolo games off and on throughout our entire five-year relationship. It all started when Janet confessed to a fantasy of being pleasured by an anonymous hunk. A man who would please her in any way she desired, then leave, never to be seen again. The mythical, voiceless fuck. It got me to thinking.

I was determined to fulfill my wife's gigolo fantasies the best I could. Naturally, I wasn't about to call Hire-a-Hunk, and being of firm body and limitless libido, I thought I could just as easily fit the bill. So about a month later, I put my game plan into action.

Janet had spent a week working late at her office, trying desperately to fulfill an impossible deadline. Tense and frazzled, I knew that what she needed was a break. But I didn't want to walk in on her and offer my services unannounced, so I arranged for one of her coworkers to give her a call and tell her she was being sent a "present" as a reward for her hard work. An hour later, I showed up.

I had prepared myself for the part, discarding my familiar jeans and T-shirt for designer clothes. I had also applied a dab of oil to my hair, combing it straight back instead of to the side. A touch of cologne completed the new me.

I entered my wife's private office and introduced myself as "Chuck, from the escort service." Janet, surprised at first, quickly fell into step.

"What a nice surprise," she said with a sly smile.

"I was told that you've been under some stress lately," I said, as I locked the office door behind me and turned off the overhead lights, leaving the room cast in the soft glow of her desk lamp.

"I have, indeed, Chuck," Janet said, suppressing a laugh.

"Perhaps I can be of some service," I said, sitting on the edge of the desk. "Your pleasure is my command." I wondered if this was how the pros did it. Sounded a bit hokey to me.

"Let me get this straight," Janet said, chuckling. "You're here from an escort service, a gift from a friend, and for the next, what, hour, you'll do whatever I want sexually?"

"You got it," I said. "That is, if you want it."

"Oh, Chuck, you don't know how long I've been sitting behind this desk daydreaming about getting it."

"Why don't you come over here?" I said. "We'll start by undressing you."

With that, my wife got up and walked around her desk to stand before me in eager anticipation. Knowing that it was more than the simple act of undressing her that counted, I praised every inch of her body as I bared it, telling her what a sexy lady she was, what beautiful smooth skin she had, and how lucky I was to be there for her.

Janet took it all in, and as I spoke I could see her embracing her fantasy, her imagination replacing her husband, Hedrick, with a stud named Chuck.

"Oh, what beautiful breasts," I whispered, running my fingers along the edge of her black lace bra.

"You like them?" Janet asked in a quiet voice.

"Oh, yes." I sighed. My wife's fantasy was working for me as well. I was getting off on the idea of bringing pleasure to a lady unknown to me. Unfastening her bra, I unleashed her firm breasts, scooped them up into my hands, and began to feast. As I ran the tip of my tongue sensuously around the edge of her silver-dollar-size areola, I felt Janet's body shiver under my touch.

"Oh, that's nice," she whispered. "You don't know how much I needed this."

Wrapping my lips around a fat nipple, I pulled that little nub of crinkled flesh deep into my mouth and sucked on it for the longest time.

"You do that so well, Chuck," Janet said with a sigh. "But don't neglect the other one."

I scooped up her other breast and smothered it with my mouth, sucking hard on her nipple while she tilted her head back and let out a breath. I really got into it, my imagination awash with the idea that I was servicing a woman who hadn't had sex in some time.

"Would you like me to eat you?" I asked.

"That would be nice," she said.

"It would be my pleasure," I said, and Janet beamed.

Sitting back in her chair, Janet pulled her panties down and spread her legs wide, her dark bush glistening with her growing passion. Kneeling before her, I wrapped my arms around her legs and brushed my cheek against her soft thigh.

"Such a nice pussy," I whispered. "It isn't often that I have the honor to eat such a sexy lady."

Knowing how much Janet enjoys oral sex, I used every trick in the book and then some. Beginning with little teasing flicks of my tongue against her engorged labia, then changing to long, luxuriant strokes along the full length of her pussy. Again and again I licked her, beginning at the very base of her pussy and sliding my tongue slowly up to her clitoris.

My "client" sat back in the swivel chair and sighed deeply, spreading her legs even more for me. And soon, with my lips wrapped firmly around her clitoris, my hands under her ass, I felt Janet's body jerk and twitch as one wave of pleasure after another swept over her. When it was done, she lowered her legs, caught her breath, and glanced at her watch.

"Fifteen minutes to go," she said in a breathless voice.

"Just enough time for me to fuck you," I said. "That is, if you wish."

"I wish! I wish!"

"I'm going to fuck you like you've never been fucked before," I said, totally involved in the fantasy.

Still kneeling before her, I held my cock in my hand and guided it into her soaking pussy. We both watched as the knobby cockhead slipped between her pussy lips.

"You like that?" I asked.

"Oh, yes," she moaned.

"Tell me how you want it," I said, my cock pulsating in her pussy.

"I want it hard, Chuck. Give it to me hard."

"You got it, lady," I said. I wrapped my arms around her waist, buried my face in the warm fleshiness of her breasts, and proceeded to fuck her like there was no tomorrow. I went deep with every stroke, feeling the full length of my shaft driving into her warm pussy.

Janet sank into the chair, her hands clutching the arms, her breathless voice egging me on. Grabbing her ass in my hands, I pulled her to me as I fucked her, slamming her pussy onto my cock with every stroke. Janet's back was arched, her head tilted back, and her face contorted with pleasure. Her cries of ecstasy filled the office. I couldn't help but think what a great fantasy this was. Here I was, pretending to service a lady's sexual needs, and I was as turned-on as she was!

A quick glance at her watch told me that our time was up, but I decided to put in some overtime. Pulling out of my wife, I turned her around in the chair, praised her for her perfect ass, and then proceeded to take her from behind. With my hands on her ass, I plunged, telling her how much I enjoyed fucking her tight little cunt.

I drove into her until my heart was pounding and my cock was packed full of the passion that screamed to be released. I pulled out, held my cock in my hands, pumped once or twice, and sent a long stream of semen splattering all over her arched back. Satisfied, I reached for some tissues and cleaned her up.

"Wow! That was excellent, Chuck," my wife said with a sly smile as we dressed. "Maybe you'll come back another time."

"Undoubtedly" was all I said. The illusion of having serviced her was still fresh in our imaginations, and I didn't want to say anything that would shatter that illusion. So, I simply dressed, bid "my client" a good evening, and left. Later that night, Janet and I made slow and easy love, our desire for each other engulfing us.

—*Mr. H.T., Youngstown, Ohio*

Horny Sailor Dreams of Sharing Pleasure with His Wife Upon His Return Home

I am currently in the navy and have not seen my wife for over three months now. Being separated like this is not easy for either of us, but we manage to cope by writing letters to each other in which we describe our dreams and desires. My last one went like this:

Now that you're ready to turn in for the evening, relax and let your imagination take over. You're probably wearing a shirt to sleep in. Go ahead and take it off. As you read this, run your fingers softly over your stomach and your sides. Imagine that it's me caressing your skin, my hands sliding smoothly up and down your body. I lift your breasts in my hands. They feel soft yet still firm. Lightly massaging them makes you moan slightly. I bend over to give each nipple a little kiss and flick it with my tongue. They stiffen.

Moving down your body, I caress your thighs and then your calves. I softly knead my way back up your legs to the top of your thighs, and you open your legs for me. Again my touches are feathery around the insides of your thighs. No, I'm not going to touch your pussy yet, but I can see that it's getting wet. You want me to rub it, to lick it, but I just keep stroking your thighs and move back up to your breasts. As I massage your nipples between my fingers, I pull on them the way you like. They look so sexy stretched out. They need my mouth on them. They need to be licked.

I take each breast in my hands and lick around the

nipples, one at a time. I lick around an entire breast and then come back to your nipples and take one into my mouth while tweaking the other between my fingers. They're so stiff. As I suck, I flick them with my tongue and lightly nip at them. Succulent. My cock is getting hard just thinking about you. I'll have to jack off later.

I start kissing each breast and move down your belly, again kissing and licking all the way to your mound. I kiss it and then skip over to your thighs. No pussy yet. Again I caress them, lightly lick them. You get goose bumps. Up and down each leg I go, licking around your knees and back up to the crease between your legs and your pussy. It's so sensitive there. Licking softly up to the small amount of hair there, I nuzzle my nose in it. I can't stand it any longer. I must taste you.

I brush your clitoris softly with my tongue. You arch your back and moan. I lick the lips first on the outside and then spread them. They're pink and wet. I bury my tongue between your folds. You taste and smell fabulous. I lick up and down, up and down. Spread those lips for me, baby. I want to eat you up. I can't get enough. I go back and forth, flicking at your clitoris, plunging my tongue deep inside your sweet pussy. I love to fuck you with my tongue and rub your juices all over my face.

But now I need to be in you. I climb up between your legs and rub my hard cock over your hot, juicy pussy. Slowly, I start to penetrate you, then push in hard. You gasp. Your silky pussy wraps around my cock like a glove. I start stroking in and out, slowly at first, but after a few strokes I speed up. You make me so hot; my cock is like an iron pipe. I hold your legs apart and pump into you hard and fast. Rub your clitoris while I fuck you. You're so wet. I have to taste you again.

I pull out, bend over and lick your pretty pussy. You drive me wild. I have you turn over on your hands and knees and then I jam my cock into you from behind. As I pump into you, I grab your ass and squeeze it. Your moans are a turn-on. You keep rubbing your clitoris and grabbing my balls. All of a sudden I hear you cry out and feel your pussy clamp down on my cock. I can't stand it any longer and stiffen as I come inside you in three powerful bursts. The feeling is tremendous!

I fall off you as we both relax, and I hold you in my arms. I rub your breasts and kiss you as you massage my softening cock. You can still taste your juices on my mouth. We rest for a few minutes, and then I take a couple of licks of your pussy and kiss it because you make me feel wonderful.

—*Mr. A.E., San Diego, California*

Domestic Bliss—Restless Single Woman Comes Up with Her Ideal Mate

I am an attractive, single, twenty-six-year-old woman who would like nothing better than to settle down with the right man. I date frequently but have yet to meet the perfect man for me, like the one my fertile imagination has conjured up to keep me happy at bedtime. Domestic bliss is at the heart of my fantasies, and so I envision a man as capable in the kitchen as he is in the bedroom.

For example, I could wash the dishes while he dried and put them away, provided he kissed the back of my neck, put his hand on my breasts, or stroked my bottom during the process, both of us knowing that later he would take me to bed and we would make love—exquisite love—raising me to the heights of ecstasy.

I want a man who will caress my body, who will want to stroke my back until his hands move right down to my bottom and his fingers find my anus. That would give me a wonderful sensation. In fact, I want him to turn me onto my tummy, open my legs wide, and play with me.

Actually, I long for him to give me an enema, taking his time over it, pausing frequently, removing the tube and then putting it in me again. It would make me very, very wet and ready for him. Then I would want him to turn me over and kiss my shoulders, moving down to my breasts, kneading them with his hands while his lips caressed them. That would bring me almost to the point of orgasm. I would be very near and almost frantic, knowing all the time he would take me completely, going deeply into me.

In my fantasy scene, my lover now moves on top of me and I open my legs for him, lifting my knees up so he can go deep inside me. He would make me come almost at once, making me feel as if all my nerves were being short-circuited. He wouldn't stop; he would go on and on and on until I cried out, begging him to stop but knowing he wouldn't until I had another orgasm—six, seven, or more in fairly quick succession. Then he would pull out of me—a devastating moment—and turn me on my side with my back toward him.

My fantasy lover now draws my knees up toward my tummy. His hands move all over my body, caressing it, holding my breasts. Then he thrusts into me from behind, and I come again. He would turn me onto my back again, put two pillows under my bottom, then slowly and deliberately open my legs, raise my knees, and go deeply into me again. We would come together, beyond control, after which we would both relax together, completely exhausted.

Where, oh where is this dream mate of mine?

—*Ms. V.B., Oak Ridge, Tennessee*

Woman Envisions Herself in the Arms of a Prima Ballerina

When I was a child my parents sent me to ballet lessons—and I hated them. I was not as coordinated as the other students, and my body just didn't seem to be as fluid. Today, as an adult, I no longer have two left feet, but I will never be as graceful as a ballerina.

And my body has settled into what is euphemistically referred to as a Rubenesque figure: wide, fleshy hips, large, heavy breasts, and many womanly curves. At least I am able to enjoy watching ballet, though, and when I do, I sit mesmerized, marveling at the beauty of the dancers. It is at the ballet that I engage in my favorite fantasy.

I am waiting backstage after a particularly moving performance of *Giselle* with a bouquet for the prima ballerina. I want very badly to see her slender limbs up close. There is a slight chill in the air as I huddle in the near dark, waiting for the door to open. Many of the other dancers have been flitting by on their way to parties or dinner, and I wonder if perhaps the prima ballerina has left through another door. But then there she is, looking directly at me as I hand her the bouquet of fragrant lilacs.

"Thank you," she says, her voice as clear as her flawless complexion. There are rose blossoms in her cheeks, forget-me-nots in her eyes, and her fine, flaxen-colored hair is wound tightly into a bun on the crown of her elegant head.

"You were wonderful," I manage to gasp, so taken am I with her beauty.

"Thank you again," she says warmly, her lush eyelashes fluttering.

"Where are you going now?" she asks. "Dinner? A party?" I admit to her that I have no plans. "Perhaps you would like to join me," she says invitingly. "I always follow a performance with a long walk . . . to relax." I graciously accept and follow her as she starts out briskly toward the river.

As we walk, she asks me about my interest in ballet and what I do for a living, and I answer her shyly. She tells me about her years at Juilliard and her travels, and I take it all in hungrily. When we come to the river, reflecting a brilliant moon, she sits down on a park bench and pats the spot beside her. "Sit, sit," she suggests. And I do.

For a few minutes we sit in silence. I am barely able to breathe because I am so electrified by our closeness. Her delicate ankles are crossed, every bone in her thin, strong legs visible through her luminous skin. Her delicate hands are crossed in her lap, and I long to hold them to my breast, to touch her tiny, firm breasts. I want to pull the pins from her hair and run my fingers through her soft curls. I am aware that my breathing has quickened, coming now in almost audible pants. I stare at her long legs, so gracefully tangled beneath her, swinging from the bench. "I'm a bit chilled," she whispers. "Would you mind putting your arm around me? I can feel your warmth from here." My tongue feels like a fat sea sponge and I am unable to answer her, but I carefully slip my arm around her tiny waist. She wriggles closer to me and leans against my shoulder. I am terrified that she will hear my heart pounding. I am so aroused. I wonder if she has any idea how her beauty affects me. And then she reaches into my blazer and cups my breast.

"I've always wondered what it would feel like to have a large bust," she says, hefting my breast and running her thumb over my stiffening nipple. "Yours certainly feel wonderful." I am still unable to speak.

"Would you like to feel mine?" she asks, turning toward me. "They're really nothing in comparison to yours."

I swallow dryly and croak, "No, no. They're positively exquisite. I've fantasized about breasts such as yours for years." And I hesitantly touch them, two tiny, firm mounds, with nipples poking stiffly underneath her leotard.

"Do you like my body?" she asks impossibly. I nod an emphatic yes, my gaze fixed on her tender breasts. "I'd like you to have it," she chirps. "But just for tonight." And she laughs. With the pulling of a few Danskin ties, her leotard and wraparound skirt fall to the ground, and she stands before me in nothing but her pale coral tights and fragile ballet slippers. I can see her dark blonde thatch through the transparent pink fabric and I press my fingers into the soft tuft.

"That's nice," she purrs. "Please, don't stop." She steps closer to me as I sit on the bench, admiring her attenuated limbs, her waspish torso, and her hip bones poking sharply through her tights. After sliding my palm suggestively between her legs, I pull at the elastic waist and roll her tights down to her ankles, revealing her pale triangle and long, slender legs. She spryly steps out of her slippers and the curled-up tights, huddling close to me. I pull her to my chest, wrapping her in my blazer, inhaling the smell of the shampoo, sweat, and hair spray in her perfect little bun.

"May I take your hair down?" I whisper.

"Of course," she mumbles into my chest, her warm breath setting my skin afire.

As my fingers search for her hairpins, I feel her fumbling at the buttons of my blouse. One by one I pull her hairpins loose; one by one she unfastens my buttons. Her blonde curls fall loosely to her shoulders and I rake my fingers through them, holding my breath as I feel her moist lips caress my cleavage.

Now I have her here in front of me, naked and unfurled. Her hands and mouth are working my nipples and skin, and I am paralyzed. She senses my uncertainty and leans up. "Is this what you want?" she asks, proffering her blonde pussy. I can smell her sex, intermingled with a sweet tang of sweat, only inches from my face. My heart is lurching crazily in my chest. "My goodness, you're shy," she exclaims, and in seconds she is climbing onto my lap. Then she stands, placing one fragile foot on either side of my thighs and turning her toes in a dainty second position. She tenses her thighs in a *plié*. The delicate hairs of her pussy graze my face. The wrinkly, pink folds of her labia are before me, and I finally overcome my reticence.

Reaching around, I firmly grip her shapely, flexed bottom and pull her forward. My nose is lost in her tangle of pubic curls, and I extend my tongue, sliding it back and forth over her tiny protruding clitoris. She squeals and squirms and urges me on. As I rock her body toward me rhythmically, she rides my lapping tongue until I feel every sinewy muscle in her body tense. I frantically flick her clitoris with my tongue until her knees shake, and she moans deeply, the tension flowing from her. With a sharp sob and one last shudder, her orgasm consumes her completely. She collapses into my lap and kisses me deeply, her tears mingling with the taste of her tongue and my tongue and the taste of her sex.

I cradle her gently, listening to her breathing. "You were wonderful," she whispers, gazing up at me, the pastel bouquet of her features now in full bloom. "Thank you," I reply.

—*Ms. S.L., Great Neck, New York* O╌▪

Computer Ace Dreams of Desktop Delights with a Coworker

I'm thinking about her tonight. I can't help it, can't get her out of my mind. I try to work. I stare at the computer screen until it goes blank and those little fish and flying toasters wiggle and slide across it.

I shake my head to clear her image, wiping my mind clean like an Etch A Sketch. I force my fingers to the keyboard, my eyes on the sheets of numbers on my desk. Typing, fingers flying, I finally stop to take a sip of coffee, but my mind fills again with another type of figure . . . hers.

I want her so bad. And how will it go? Yes, I'll take her panties down, pull them way down to her ankles, bend her over the desk, and oh, feel how wet she is, so slippery. Sliding into her feels so good, my hand in her hair, touching the back of her neck, the fine little curls that get damp as we move.

Or maybe I'll bend her over first, press my lips to her pussy through the thin cotton of her panties, reach my fingers inside the waistband to tease the lips of her flower until she moans and arches her back, begging for it, begging me to put my cock inside her, to plunge it deep where it's velvety soft and hot.

I know she's hot for me. In the office, when she passes my desk, she's always just looking away when I turn to face her. Her eyes were obviously on me only the second before. I can feel her eyes on me, moving over me, trying to get in my head and tell me what she wants.

I know what you want, sweetheart, I know that you need my cock pulsing inside you. Dancing inside you. I'll make love to you so nice, baby, so fucking nice. I'll make you moan, low, like an animal. I'll make you beg me to do you harder. But I'll keep it nice and easy, back and forth, steady now, steady, and then . . . I'll ravage you. I'll thrust it in so deep that you'll gasp and close your eyes, and you'll scream.

I know what she wants because she touches herself when she looks at me. She runs her hands down her thighs to smooth her skirt. She fingers her necklace and then lightly, so lightly, traces her fingertips over her breasts, as if she's adjusting her vest, as if she's not wishing that my fingertips lingered there or that my mouth was kissing her there.

Oh, yes, baby, my mouth on your perfect breasts, licking and sucking. I'll clear away the papers on my desk—I'll take you face-up, pull that little business skirt off your naughty body, peel your stockings down, grab your wrists and tie them together above your head. You want it like that, don't you, baby?

How deliciously helpless and vulnerable you would be like that, sprawled atop my desk with your clothes in disarray, your purring pussy on display, your beautiful face a mask of desire as whimpers of lust bubble up from your throat. How wonderful it would be to see you so turned-on that you couldn't think straight. And to know that I have what you crave.

$657 on business lunches. $3,200 for rent. $235.50 at the copy shop. Flip the page. $1,300 professional services. $125 for parking. $340 telephone. Late on invoice #109 to freight. Fuck 'em. Let them wait. I need her.

She's like a kitten the way she tilts her head forward when she talks to me. I know she wants me to kiss her, to brush her bangs away from her eyes so that I can study her face. She's so composed, so official-looking in those business pumps...

Baby, I want you in fuck-me pumps, five-inch stiletto heels and a cutaway teddy that leaves your nipples exposed. I want to bite them, nibble on them while you're tied there, helpless. I want to make you come like that, by sucking and biting on your nipples. I want to feel your body grow rigid right before you come.

On Friday, when she stopped by my desk, she called me Matt for the first time.

I want to hear you call my name as you come, begging me to take you all the way, take you over the crest. I want to hear you say it, "Matt, please," desperation in your voice, "Oh, Matt..."

I know how she'll look when she comes. I've fantasized about it for hours. Her serious expression relaxes. Her long lashes flicker against her cheeks—she's trying to keep her eyes open to watch me, but with the thrusting of my cock inside her she can't help but close her eyes and lean her head back. She bites her full bottom lip with her teeth.

With your head back, exposing your lovely long neck for me to kiss, I can feel your heartbeat in your throat, that lifeline telling me how excited you are, speeding up, beating so fast, so hard, while I fuck you until we explode together amid the crumpled papers on my desk, the coffee cups, the manuals, the stacks of books and ring binders. Your curls spread over my keyboard, your tied hands rest on my monitor, your legs spread apart on the edge of my desk, one foot dangling over my briefcase.

I'll be the one to say it, to beg, "Please, baby, will you please come?"

I'll be waiting. And daydreaming.

—*Mr. M.S., Seattle, Washington*   ⊙┼▪

Imagining the Joy If My New Girlfriend Ever Reveals a Desire to Dominate Me

Several months ago, I started seeing a statuesque beauty named Amelia and almost immediately began fantasizing about her tying me up and doing all sorts of wickedly wonderful things to my helpless body.

I imagine that I have invited her out to dinner at a fancy restaurant. When we get to my Jeep, Amelia says that she's not really hungry and suggests that we pick up something at a fast-food place. I can tell by the mischievous look in her eye that she has a special evening planned. My heart flutters in anticipation of what may come. I order dinner at the drive-up window, and as we pull away she instructs me to park in the rear of the restaurant's parking lot. Amelia then reaches behind the seat and produces a small bag of toys. She demands that I remove my pants, then hands me a leather strap with a lock on it and tells me to wrap it around my cock and balls. I comply with my heart beating fast and blood pulsing into my cock. Amelia orders me to drive to a secluded spot.

As I drive through the city, she reaches over to my crotch and plays with my hard-on while informing me that I will be her slave for the evening and must comply with her every wish. She lifts her skirt to show me that she has on red thigh-high stockings and the red panties that I gave her for Valentine's Day. As I turn off the main road and head up into the hills, she demands that I remove my shirt, which leaves me totally naked.

I pull off the road into a stand of trees overlooking the city and stop the Jeep. Amelia tells me to get out and hand her the keys. I open the back of the Jeep, lay the backseat down, and spread out a blanket. Amelia takes a rope and attaches it to the strap on my balls, using it as a leash to walk me around the Jeep. She then hands me wrist cuffs and a collar and instructs that I put them on. My hands are shaking in anticipation of what lies in store for me. Amelia runs the rope through the crack of my ass and secures it to the collar. She then opens her bag and produces a riding crop. As I stand at attention, she runs the crop over my body, occasionally swatting my ass.

Amelia then instructs me to bend over as far as I can and I comply. In this position, my balls are pulled up even tighter against my crotch. She then states that I am to call her Mistress for the rest of the night and that if I forget I will be subjected to five swats for every infraction. To let me know she is serious, she proceeds to administer five sound swats to my upturned ass. The pain sends waves of sharp pleasure throughout my body.

Mistress goes back to the Jeep, reclines inside, and orders me to prepare her dinner. As I lay out the fast-food items for her, she barks, "Where is my drink?" She orders me to get the wine that is in the ice chest behind the seat. As I pour her wine, she lifts her dress to expose her pantied crotch. Rubbing her finger over her swollen lips, she informs me that her pussy will be my appetizer. I crawl into the Jeep and proceed to lick her pantied crotch while she eats her meal. After a while, Mistress instructs me to get on my back and then lowers herself onto my mouth. I know she is close to coming when she starts to rock back and forth across my face. But suddenly she stops and says, "I did not tell you to make me come, did I? Now eat your dinner."

I am required to stand outside and eat the cold

food while she oils up my still-hard cock. Mistress milks a small amount of sticky fluid from the end of my cock, catching it on the tip of her finger. She holds it to my mouth and instructs me to clean her finger. Mistress then asks me if I am thirsty. I answer yes, but I forget to end with "Mistress" and get five swats of the crop. After that, she holds up a glass of wine. I am told not to miss a drop as she starts to pour it into my mouth.

She orders me to kneel as she removes her panties, slides into the back of the Jeep, and spreads her legs so I can eat her. Her aroma and flavor are driving me crazy. Mistress grabs my head and pulls it toward her as she shouts, "Don't stop!" She comes intensely and then pushes me away.

Mistress instructs me to bend over and grab my ankles. She asks if I want my punishment now. I reply that I do, and she pours oil on my upturned ass and rubs her hand down the crack. She takes a small butt plug from the bag and inserts it in my anus. I am instructed to keep it in place, move to the side of the Jeep, and stand facing the door. She proceeds to give me ten lashes with a riding crop, pausing in between to pull on my cock and rub oil on my ass. Mistress then states that she wants to try something else.

She releases me and orders me to climb into the Jeep on my knees with my ass in the air. I am not to move under any circumstances. She finally removes the butt plug, saying that she is going to test her new vibrator. As she inserts it inside me, she reaches between my legs and pulls on my swollen cock. "You had better not come," she warns. She continues to fuck me with the vibrator until I am begging to climax.

Mistress picks up a black paddle and rubs it against my upturned ass. I am told to count the blows as she brings the paddle down hard on my ass over and over again. Next, I am instructed to get on my back on the blanket that has been placed on the ground outside. Mistress, who is still wearing her dress, stands over my head. I can see her beautiful crotch above me as she pulls on the leash attached to my balls. "You like what you are looking at, don't you?" she asks. "Do you want to eat me?" I reply that I do, and she slowly lowers herself onto me.

I eat her for a while, enjoying her taste and aroma, and then she stands and repositions herself so she is straddling my cock. She places the head of my cock at the entrance to her cunt. "How bad do you want it?" she asks. I beg. I beg like I have never begged before. Finally, she lowers herself onto me, enveloping my cock in her warmth and wetness. My orgasm builds quickly, and then I'm coming, my semen spurting up into her pussy.

—*Mr. W.B., Bismarck, North Dakota*

What She Wouldn't Give to Know the Passion He Harbors for Her

I've been happily married for two years, but every now and then I fantasize about having sex with different men. It's perfectly normal, and I know I'm not the only married woman in America who thinks this way.

The star of my dreams is a friend of a friend. Dominick is a total player and not someone I would risk my reputation for, married or not, but he's got to be the most attractive guy I've ever seen, the perfect female fantasy. He's a tall, lean Italian with dark hair, dark eyes, and a smile that gets to me. He looks like the type of man you'd see in a fashion magazine.

Dominick is such a guy—he practically breaks his neck to glimpse beautiful women every chance he gets. He loves attention, too, just as much as he admires his own good looks. In my fantasy, he's at the beach with friends when I approach in my French-cut bikini and greet him with a very friendly hello. Of course, Dominick gives his friends something to envy as he affectionately kisses my cheek and gives me a hug, as if we're intimate already.

I have to say that I'm looking mighty fine in my new bikini and my eye-catching tan, although I'm not nearly half as dark as Dominick. Then again, when it comes to the sun, my Irish paleness can't compete with his Mediterranean complexion. Looks-wise, I've been told I'm "real cute," and I'm confident with my small, firm frame. My hazel eyes are my best feature, I think. They change colors.

Dominick and I go for a walk along the water and, teasing his friends, he gives them a little good-bye wave. I decide I really want to shock him, so I turn to him and say, "I've always wanted to fuck you, Dominick. What do you think about that?" He tries to act suave, but I can tell he's been knocked for a loop. "Then I think we should fuck," he finally says with a sexy smile.

We continue walking barefoot along the water's edge, our arms now wrapped around each other's waists, until we reach what looks like the end of the beach. "My beach house is over there," he says, pointing in the distance. I'm glad he has a place for us to go, because by this time I'm really aching for him.

He rents the house for the summer with a couple of his friends, the ones we left back at the beach. And, because I'm controlling this fantasy, that's where we'll stay. We walk in through the front screen door and enter the living room. Men's tennis shoes at the foot of the couch and a copy of *Penthouse* that's opened to the centerfold give the bachelors away. We continue to the back of the house to Dominick's bedroom.

I get comfortable on the bed, and he stands there for a moment, drinking me in. "Well, what are you waiting for?" I ask innocently. He joins me on the bed and kisses me, cupping my breasts in his hands. I feel weak from his touch, but I keep my composure. Dominick reaches behind my neck with one hand to untie my straps, and my bikini top falls forward. Next, he's squeezing my baseball-size breasts and sucking my pert nipples. I'm looking down at his head, running my fingers through his wavy hair.

Dominick lays me down on his bed and gets on top of me, kissing me deeply. He's so big that I nearly lose my breath. But I can't interrupt him now, not when his harder-than-hard cock is pressing up against my thigh. Our kissing grows more impassioned, and I pull away to plead, "Fuck me." He starts pulling off the biking shorts that fit his muscled legs so well. I pull off my own bottoms, not surprised to see the big wet spot in the crotch area. Dominick groans and slides two fingers in and out of my pussy a few times before diving in with his nice, big cock.

"Uuuh…" I gasp when he enters me in one long, smooth movement. It's a delightfully tight fit. Right away, we're going at it like two cave people desperately rubbing two sticks together. The mounting friction causes our bodies to heat up, and soon I smell a mixture of sweat and beach. Dominick's tongue teases mine, turning me on even more, as he plunges in and out of my excited pussy. "Fuck me harder." I'm barely able to get the words out because I'm so overcome with lust.

The fire is building, and pretty soon I can feel it all over. I scream with the beginnings of a powerful orgasm, writhing underneath Dominick's still-thrusting body. Suddenly, I know not where I am, who I'm with, or even my name—only that I feel glorious and free. Then I am jolted back to reality by a hot stream of Dominick's come inside my pussy.

We hardly rest before I start stroking his cock back to life. But this time I tell Dominick I want him to fuck me doggie-style. I position myself on my hands and knees with my ass facing him. "I like it," he says, as he grabs a handful and smooches it. Then he is guiding his revived cock inside me. We decide to take it a little slower this time, and I try to hold on as we move back and forth. I feel the mushroom-shaped head of his cock almost pull out of my hole, then drive right back in. My entire body is rocking with the rhythm of our thrusts. I look down to admire the cleavage between my hanging breasts.

My fantasy lover's really slamming into me now. I stick my ass out farther and get down on my elbows, resting my head on the mattress. Dominick grunts with each thrust and, again, we're coming together, Dominick holding his cock deep inside me. We collapse, but before we fall asleep, Dominick looks into my eyes and asks, "Did I make them change color like that?" I tell him he sure did.

It's funny, whenever I see Dominick in real life this fantasy starts playing in my head. And I wonder if he sometimes fantasizes about one married woman in particular...

—*Ms. B.D., Islip, New York* ⊙━▪

Modern-Day Pleasures for a Victorian Lady in a Satin Corset and Lace-Up Boots

I lay on the rose satin sheets beneath the ruffled canopy of the four-poster bed, waiting for a fantasy to take shape in my mind. My fingers were gliding idly across my smooth abdomen. My red nails were a vivid contrast to my lightly tanned skin and the white lace of my garter belt. Sliding through my neatly trimmed pubic thatch, one finger eased in between the pouting lips of my pussy and rubbed slowly back and forth.

A picture of a Victorian couple in the stateroom of a ship came into focus—one of my favorite fantasies. Perhaps it came from the memories of being back in the old house that five generations of my family had occupied. Perhaps it was the garters and the old-fashioned bed. Whatever inspired my fantasy, I gave a moan of joy to welcome the phantom couple.

He was a distinguished-looking man in a white tie and tailcoat. As always, she was not yet fully dressed, and her face was obscured. She wore only silk stockings and black high-heeled lace-up boots rising to mid-calf. The heels of the boots were gracefully curved, the toes pointed, the calfskin glistening. The black silk stockings were drawn about halfway up her shapely thighs, leaving a gap of alabaster skin between them and a black satin corset she had just finished wrapping around her waist. She was connecting the fasteners in the front, but the garter ribbons still hung beneath the corset. Slack laces dangled from the back until the gentleman pulled them, transforming her cylindrical form into an hourglass as the whalebone stays flexed inward.

My fingertips massaged my clitoris with short strokes. Slowing down to make it last, I withdrew my hand and licked the thick, musky juices from my fingers. I wriggled my toes inside my pointed shoes and felt the snugness of my garter belt and its taut straps holding up my stockings. I imagined that the Victorian corset was around my own waist and that the steep arch of my foot was being caused by those laced boots—I could feel their pressure on my instep and ankle.

The woman bent over a sticker-covered steamer trunk to steady herself as the gentleman worked the laces tighter. Memories stirred. Had I seen a trunk like that? Where? But I focused again on the tightening corset, drawing in my breath as his pull on the laces constricted her waist even further, accentuating the hourglass effect. He knotted the laces and fastened the garters, drawing up her stockings. His large hands traced the tops of the silk stockings and gently kneaded her fleshy buttocks.

She did not protest when he slid a finger between her legs—indeed, she spread her legs further to let him probe without restriction. His hands moved to her pinched waist and turned her so that she sat facing him on the top of the trunk. The gentleman dropped to his knees, spread her creamy thighs, and buried his face between them, his hands massaging the luscious globes that pouted over the top of the corset.

My finger moved faster and my breathing grew rapid. My other hand caressed my breasts; I clamped a hard nipple between my thumb and forefinger so that the pressure enhanced my pleasure. I licked my parted lips, and the muscles of my jaw tightened as I tried to postpone the explosion. I held my breath, knowing that if I released it, I was gone. Then I could control my body no longer and my hips bucked as my breath burst from my lungs. I lay there savoring the aftershocks, eventually falling into a deep sleep.

Curiosity about the steamer trunk prompted me to drag my husband, Craig, up to the attic the following Saturday. He obligingly shifted generations of surplus belongings until I spied the trunk. He couldn't fathom my excitement until I dug into its depths and came up with a black satin corset and a pair of high-heeled lace-up boots. To Craig, the boots and corset had a different symbolism.

"Is Mistress Anna ready to retire to her boudoir?"

I was indeed, and I arranged the lighting and the draperies to suggest a Victorian boudoir. I piled my hair on top of my head and painted a thinner, more demanding mouth over my generous lips. Turning to Craig, I commanded him to strip, kneel, and smooth my stockings along my legs, kissing my feet farewell before he did so. I teased his cock and balls with my one foot as he paid homage to the other. His erection was ample proof of his excitement.

The ninety-year-old boots were still soft and supple, and I admired their workmanship. Even the tiny nails of the heel were perfectly arranged. I imagined the lovely click they would make on a hardwood floor. Dangling them before Craig's face, I indicated that he should slide them onto my feet and lace them. The coolness of the leather contrasted with the heat of my growing passion as they encased my toes and ankles. I used Craig's thighs as a temporary footstool, and I was pleased to see that those little nails had left their imprint on his flesh.

"Tighter!" I demanded, as he pulled the corset laces, drawing my waist in to an even smaller size. My image in the mirror gazed back at me—the Victorian lady of my fantasy, but this time in command, no longer submissive to her mate. Craig stood behind me, his cock straining, its tip glistening with precome. He understood that I was in control, but clearly our different takes on this fantasy were beginning to merge into one.

I lay back on the satin sheets, their rose a stunning contrast to the black of my corset and stockings. Without urging, Craig dropped to his knees between my legs. Delicious moments later his muffled voice inquired, "Does this please Mistress Anna?" Yes, it did—it pleased me very much to have my fantasy come so vividly to life.

—*Ms. A.U., Trenton, New Jersey* O┼▪

Apprentice Jockey Would Love to Mount "Ponytailed Princess"

I'm a young guy trying to make it in the tough, competitive world of horse racing. I'm what is known as a "bug rider," which means I ride with a weight allowance, as do all the guys starting out. The idea is to help make us more competitive with the experienced jocks. It's also an incentive for trainers to give us mounts, since a weight allowance, which in my case is five pounds, gives a horse a bit of an edge. If he happens to be talented, a jock with a bug can become a popular guy around the horse barns.

But enough about my budding career; what I want to tell you about is this great erotic fantasy I have concerning a really cute female jockey I'll call Melanie. She arrived on the scene a couple of months ago, and ever since, she's been dominating my thoughts. Melanie's been around long enough to have lost her bug, so she rides on an equal basis with the other jocks. She's darn good, too, and even though there's still some prejudice against girl riders, Melanie has earned the respect of a lot of knowledgeable horsemen.

Of course, it doesn't hurt that she's a pint-size package of female pulchritude with her curvy little figure, sparkling blue eyes, and shiny blonde hair, which she always wears in a ponytail. A lot of the guys, including some of the older, married ones, have said that Melanie could ride them to the finish line anytime. That's the kind of effect she has on a fellow.

Problem is, she knows she's special, on and off the track, and she walks around like she owns the place. The only people she really talks to are the trainers, and her agent, of course, because without them she goes nowhere fast. As for the rest of us, forget it. The only time we get some attention is when she has won a race and comes back to gloat. Sexy and snooty, that's the ponytailed princess.

In my favorite fantasy, however, it's an altogether different story, at least as far as I'm concerned. Although Melanie still keeps her distance from the others, with me she's warm and friendly and forever flirting. My charm, sense of humor, and great smile have won her over. We're still fierce competitors on the track, but away from it we're friends. She's very attracted to me, for sure, but I tell her that I won't sleep with her until she's won three races on the same day. This challenge is difficult but not impossible.

Well, Melanie becomes an even more aggressive rider, surging to the front whenever possible, gunning her horse through the smallest opening on the rail, using all the cunning she's accumulated so far to out-distance her rivals, taking chances even a veteran jock might think twice about—and all because she's dying for me to fuck her! That makes yours truly, who's just a shade over five-one, feel ten feet tall.

Finally, Melanie attains her goal, winning the first, fifth, and seventh races on a nine-race card. She's all smiles as she prances back to the jockeys' quarters. As I don't have a mount in the eighth or ninth race, I'm in street clothes and relaxing in the lounge. Melanie bursts in and practically jumps into my arms. "I did it!" she says excitedly. "Did you see me on the monitor?" I tell her that I did and that my cock started swelling the second she crossed the finish line. She laughs and snakes a hand down between us to squeeze my cock through my slacks. "When do I get this?" she asks pointedly.

"How 'bout right now?" I say with a grin, my cock getting longer and harder by the second. "We'll go over to the barn area, find an empty stall, and screw ourselves silly."

Once she's convinced that I'm serious, Melanie warms to the idea in a hurry. In fact, she confesses to harboring a "really wild" fantasy of being ridden to orgasm in a horse's stall. Giving my cock one final squeeze, she tells me to wait for her while she changes out of her jockey silks into street clothes. She's back in no time, looking really sexy in a snug-fitting pink shirt, lemon-yellow slacks, and white sneakers. "Let's go," she says, taking my hand and pulling me after her as she starts for the door.

In real life, of course, this would be virtually impossible to pull off, but because it's my fantasy, we have no trouble finding an empty stall in a shed row at the furthermost part of the barn area. Melanie swings open the gate and steps inside, inhaling the earthy aroma of hay and horses. "God, this is heaven," she sighs. "No man's cologne turns me on as much as this does. Hurry and get naked for me. Please."

With the summer sun still shining brightly, I quickly shed my clothes and spread a horse blanket over the bed of straw covering the floor of the stall. When I straighten up, I am greeted by the sight of Melanie looking like a very pretty doll whose clothes have been removed. My eyes zero in on her pert breasts, the rosy nipples already erect; then my gaze drops to her adorable blonde bush. Smiling, she turns around and bends over to show off her delectable bottom. She's even more desirable naked than I'd imagined her to be.

Melanie steps over to me, sinks to her knees, and, in one easy, fluid motion, takes all but a half inch of my cock in her mouth, causing me to almost lose it right then and there. But I hang on and savor the wonderful caress of her lips gliding over my shaft, her tongue slithering along the sensitive underside. I grab her ponytail and playfully hold it up as she continues sucking on my cock with sluttish delight. Her hands travel up my legs to cup and squeeze my buttocks, and one of her curious fingers probes my asshole.

Eager to return the pleasure, I tell Melanie to get down on the blanket so I can eat her. As soon as she's ready, I plaster my face to her inviting little pussy and commence feasting. She mewls with pleasure as I lap up her flowing juices. I slide my hands under her ass and cup her sweet cheeks, lifting her up off the blanket as I curl my lips around her aroused clitoris and suck it gently. In the distance a horse whinnies, and this seems to fuel Melanie's passion.

After I've brought her to orgasm with my devilish tongue, she orders me onto my back and promptly climbs aboard my cock, moaning with joy as her soaking pussy slides down my pole of flesh. Up and down, up and down she bounces, her head thrown back, her cute pear-shaped breasts bobbing on her chest. Her pussy is deliciously tight, a warm, wet cavern for my engorged member. Somehow I manage to hold back my orgasm as she cries out that she's coming. Her body stiffens, and her nails dig into my chest as the pleasure of her climax envelops her. It's orgasm number two for my favorite female jockey.

Recovering quickly, Melanie positions herself on all fours and tells me to do her "horsey-style." Happy to oblige, I get behind her and slide balls-deep into her pretty pussy. Melanie lets out a groan and rams her ass back against me. She spurs me on with dirty talk, telling me exactly what she wants and how she wants it. With lust churning inside me, I grab hold of her ponytail and use it like a rein to jerk her head back and up. This surprises her and she cries out, and I know for certain that she likes it when she asks me to pull her hair harder.

I'm giving it to her good, fucking her hard, getting closer and closer to the finish line. And then suddenly I'm there, groaning loudly as semen starts spurting from my pulsating cock into Melanie's convulsing pussy. She, too, is at the finish line, a cry of triumph bursting from her throat as she comes for the third time.

After resting for a while, we put on our clothes and walk together to the parking lot for our cars. "Wow, three orgasms for three races won," says Melanie. "What would you give me if I won all nine races?"

"Guess," I say, grinning.

—*Name and address withheld*   ⚷

Their Wild Imaginations Put Extra Zip in Couple's Love Life

My wife, Jean, and I have great sex, full of experimentation and fantasy, to which *Penthouse Variations* has been a major contributor. One of our favorite games is to put a stack of back issues on the bed and for one of us to put a finger into any of the magazines. We then turn to the nearest photo of some beautiful body, and Jean imitates the action on the page.

If it is a single girl shot, Jean will strike the same pose, but she continues the action as if anticipating what the model's next move would be. If the girl is holding her breasts, Jean will hold hers and then massage them, pinching and pulling her nipples several times or lifting them up for a quick lick. Our rules say that the action has to last for at least one minute before we go on to another photo spread.

A few weeks ago, after several exciting scenes were unfolded before me, it was Jean's turn to pick. Flipping the pages very slowly, she stopped on one of your beautiful girl-girl layouts. I can't count how many times I have pictured my wife as a lively participant in action like that depicted on the page. She assumed the position of one of the girls, lying flat on her back, her knees bent and her long legs spread to expose her neatly trimmed pussy.

I could tell that the previous little dramas had made her wet, and I asked her teasingly how she was going to act out a scene that showed two girls. She replied that she'd talk to her imaginary partner as if she were there, instructing her to do what the other girl in the photo was doing.

To my surprise, she called out the name of one of our best friends as she gently rubbed her own clitoris. The minute was up, but she showed no signs of wanting to stop. There was no guy in the picture, but I didn't care. I had to stroke myself as my wife went harder and harder over her swollen button, dipping her fingers deep inside herself to bring up more juice.

As she started to squeeze her nipples, she continued

to tell "Franny" what to do: "Lick me harder, please, Franny. Make me come, my beautiful girl." She finally did come, her hips bucking up and down, her hand grinding flat into her pussy.

Jean then told me she wanted her imaginary friend to make me come. She told me to lie down, continue stroking my cock, and talk to Franny. Just listening to her, I was ready to shoot, but I stroked harder and harder, telling her how good it felt. Jean said that when I was ready to climax, I was to let go of my cock as the come started to rise up from my balls. She said Franny would want it shot all over her, and I did as I was told.

I let go of my cock, and with no movement on my part, my semen surged out, shooting everywhere. I moaned Franny's name as I continued coming into the air. It felt as if someone was really milking it out of me, yet I know Jean didn't touch me. She was too busy stroking herself, climaxing for the second time.

That was several weeks ago. This past weekend, Jean had a girls' night out with Franny, and she still wasn't home when I went to bed at three in the morning. I was feeling kind of hot, so I got out the last *Penthouse Variations* and started thumbing through it.

Between the pages I found a note from Jean, tucked next to one of the hottest girl scenes you've ever published—one where the girl with the big breasts has the same short blonde hairstyle Jean wears, and her tongue is actively licking her partner's clitoris. It also shows her partner tugging with long fingers on the blonde's stiff nipples, just the way Jean likes hers pulled. The note said, "I enjoyed the rehearsal, but tonight's opening night."

—*Mr. L.A., Pittsburgh, Pennsylvania* ⚷

An Incredible Night of Unbridled Lust for Outrageous Show-Off

Six months ago, I met the most wonderful man, and he quickly became my lover. He is tall, dark, and handsome, with a marvelous personality. What I love most about him, though, is his wild sexual imagination. His job requires that we be apart for weeks at a time, but he never fails to write to me. In his letters, he often describes a fantasy that he wants us to act out, like the one that follows:

You've always loved to dress naughty so you can show off your fantastic body. You wear tight, low-cut dresses and rarely wear any underwear. So, as a gift, I've planned a night for you to indulge in your exhibitionism.

You come home, and I tell you I've invited three friends of mine over for poker. When you ask me what you should wear, I tell you to be daring and knock their socks off. You choose a short, black leather miniskirt and the sleeveless black top you bought from Victoria's Secret.

My friends arrive and the game begins. You are playing the part of the perfect hostess: bringing drinks and sandwiches and leaning low to serve the players. The game comes to a halt every time you walk into the room, and you are enjoying the attention. When I sense the time is right, I steer the conversation toward women's bodies. You are sitting beside me, sipping your drink. One of the guys comments on how nice you look, and you give your characteristic modest smile.

One of the men, Pete, suggests that having you as our hostess is the next best thing to having a topless waitress.

"Maybe that can be arranged," I say, taking your arm and guiding you into a standing position. Moving behind you as you face the table, I lean against you and whisper, "Is this okay?" You nod with a smile as I unbutton your sexy top. All eyes are on you, and though you blush, you make no move to hide your exquisite breasts, which are now in full view.

"Now we have our serving wench," I say. I sit back down and pick up my cards. But the game is truly over. You gather some empty glasses and go to the bar to refill them. The three men keep looking at me questioningly, but I say nothing. As you hand Al his drink, he remarks, "Next best thing to a nude barmaid."

You look at me and unzip the side of your skirt, letting it fall to the floor.

"Her pussy gets really wet when she has an audience," I comment. I stand behind you and guide your hands to your breasts. "Let's give them a show, my love."

You begin to squeeze your breasts, pinching and

rolling the nipples between your fingers. The three men turn their chairs to face you. The bulges in their pants are distinct.

"Ready to show them your ass?" I whisper hotly into your ear.

You turn around and stand with your feet apart, slowly bending over so that your pussy is exposed. I put my hands on your shoulders and guide you, still bent over backward, until your pussy is in front of Al's face.

"She has the best-tasting cunt in the whole world," I say. He needs no further urging as his tongue darts out, and he begins to eat you wildly, running his tongue over your clitoris and in and out of your pussy. I see your knees buckle, but you catch yourself and grind your cunt against his mouth.

Nick walks over and kneels next to you. He grabs one of your breasts and begins to play with the nipple like he's milking you while he sucks the other nipple into his mouth. Pete walks in front of you, leans down, and grabs a handful of your hair. He arches your neck back and thrusts his tongue into your mouth. His jaw and head move as if he is eating your tongue. You quiver with arousal. After watching the scene for a few moments, I suggest that we all move to the bedroom.

Once upstairs, you notice the closet door is ajar and wonder if I have the video camera running. I do, and I answer your questioning glance with a nod. You sit on the bed, and I direct Pete to stand in front of you and strip. As he finishes undressing, I have you stand

and kiss him as you rub your body against his. Then I make you kneel and take his cock in your mouth for a minute. I have you repeat the ritual with the other two men, one at a time.

"Let's see if we can give her a night to remember," I say. I tell Pete to lie on the bed. He is stroking his fully erect cock as you walk over and straddle him. My own cock hardens as I watch the woman I love grab a stranger's cock and guide it into her soaked pussy. Pete groans as you take the length of him inside you. Nick and Al move to either side of the bed and begin to play with your breasts.

After a few minutes, I ease you down so your breasts are crushed against Pete's chest. I suggest to Al that your ass needs some attention, and he quickly moves behind you. You're rocking back and forth on Pete's cock as Al begins to finger your asshole. I see you shudder, and I know you are coming. Al gets on his knees behind you, and you gasp as he slowly works his cock into your ass. When he's fully inside you, Nick pulls your face toward him. He is kneeling next to you and, before another moment passes, he feeds you his erection.

I watch you lick the head of another man's cock, slide your tongue up and down its shaft, weave your tongue around his balls. I see your neck muscles work as you open your mouth and push down on him until his entire length is in you. You begin pumping him in and out of your mouth to the rhythm of Al and Pete pounding their cocks into your ass and cunt. You whimper as you tremble through a monstrous orgasm.

Pete empties himself into your pussy, Al comes in your ass, and Nick finally shoots his load into your greedy mouth.

The men slowly pull their softening cocks out of your body and the four of you collapse, laughing and panting on the bed. You get up and disappear into the bathroom to wash up as I pass out towels to the grinning, still-disbelieving men. It's such a turn-on, watching you taking on three strange cocks. I smile, because after their good-byes, you'll still be here with me. And as you stride into the room proudly naked, your skin glistening from your shower, I know you are all mine.

—*Ms. D.V., Silver Spring, Maryland*   ⚷

Wild Jungle Dreams for Gal
Who Craves Savage Thrills

Sex and music are inextricably entwined for me, even in my fantasy life. Music with a primitive driving beat especially turns me on, releasing something primordial, something savage that rarely gets to show through my everyday corporate exterior.

In my dreams I have shed my suit and pearls and am wrapped in a clinging tribal garment that reveals my taut thighs and lets my breasts show off their arrogant tilt, nipples tingling and erect. I always have flowers in my hair in these dreams, and the scents of the jungle perfume the air.

Last night the drums were beating, and I swayed to their rhythm. The whole village was dancing, hypnotized by the slow beat that captured the soul. There was a singsong chant in the background, but the drums controlled my movements. As my hips swayed, I ran my hands over my breasts, the erotic movement tightening my already-erect nipples.

I slid my hand down over my flat stomach and felt that the cloth over my pussy was already wet with excitement. Someone else's hand was on my thigh. A muscular body swayed behind me. His movements werc compelling and reminded me that solitary pleasure was not the purpose of this ceremony. His hand slipped under my sarong, his fingers finding the dampness of my pubic hair. He pulled me back against the hardness of his cock. I wanted exactly what he wanted. The smell of his sweat only heightened the moment, and when we both began to grind to the steady beat, his hot breath on my ear had me on the verge of coming.

Another man joined us, leaping in front of me, his eyes asking my permission as his hands moved over my breasts. Grabbing my waist and thrusting, he made me aware of his huge erection pushing toward my hot pussy. I was in ecstasy as the pressure was applied simultaneously to my buttocks and to my juicy cunt. The man in front was pulling hard on my nipples and then releasing them, while the grinding reached the point of frenzy. I didn't know which man slipped his finger into me as I was still caught between them. All I knew was that a series of shudders coursed through me as that finger fucked me until the music stopped.

We all turned toward the bonfire in the middle of the clearing. Through the haze of heat appeared the biggest man I'd ever seen—massive chest, every muscle outlined by the glow of the fire. His eyes pierced my very soul as he came toward me, stepping over the other couples strewn around the fire.

At his gesture, the two men with me lifted me in their arms and carried me to a pile of animal skins beside the fire. They stripped me as I danced for my new master, exposing my body to the eyes of the whole assembly. The fragrant wood smoke added to the erotic sensuality of the moment. My nostrils flared and my breasts heaved as the giant examined me with undisguised lust. The drums started again, softly and rhythmically.

The other two men laid me back on the soft and pungent skins. The giant's eyes held me spellbound, and his massive hands stroked my cunt. Every beat of the drum intensified the corresponding pulse in my body and brought more wetness to my soaked pussy. I wanted him in me, wanted to be invaded by his massive maleness.

He pulled my legs apart and pushed up my knees, but it was not my pussy he wanted just yet. His enormous cock loomed before my face, and I tried to open wide enough to swallow it, knowing it was far too big for me to take to the root. His thrusts and mine got most of it down my throat, and I sucked the delicious taste of him for all I was worth.

One of the other men had bent to lick my pussy, and his tongue deftly found my clitoris, moving from gentleness to roughness in a heartbeat. I squirmed with a pleasure more intense than I had ever known in my life. Other mouths sucked my fingers and kissed my flat stomach as I sucked the enormous root of my desire. Only its bulk prevented my moans from echoing around the clearing.

He withdrew his organ and knelt farther back, between my legs. The huge organ that had invaded my mouth began to ravage my cunt, entering and filling me inexorably, fuller than I could have believed possible. I was impaled on his cock. I could smell his manliness and taste his sweat as he picked up speed, pounding into me and driving me crazy with orgasm after orgasm.

Again and again I rose to the peak of ecstasy. My body was a mindless animal, craving more and more, even as it was exhausted by so much pleasure. With a wild cry, he came after one last lunge, and I felt his seed gush into me. The primeval ritual completed, we collapsed onto the furs, sticky with sweat and sex juices.

When I took my hand away from my sated pussy, I missed his warmth and power, but I knew he would never be far away. The drums would surely bring us back together, anytime I wanted.

—*Ms. O.H., Philadelphia, Pennsylvania*

Ode to a Woman Whose Beauty and Grace Fuel a Wild Desire

A few months ago, while traveling abroad, I met a wonderful woman named Marie at the French embassy in London. Fiercely attracted to each other, we began a torrid affair that ended abruptly when I was summoned back to the States by my employer. I miss her tremendously and have taken to writing her detailed letters conveying my passion for her. I would like to share with you my last letter to her:

My Sweet Marie,

I ache to make love to you. I dream of you, of your breath on my face, mingling with mine. My hands holding your face. Your eyes looking into mine. You know the most sensitive part of your body is where I want my hot breath to reach. That wet, dark place. Wet with thoughts of me. With the tip of my tongue I want to disturb its peace, awaken it. I am here, next to you now, and you are so close to me. Ultimate intimacy, I devour you. I will drive out every thought, every rational sense, so that only the pleasure of my touch fills you.

Oh God, the first taste of you will surely be too much, I know. After the kiss, with my lips on you: There is my tongue, erotically parting your sensuous lips. Exploring you. Finding those places you want me to find.

Then I must stop to savor the musky pleasure of you. It is then that I will find your face again and kiss you deeply. The taste of you on me becomes something else—the taste of us. It is unforgettable.

I will undress you and look at you. And tell of the beauty I see. When I remove your top, I will kiss your shoulders, your arms, your hands—each delicate finger. When you help me take off your bra, your breasts will not be unsupported. For I will hold them both and gently kiss each one. Your arms are around me, and my mouth is on each breast in turn. Then you open my shirt and use your lips and teeth on my tiny nipples.

You are wearing a skirt, long and black. We move together again, standing close. Your naked breasts on my bare skin. My hands on your hips pull you tight to me so you feel the hardness of my excitement against your belly. I kneel in front of you to kiss your bare stomach. My arms surround you. I hold you tight to my face, and through your skirt I smell your rising passion. You push hard against my face as I cup your firm ass and hold you there. Your hands on my head turn my face up to yours, and we smile again. My hand under your skirt brushes you through your panties, feeling the cleft of your pussy—you squeeze my hand with your thighs.

I unbutton your skirt, and it drops to the floor. Still kneeling, I press my face into your crotch and let my breath warm you there. All the while you hold me close and tell me that you love me. My fingers slip under the waistband of your panties, and I slide them down your legs and help you step out of them. I stand, and you embrace me tightly and then kneel to pull down my trousers and briefs, helping free my painfully erect penis from all restraint. Then, taking your hand, I lead you to the bed.

You are a feast, and I know not where to go next in the savoring of you. Do I lose myself in your voluptuous breasts? Or cast all foreplay aside and plunge my cock between your open legs? Or do I guide your lovely mouth to my nipples and then lower, to my bursting erection? Or should we face each other head to toe and use our mouths on each other? Or maybe I should ask what you most want, soliciting your inner secrets and desires for me to fulfill. Or do I want to look at you from across the room, gather the entirety of you with my eyes while I'm stroking myself and watching you do the same. These are fantasies within the fantasy, darling.

A kiss is most true for me at this moment. And there is never too much kissing of you. So I gather you to me once again. The force of my kiss is strong, and you return my passion fully. We pause to breathe, and I suck on your nipples together, your breasts held close by my hands.

Now you put your hands on my shoulders to push me back, kneeling between my legs. You straddle my chest, your heated wet crotch scorching me. Then you slide forward and lower yourself to my lips. Your eyes close and you toss your head back as I thrust my tongue into you. I hold your hips firmly as you slowly move your deliciousness back and forth over my mouth. I reach for your breasts, cup each one and fondle your hard nipples with my thumbs while tasting the richness of you.

Just as we pause between kisses, so we now separate

to recharge. I see you with those smoky eyes, looking deep into me. You lie back on your pillow and sigh that angelic sigh I love so. I lie with you and hold you from behind, my arms enveloping you as I kiss your neck and back. I describe the goodness of you: your pure heart and soaring soul. And you tell me, too, my darling, why you love me.

Now you turn in my arms and your open mouth approaches mine. You kiss me deeply. I use my tongue to explore your mouth, your teeth, your lips, as your hand finds my crotch. My mind can forestall orgasm, but my body has been filled to overflowing with you. You hold my cock at its base and bend to take me in your mouth. Oh, you take me in, your lips and tongue seeking all of me. I can only gasp for breath and revel in the sensations you create. Then you stop, your tongue giving a last caress to the tip of my desperate organ as it throbs upward with each beat of my pounding heart. You rise up and speak so softly into my chest that I barely hear your words.

I get up and stand next to the bed. I turn you on your stomach near the edge of the bed and put a pillow under your head. I stand over you and, starting at your neck, use my fingers and thumbs to loosen the muscles. Then your shoulders with the heel of my hands, moving down your back. I then work the center of your spine and end at the small of your back. I kiss there, too, and go lower to the top of your ass. I massage your tight buttocks, spreading and kissing them. My breathing is fast now, and I finally bury my face between the sweet cheeks of your ass.

After a while, you sit up at the edge of the bed as I kneel on the floor between your legs. Your face is full of desire. I put my hands on your shoulders and gently push you on the bed, with your feet on the floor and your bottom at the edge. You are open to me, and I lick you from your ass to your clitoris. Your clitoris, your whole body, responds to each caress of my tongue and lips.

I sit up and touch my stiff cock to your clitoris. I go back and forth with the tip, pressing gently on the sensitive spot while caressing your breast with my other hand, all the while watching your beautiful face. Your breathing becomes shallow and rapid. I keep my cock on your clit, pressing, rubbing, smooth and rhythmic, a hand on your breast, eyes on your face, until you come. The beauty of your orgasm is my fulfillment. I do not move for a while, nor do you, until at last you sit up to kiss me. My throbbing cock, still touching your body, slips into you easily. Oh God, you are so fine.

And there we are, connected at last. We kiss each other as our genitals beat together with our pumping hearts. When my face is close to yours, I cannot concentrate on anything else. You lower your head to suck on my nipple. I push hard into you. Your hands go around me, holding my ass. You pull me toward you with each thrust of my body, your eyes connected to mine. I tell you that I love you, that you are my beautiful Marie, and that I must come now. We slow down, but keep moving to make my orgasm happen with infinite, acute, almost tortuous deliberateness. I ask you to look into my eyes while you kiss me, while I come. I want everything all at once, and I get it with you. We gaze, we kiss, I come.

I'll end with a kiss on your sweet lips. I now close my eyes and I am sure I hear your musical voice and that soft sigh of my Marie who loves me.

                —Mr. M.D., Washington, D.C. O⊢▪

Tropical Island Queen Enjoys Her Harem of Virile Slave Boys

Sometimes late at night, when I'm horny and don't have a lover to help satisfy me, I lose myself in the rich world of my imagination. I turn off all the lights except for the lamp with the blue bulb by my bed, and then I let my brain run wild.

Over the years, I have concocted countless erotic scenarios that have served to spur me on to tremendous orgasms while masturbating. My particular tastes about what to envision change from week to week, but there has been one particular fantasy that has stayed with me throughout the years, being refined and expanded each time. It goes something like this:

I am the breathtakingly stunning queen of some faraway desert island in the balmy tropics. I have assigned the day-to-day political workings of the island to my well-trusted high-ranking female officials, leaving me free to spend my days basking in the sun, eating gourmet food, and enjoying other pleasures of the body. I slink around in bejeweled bikini tops and short silk skirts, or sometimes I go topless if I am so inclined, allowing the masses to gaze upon my perfect breasts and erect nipples. While there are many beautiful women on the island, I am unquestionably the most gorgeous and am worshipped as such by all the inhabitants, both male and female.

Sometimes I take my pleasure with attractive civilians of both sexes, but for the most part my sexual needs are attended to by my harem. This is a group of about forty young, smooth, muscular, tanned, long-haired men who parade around only in the skimpiest of G-string-like loincloths—by my command, of course. It is the greatest honor to be selected as a member of my harem—only the most physically exquisite of candidates are chosen. They are well compensated for their work, but their primary reward is that they are allowed to be in my presence and tend to my body's every whim and need.

Sure, I have my servant boys fan me with palm leaves and feed me grapes and the like, but their duties go far beyond that. I must have a full-body massage with oil at least six times a day, and I also have my boys give me mud baths and do my hair and nails. And believe me, being attended to day and night by all those sexy young studs makes me pretty hot, and who better to satisfy my cravings than my bevy of boys? (I may have neglected to mention that my boys are also selected on the basis of the skill with which they can use their hands, mouths, and cocks, and rest assured, the testing process is quite rigorous.)

A typical massage session starts with me on my

stomach on a cushioned table, with a boy positioned at each corner. I take a moment to inspect my four gifts from the gods. Ah, they are truly beautiful and all mine—but then again, aren't they all? When I give the signal to begin, they pour warm oil all down my back, and I moan as soft hands grasp each of my limbs, working the knots and easing the tension of my oh-so-stressful lifestyle. Gradually, two pairs of hands work their way up my thighs while the others' hands run down my back and over my firm buttocks. Soon the eight hands are joined by four tongues, which slurp and slide over my thighs and buttocks, simultaneously working their way dangerously close to my burning core.

When I can't stand the sweet torture another minute, I give the signal—a sharp whistle—and two tongues go straight for my pussy, dueling one another to slide inside my satiny pocket. I arch my hips upward, allowing them more room to maneuver, while my other two Adonises move up toward my head. One kneels down and begins to kiss me deeply, while the other takes my hand and runs it down his chiseled, well-oiled abs until it reaches his cock. I grasp its hardness in delight, squirming like a fish as the plunging tongues below send a flood of warmth racing throughout my body.

Just when I am about to come, I give the second signal—a quick tug on the cock I am holding—and the four men stop what they are doing and gently turn me over. The two guys near my head immediately bend, and each one takes a pebble-hard rosy-brown nipple in his mouth. They suck mightily while their hands roam along my taut abdomen. I am moaning aloud in ecstasy, lost in a swirling sea of soft hands and tongues.

I need to be filled up inside, and my boys aren't about to disappoint me. I spread my legs wide, and the lucky contender hops up on the table, kneels down, and raises my hips, then quickly thrusts his huge cock (one of the requirements for the job, of course) into my slippery hole. I coo in delight as he begins a slow, deep penetration, the way I like it best.

Now I'm just about at heaven's gate, with two talented tongues nuzzling my nipples and one sizable cock thrusting in and out of my velvety walls. Only one more thing is necessary, and the unoccupied slave boy knows what to do. Maneuvering around his compatriot's thrusting member, he somehow manages to plaster his lips around my swollen clitoris. I have taught all my boys the precise way I like to be licked— hard sucks with the lips alternated with quick flicks of the tongue. The lucky boy is always swooning when given the honor of licking my royal pussy, and soon I am swooning under his talented touch.

The oral ministrations, combined with the deep, hard thrusting of a solid penis and the light sucking of my nipples, never fail to bring me over the edge. I begin to float away from myself as colors swirl behind my closed lids and my pelvic region explodes with all the brilliance of a Roman candle. I am always very vocal through my climaxes, and my voice rings out, informing the entire island that I have been satisfied once again.

When I regain my senses, I loosen my limbs and

release my beautiful slaves from my grip. They know they have done well, and now they will be treated to the pleasure of cleaning my exhausted body. First, they clean me top to bottom with their soft tongues, paying special attention to my pussy, especially if the boy who had been fucking me shot his load inside me. Once I have been thoroughly cleaned and licked to at least one more orgasm, I am given a light sponge bath and dressed in some flimsy little garment.

Then, as I recline on my plush queen-size bed right on the beach, I order my four boys to strip off their loincloths (if they still have them on) and show me how turned-on they were by pleasuring me. As they reveal their proud erections glistening in the brilliant sunlight and then begin to stroke them, I bask in the knowledge that I am the sexiest woman alive.

I watch with glee as my four young gods shoot their creamy seed on the sand. Then I send them off to their quarters to get cleaned up, while at the same time I summon for a fresh new quartet. It's almost time for my second massage of the day.

—*Ms. S.I., Little Rock, Arkansas*   O⊢■

A Trip into the Past Gets Exciting When They're Abducted by a Pair of Bandits

Steam hissed from the cylinders and smoke belched from the stack as the vintage steam locomotive clambered up the grade. It was pulling a short string of cars that included several Pullmans, a snack car, and an old wooden caboose. We could hear the ties creak and nails pull as the heavy coach in which we sat rolled over the tracks.

No one was more impressed by all this than my husband, Thomas, who sat excitedly beside me, completely smitten with the whole experience. He watched intently as the train traveled through the countryside, enjoying our fun-filled trip into the past.

For me, the train ride was a chance for us to be together. Knowing how much the history of the railroad fascinated Thomas, I'd worn an outfit I was sure he would appreciate. As close to authentic as I could get, my muslin dress consisted of a cinched bodice and a long, full skirt. I could hardly breathe in the tightly laced corset I had on beneath it, but it was worth it. Thomas's eyes widened when he saw the way it pushed up my breasts and created a deep cleavage (which I normally did not possess). As he ran his hand along my muslin-covered thigh, I could tell he was pleased. Suddenly, his gentle caress turned into a squeeze, and I followed his gaze to see what had caught his attention.

Two men on horseback were galloping toward the tracks from out of the trees. They were riding alongside the train close enough for us to see that they were toting pistols and wearing masks over their eyes. It was a staged robbery for the pleasure of the tourists. The train slowed and then came to a stop as the bandits stepped into the coach to demand money and jewelry. As they neared us, Thomas nudged me and suggested that for some added drama I should act reluctant to give them anything.

"Hand over your purse, lady," the train robber demanded.

"I don't think so," I replied, and to my utter surprise, the man grabbed me tightly by the waist, hefted me up, and dragged me out of the coach. Thomas was also taken along as I was set on top of a horse, firmly planted in front of the bandit, and tied effectively to the saddle. I looked over at my husband, and when he smiled at me I realized that he'd set this up to make our experience as realistic as possible. He'd been hinting at a special surprise for weeks, and I guessed that this was it.

Thomas was handled as roughly as I was, and then we were galloping away for what seemed like a long time. We came to a stop beside a small log cabin nestled in the countryside and were carried inside. Soon, the horses weren't the only things that were hitched. Thomas was bound with rope to a wooden chair, and I was tied to the bed in a spread-eagled position. When the bandits went out to feed the horses, I asked my husband what was going on here.

"This is my gift to you," he said. "It's that fantasy you've always talked about." I could hardly believe that it was happening, and I probably wouldn't have if I hadn't been tied to that bed. I was also extremely thrilled, so when the bandits reappeared I played along.

"If you let my husband go, I'll let you do anything you want with me," I said. They looked over at Thomas, who nodded in agreement.

"Anything?" the one who appeared to be the leader asked. "You should be careful with your choice of words, bound as you are." He told his young partner to cut Thomas's bonds, and my pussy grew damp as I watched him do it. But when he came over to cut mine, he was stopped.

"Retie this spitfire after she strips," he was told. "I think she likes it." He was right; I had sported handcuffs many times for Thomas, but I had never felt the thrill that I felt now. My excitement grew as they undid my bonds and had me do a sinfully slow striptease for them, first removing the muslin gown, then the snug-fitting corset. When I was completely naked, I checked for their reactions and saw growing bulges in the fronts of their jeans.

"I guess I'm the only one who isn't shy," I said, a hint that both men got. Watching two strangers strip was exciting, especially since I knew they would be pleasuring me in a matter of minutes. Both men had hard, firm bodies and were well tanned. The older one, Jesse, had short black hair and big blue eyes. The younger one, Clark, had reddish hair, a mustache, and green eyes.

I was more than willing to play my role, so I sank to my knees at Jesse's command. Using their discarded clothing for padding, I made sure Thomas could get a clear view of me as I acted out my fantasy for him.

It had been a while since I'd seen anyone else's cock up close, so I devoured Jesse's inner thighs, balls, and the base of his cock with relish. He groaned with disappointment when I moved to Clark to do the exact

same thing to him. Both men were thrilled with the
gentle teasing of my mouth, but I could tell that it was
Thomas who enjoyed it the most. It brought out the
voyeur in him, and he stroked his dick while watching
me suck the cocks of two strange men.

I went back and forth between the bandits, taking their erect cocks deep down my throat. I ran my
tongue along the undersides of their hard shafts as the
roof of my mouth stroked along the tops. Jesse seemed
content to stand still while I bobbed my head up and
down over his dick, while Clark preferred to hold my
face steady and thrust into my mouth.

Though I truly enjoyed sucking the train robbers'
cocks, it wasn't long before I was yearning to have
them both inside me. Sensing this, Jesse pushed my
mouth off his dick to pick me up, and I melted into his
strong arms. One encircled my waist while the other
gripped me by the crook of my knees, and I could see
his muscles ripple as they went taut with my weight.
While he carried me to the bed, I peppered his chest
with kisses and flicked my tongue at his nipples. Then
he lay me down upon the mattress, and I once again
felt the rough texture of the rope as it was wrapped
around my wrists and ankles.

I was on my stomach this time, facing the foot-
board. This seemed strange until Clark moved in front
of me with his twitching cock positioned right at my
mouth. As I opened my lips and took him inside, his
partner moved onto the bed behind me and raised my
ass as best he could, tied down as I was. I quivered,
knowing that I was about to feel another man's cock in

my pussy for the first time in twelve years. Just then, from out of the corner of my eye, I caught a glimpse of my husband slowly masturbating at the sight of me with the two men.

That's when Jesse grasped my hips in his strong hands and slid his steely erection into my cunt. As I opened up to receive him, I moaned around the stiff cock that was planted firmly in my mouth. Everything came into sharper focus as the strangers fucked me from both ends. I could feel their bulbous cockheads and every protruding vein on their shafts as they slid in and out of my mouth and pussy. All the while, I could hear my husband's groans from the other side of the room as his hand flew over his dick.

When my teeth accidentally raked over a sensitive spot on Clark's cock, he groaned and threaded his fingers in my hair, holding my head still so he could fuck my face. A moment later, he let go and I tossed my head about, pulling his cock this way and that to give him as much pleasure as I could with my hands bound. It must have been too much for him because I soon felt his dick harden and twitch against my tongue. Our eyes met, and then a second later his hot seed shot down my throat. I swallowed it with a wantonness that any man would have loved, adding a little drama for my husband's benefit by repeating the action a few more times than was necessary.

As Clark's cock softened in my mouth, Jesse continued fucking me with steady, forceful strides. His hands snaked over my hips until they were on my breasts. He palmed them delicately, letting his callused fingers flick each nipple as I shook with desire. My tremors grew even stronger when he slipped his fingers against my slippery, engorged clit. I started convulsing on the mattress, pulling at my bonds and moaning loudly until I came in an explosion of lust. Jesse stayed inside me, fucking me hard with short, shallow thrusts as my quivering cunt drew him inward.

When I glanced over at my husband again, his look of rapture mirrored my own as he pumped his cock in his hand while watching the bandit fuck me. Then all the muscles in his body went tense, and I knew he was going to come soon. He grit his teeth and closed his eyes as the semen shot from the tip of his cock in a thick white rope that landed on his stomach. Then Jesse's hard cock twitched inside my cunt and he filled me up with his own hot load.

Thoroughly exhausted, I barely noticed when Jesse pulled out of my well-fucked pussy. He kissed my cheek and spoke tenderly to me, breaking out of character for the first time that day.

"We'll let you and your husband be alone now," he said, and then I heard him and Clark ride off on their horses. Thomas and I spent the remainder of the weekend at the cabin he had rented as part of my surprise. We acted out all sorts of sexy fantasies and created more than a few new ones. It was a weekend that I'll never forget.

—*Ms. M.T., Grand Junction, Colorado*

A Stay at a Spa Was a Real Treat, Though Not as Relaxing as She Had Expected

I'd gotten to the point where I could hardly function because my job had overwhelmed me completely. I was in desperate need of a long stay at a spa, but unfortunately, I couldn't get the time off from work. With nothing else to do and no other way to relax, I decided to use the little free time I had at home to send my mind on a vacation. That's how I came up with the following fantasy.

I arrived at the spa and the concierge took my bag before leading me to a changing room. Once there, he handed me a robe and assured me that he would take care of checking me in and bringing my belongings to my room. Then he left me, and when I entered the room, I discovered a woman who was completely naked and frantically searching for her robe. Consequently, I opened my locker and discovered that I had an extra one. I turned to the tall, voluptuous blonde and held out the robe for her to slither into. While doing so, one of her large breasts rubbed up against my hand, and I saw a smile appear on her face. She tied the robe, said, "Thank you," and disappeared out the door. My first thought was that I'd definitely have to find her again later on.

Later arrived sooner than planned, because we were inadvertently scheduled for a massage at the exact same time with the same masseur. Not a problem, we agreed, as Frank, our well-proportioned and well-endowed masseur, suggested that we could take turns. I got on the table first as Juliet, the woman from the locker room, stripped off her robe. I was really excited that I got to see her beautiful body again so soon.

Frank removed the sheet that covered me, revealing my naked body. Juliet smiled, and I could tell that she was as attracted to me as I was to her. Then, to my delight, Frank began by moving his soft, large hands up my legs to my inner thighs, all the while tantalizing me with the sight of his hard cock, which was visible through his thin linen pants.

As my clit hardened and my pussy grew damp, I glanced over at Juliet, who was sitting in her chair and twisting her nipples until they were completely erect. Noticing my glance, she slowly ran her hands down her torso until they reached the blonde hair that covered her mound. Teasingly, she inserted her fingers deep into her wet pussy while stroking her clit with her thumb. Then, to my ultimate pleasure, she removed her fingers from her cunt, sucked off her juices, and asked Frank, "Mind if I help out?"

Frank was happy to oblige as he took her wrists and filled her hands with hot scented oil. Then he placed her hands on my breasts. As he went back to work, continuing up my inner thighs, Juliet massaged my tits, and I relished every touch. Just then, Frank's fingers entered my body at the exact same moment that Juliet's lips made contact with my well-lubricated skin. She sucked my nipples, softly and slowly at first, but soon building to long, hard tongue motions that had my entire body begging for more. And all the while,

Frank thrust his finger in and out of my steamy cunt, even as he started to eat me, lapping at my throbbing clit.

Soon I couldn't tell who was sucking my erect nipples and who was licking the juices from between my thighs. I knew that there had to have been a switch in positions because I had Juliet's head in my hands as she sucked on my clit while Frank's hard cock was in my mouth and his hands were caressing my breasts. Then I lost control of my body and felt the waves of my orgasm pulsating through me.

After I had returned to earth, Juliet stood up, threw her hair back, and took my spot on the table. I immediately dove between her thighs as Frank massaged her swollen breasts. When he couldn't resist any longer, he pulled her up and kissed her passionately. Now his tongue was in her mouth while mine made circles against the knob of her clit. Then Frank straddled her body right there on the massage table and inserted his hard, well-oiled cock between her breasts, which she pressed tightly around his shaft with her hands. I leaned over Juliet, alternating between receiving her long, luscious kisses with my mouth and feeling her lips sucking and nibbling at my breasts. Frank began sliding his cock between Juliet's breasts, and all the while she and I each frantically rubbed our own dripping pussies.

Frank continued to press Juliet's tits firmly around his cock as he fucked them hard. Soon his shaft flushed with color and he shot his load onto the nape of her neck, which I was ready and willing to lick up. We then decided to let Frank rest and watch for a while, and Juliet and I moved into the sixty-nine position to finish the job he'd started. I plunged my tongue into Juliet's cunt and rubbed her clit as she mimicked my actions on my cunt. Soon we were screaming out our orgasms, which lasted for what seemed like hours. Our muscles constricted and our bodies quivered uncontrollably.

Finally, we returned to Frank, taking turns with his cock in our mouths. When I felt his dick start to swell, the vein on the underside of his shaft pulsating against my tongue, I straddled his body and lowered my cunt down over his length, constricting and releasing my juicy core until he filled me with his hot come. At the end of our session, we all felt satisfied yet exhausted. Then Juliet and I left Frank to recover for his next appointment and headed off to the sauna to wind down. Our "massage" had been fun, but it sure hadn't been relaxing!

As we entered the sauna and stripped off our robes, we discovered that we were not alone. We introduced ourselves to the man who was sitting on the cedar bench and learned that his name was David. He was really cute, with curly brown hair and green eyes, and exchanging a glance with Juliet, I knew that she was thinking the exact same thing that I was. I told David that we had just returned from a massage and were feeling quite rejuvenated. Juliet giggled, and then I placed my hands on his shoulders and said, "Let me show you what we learned about relieving tension."

I began massaging David, gliding my hands from

his shoulders and neck slowly down to his chest, where I circled his nipples with my fingertips while pressing my breasts against his back. As I enjoyed his chiseled six-pack abs and erect nipples, Juliet kept her eyes on the handsome package that was protruding from his towel. She then dropped to all fours, crawled between his legs, and removed the towel with her teeth, exposing his erect cock. We knew at this point that he was ours for the taking.

Juliet lingered between his thighs, caressing his cock with her hands until David could no longer take it. Holding Juliet's head, he guided himself into her mouth. To his obvious delight, she took in every inch of his length and began sucking him enthusiastically. David's hand remained on the back of her head and guided every lunge as she licked his shaft of the pre-come that was oozing from the tip of his cock. Then she pulled away and I moved quickly into place, straddling him so that his cock could easily find its way into my throbbing pussy.

I was already so wet that David's dick slid in and out of my cunt like a well-oiled piston. I began to lean back, but David grabbed me and forced our bodies together in a passionate embrace. I reached out to Juliet, and she straddled David from behind, kissing his neck and working her way around to his mouth. As she locked her lips to his, I leaned back again with one hand on his knee until I was riding his cock with determination. As David yelled out, "Fuck me, fuck me hard!" I lost control and could feel my own juices run from my body, covering his cock and thighs. His endurance was amazing, but he finally yelled out as his hard cock spewed its juices into my cunt.

Now Juliet told David that it was time for him to return the favor. He gladly obliged and began licking her pussy. I could almost swear that she was purring as he plunged his tongue in and out of her cunt. Eventually, she moaned and shuddered, lying helpless on the sauna room bench. Now we were all spent and dripping with sweat, pussy juice, and come. After taking a moment to catch our breath, we toweled off and slid back into our robes. We said good-bye to David, who thanked us for a good time.

Then we headed to the Jacuzzi, where Juliet and I got to know each other better on a more personal level. While gently massaging each other's bodies, we enjoyed the warm, bubbly water. Once we were relaxed and the skin on our fingertips was starting to pucker from the prolonged soak, we decided to shower and then meet in my room for drinks.

If I tell you what happened next in my spa fantasy, I'm going to need at least another ten pages or so. Let me just say that things with "Juliet" got pretty hot and heavy! As you can see, even though I never actually made it to a spa for a much-needed week of relaxation, I had a really fun time during my imaginary stay. And I plan on returning there really soon, and as often as possible!

—*Ms. E.G., Stamford, Connecticut*   ⚷∎

What's that Noise from the Basement? It's Our Tenants, Playing Their Games

Standing in my kitchen the other day, I heard a groan from the basement apartment and rushed down to see if something was wrong. I knocked on the door, and Wendy, one of our tenants, answered and told me that everything was fine, so I left. Back upstairs in my living room, I sat on the couch and imagined the scene that might have greeted me if the fantasy I'd had so many times in the past had been reality.

I knocked and entered the apartment the three graduate students have rented from my husband, Tom, and me for the past two years. Wendy met me in the hallway dressed in a classic harem dancer's costume, so different from the simple clothes I normally saw her in. "Please join us," she said, apparently not self-conscious of her exotic appearance. "Sue and I are entertaining Bruce."

I followed her down the hallway. Bruce is Wendy's husband, and Tom and I suspect that the voluptuous Sue is their lover. As we walked, I studied Wendy. A golden band held back her waist-length jet-black hair. A tiny golden ring pierced her belly button, and a jewel of some type was pressed deeply into her navel. Her silky red pantaloons were belted by a thin band of gold that accentuated her narrow waist and swelling hips. The crotch of her pants was split, and the belt's chains played between her thighs, alternately revealing and concealing a patch of curly black hair as she moved.

She wore no other clothes besides a multitude of gold chains that covered her bare breasts. I could hardly help noticing her full, heavy mounds, each supporting a tiny bell tinkling from her pierced nipples. Her naturally dark eyes were made up even darker, and her full lips were painted a glossy red that matched her long nails. A small, dark jewel flashed on her forehead.

I followed her to the bedroom as she apologized for her appearance. "You can see that Bruce is okay," she explained. "In fact, he is most definitely enjoying himself." I looked over at her husband as she guided me to a chair and asked me to sit. A glass of steaming tea appeared in my hands and Sue, dressed in a costume identical to Wendy's, smiled at me and then continued her dance.

Bruce didn't speak. His normally well-groomed black hair was a tousled mess. He was kneeling, and his thighs were bound together with red bands of fabric. His arms were tied behind his back with more of the same material. Otherwise, he was naked, and his widely spread legs and hairless groin made his hugely erect cock seem even thicker and longer.

Smiling at me with mischief in her eyes, Wendy knelt beside Bruce and lifted his balls for my inspection, weighing them in her palm. His uncircumcised cock seemed to grow even more when Sue danced closer, her heavy breasts swaying only inches from his open lips. I asked how long he'd been tied up.

"Three hours" was Wendy's response, and she explained that he hadn't been allowed to come in all that time. Bruce's eyes were dark with the superb agony of his need, and I could imagine how he must have been craving the relief that the two women had enjoyed denying him through three hours of constant teasing. By that point, his balls must have been boiling with come. I sat quietly, sipping my tea, and watched to see what they would do next.

Kneeling beside Bruce so as to allow me a good view and not be in Sue's way, Wendy tickled his balls with her long fingernails. She picked and pulled the tight skin, causing his cock to darken visibly. She purposely avoided touching his hard shaft, enjoying teasing him instead.

As Wendy tortured her husband's cock, Sue danced for him, swaying provocatively, the slit crotch of her pants falling open periodically so that her glistening pussy was exposed. Reaching down, she opened herself with her fingertips like she was spreading the petals of a fragrant, dewy flower. Then she arched her back until her nipples pointed toward the ceiling and played her fingers over her wet cut, moaning. She seemed to come several times in the minutes that followed, writhing and thrusting her hips while holding her pussy open for Bruce's gaze as Wendy continued to tease his helpless cock with her prolonged tickling. His tongue darted out over dry lips.

Then the two women knelt on either side of him, and he glanced at me, his eyes filled with desire. I gave him my best "poor baby" pout and blew him a kiss. My nipples were erect under my thin sweater, and I know that he noticed. I arched my back for him, thumbing my breasts to be sure he could see my hard points, proof of how arousing I found this scene.

With their hands on their thighs, the girls leaned toward Bruce's chest, each sucking a nipple between her lips. His eyes shut tight and his chin dropped as a low groan sounded from deep in his throat, the exact same sound that first drew me to the apartment. As they pulled their heads back slightly, I could see his nipples stretched tautly between their teeth.

I watched in a delirium as the prolonged arousal and stimulation continued. My hand had roamed up my skirt and between my legs, pressing on my throbbing, swollen clitoris. Then Sue was speaking softly to me, guiding the movement of my hand over my cunt. Soon I was rubbing and thrusting inside myself with the fingers of both hands. My panties were soaked and hung around my ankles. I didn't even bother kicking them off; I was so hot. And as I played with my pussy, I watched Sue, who was now lying on the floor facing Bruce, with her knees pulled back to her shoulders, masturbating as she begged him to come fuck her, which of course he couldn't do, bound and immobile as he was.

It took only seconds before I shattered into a thousand pieces as the first of a long series of orgasms washed over my body. My juices coated my fingers as they slid over my throbbing cunt. My hips came up off the chair as I fucked myself to climax again and again, drawing out the pleasure as all the while I continued to watch the show still unfolding before me.

Sue remained on the floor and was soon joined by

Wendy. They met in a long, hot kiss, hands groping each other's breasts as their tongues slid in and out of each other's mouths. Even though they were no longer touching Bruce, it was obvious that watching them was torturous to him and that he longed to be part of the action. Then, the next thing I knew, Wendy was stretched out over Sue's body so that they were mouth to pussy, each lapping hungrily between the other woman's legs.

My fingers were still busily working my cunt, and I came again at the sight of their sixty-nine. I glanced over at Bruce and could see what a difficult time he was having holding back his orgasm. Three long hours of teasing caresses and now he had to watch his wife and his roommate give each other such exquisite pleasure. I thought this was the sexiest thing I'd ever seen.

Because the girls were wrapped up in each other, I decided to do something about Bruce's situation, wanting to get in on the action. I got up out of my chair, approached him, and quickly undid his bindings. He looked so relieved that he was finally going to be allowed to come. I quickly helped him onto his back and then straddled his legs. Kneeling over him, I leaned over and took his cock in my mouth.

Just then, Wendy looked up and caught my eye. I stopped what I was doing, my lips halfway down Bruce's shaft. But I knew I had her approval when I saw her flash a mischievous grin before she resumed eating Sue's pussy. Now that I had her go-ahead, I went back to my work with renewed fervor.

Lowering my head, I took Bruce's cock as far down

my throat as I could. Then I swallowed, letting my muscles contract around his shaft. He groaned at this, and I could tell it wouldn't be long before he came, especially considering how long the two women had been teasing him. Reaching up, I mimicked Wendy's actions from earlier and tickled his balls with my fingertips. He shuddered and his hips arched, driving his dick even farther into my mouth, as from beside us I heard the squeals and sighs of Wendy and Sue enjoying their sixty-nine.

I gave his balls a good squeeze and that did it— Bruce could hold out no longer. He grabbed my shoulders tightly, his fingers digging into my skin as he sent a torrent of hot, thick come down my throat. I swallowed his entire load, which had to be the largest amount of semen I had ever experienced at one time. Then I licked his dick clean and sat back on my haunches, smiling at him. Bruce looked both satisfied and relieved to have finally come. Just then, we heard a yelp, and we both turned to see what was going on.

Wendy was coming now, too, grinding her cunt on Sue's face. She writhed through her orgasm, and when she was finished she went back to eating her friend, who soon reached her own climax, grabbing Wendy's ass cheeks and holding on tightly as her body was racked with spasms. As soon as she was done, Wendy rolled off her and onto the floor, her eyes closed tight in exhaustion. I realized then that I was tired, too, and closed my own eyes.

When I opened my eyes again, I was alone in my apartment. I was sitting on the couch, my hand still in my panties, resting on my moist pussy. *That was some fantasy,* I thought to myself as I tried to pull myself together before my husband came home from work. I couldn't wait to share it with him, as I knew how sexy he thought those two girls were.

—*Ms. B.P., Cambridge, Massachusetts*

The Hawaii Five—Oh! Exotic Quintet Seduces Urbanite with Tropical Charms

It was the postcard that got me thinking. It arrived yesterday from my friend Stan, who was on his honeymoon in Hawaii. Meanwhile, I'm stuck in Chicago, trudging through slush and snow and freezing rain just to get to and from my office. The note scrawled on the back read, "Wish you were here," and I couldn't agree more.

But it was the front of the postcard that really grabbed my attention. It was one of those pictures that you tilt back and forth to make the image move. It featured a Polynesian beauty on a sunlit beach, the Pacific Ocean sparkling behind her. Clad only in a long grass skirt and bikini top, she was in a classic hula pose, both arms extended to one side. When I moved the card back and forth, her hips shifted suggestively from side to side, doing a little dance, and she seemed to wink at me. Stan's really got my number and knows just what to do to get my juices flowing.

I stuck the postcard on the bulletin board and made myself comfortable on the couch to watch the news.

There were all sorts of reports of the day's happenings, but my eyes kept straying to the hula girl staring provocatively at me from the wall. Closing my eyes, I imagined that I was the one basking in the Hawaiian sun, a frosty piña colada by my side. The beach was deserted, and the only sounds were the waves lapping softly against the shore and a gull or two flying overhead. Then, from far off in the distance, I saw a figure moving slowly in my direction.

As the figure came a bit closer, I could make out that it was a pretty woman, accompanied by the sounds of drumming and a gentle rustling. The whole thing was very strange, since there was no actual drummer to be seen. When I finally got a close look at her, I discovered the source of the rustling: She was wearing a long grass skirt that hung low on her hips and stopped right above her slender ankles. Her only other covering was a red and yellow floral bikini top and an orchid lei around her neck. She was a sight to behold, with raven locks cascading down over her shoulders, deeply tanned olive-toned skin, and dark, almond-shaped eyes.

The drumming got louder as she approached. About two feet away from me she stopped, then began moving her hips and arms to the rhythm of the music. I watched, entranced, as her body writhed before me, her hips shaking back and forth, allowing me glimpses of long, slender legs through the parting strands of grass. My cock throbbed as I thought about what else was under her skirt, so I reached out to my beautiful apparition, wanting to find out the answer.

The dancer stopped me with a flash of her eyes. She

removed the lei from around her neck and placed it over my head, the soft petals brushing my bare chest. Then she disappeared as suddenly and mysteriously as she had arrived. I looked all around, the smell of orchids strong in my nose, but she was gone, and as far as I could tell, without a trace. I was wondering where she could have gone when a sand crab skittered over my foot. I looked down and saw an arrow drawn into the sand, pointing away from the surf. Curious, I set out in that direction.

As I walked, the sound of drumming once again reverberated in my ears, growing louder as I approached a grouping of palm trees and small grass huts. Right in the middle, people were gathered around a fire, men on drums with their broad chests adorned by necklaces made of bones, and more hula dancers. My beauty from the beach was among them, and she and the others beckoned me closer. Their dance grew more erotic as I approached, their arms reaching out to me. All I wanted at that moment was to feel those hands upon my body, finding my most sensitive spots and bringing my arousal to that point of no return. Instead, the hula dancers drew their arms away, though only to reach behind their backs and remove their bikini tops.

I couldn't believe my eyes. Right before me were five pairs of the most perfect breasts I had ever seen, round and firm and crowned by rosy nipples growing harder in the cool evening breeze. I reached out, touching first one, then another, and soon I was surrounded by the dancers and carried to a pallet made from straw.

The drummers disappeared as I was set down, though the beat continued its rhythm.

One dancer fed me bites of papaya as another fanned me with a banana leaf. My cock sprang free as my shorts were pulled down my hips, and before long someone was taking care of that as well. Wet lips wrapped around my member, sliding up and down over the pulsing shaft. Another mouth attended to my balls, sucking on them. I closed my eyes to savor the intense sensations and soon felt fingers playing with my nipples, tickling at first, then pinching and squeezing them to hardness. As I gasped with pleasure, the numerous hands and mouths, all extremely talented, saw to my every need.

The juice from the papaya ran from my lips and down my chin, and a moist tongue darted out to lick up the sticky liquid. Soon the taste of the fruit was replaced by another flavor, this one tangy and strong, as a wet pussy lowered itself over my mouth. I dined voraciously upon this delectable treat, reaching up to grasp a pair of firm thighs as the dancer's body writhed above my face.

The mouth on my cock grew more insistent, sucking harder, as did the one on my balls. I could no longer hold back the growl, long and loud, that escaped from my throat, vibrating against the pussy at my mouth. Soon that dancer's cries were echoing my own, practically drowning out the unceasing drumming beat. When her sobs subsided, she got down on her knees beside me and gave me a passionate kiss, offering me her tongue to suck.

Mouths were everywhere, covering my cock and

my balls, licking and sucking every available expanse of skin, teasing my nipples into a frenzy. My nerves went electric with pleasure as the hula girls brought my arousal higher than it had ever gone before. The pounding surf and the beating drums hammered faster and faster in my ears as the blood rushed from my appendages, making a beeline for my throbbing cock. I got harder in the dancer's mouth, growing longer and thicker, but still she took it all, swallowing my entire length. She must have signaled to her friends, because I soon felt added pressure on my balls and nipples, urging me even closer to my orgasm.

Blindly, I reached out, searching for soft breasts, and finally settled on a pair. Kneading the smooth skin, I jerked my cock into the wet mouth of an exotic Polynesian beauty. She didn't miss a beat, and I felt the familiar tightening in my balls that signaled the approach of my release. I clenched my ass tightly, feeling the heated bodies swarming around mine, and prepared for the inevitable.

All at once, everything seemed to melt. The scenery around me turned to liquid as hands, breasts, and lips brushed against my body, urging my climax. I opened my eyes and locked onto a pair of deep brown ones— my original hula girl—as her lips drew down over my cock one last time. That was all I needed, and I shot my load into her mouth, pumping what seemed like a gallon of semen down her throat.

She took it all, swallowing each considerable shot, although she let some drip down my shaft to be licked up by one of her friends. This was too much for me, and I came again, something I'd never done before. When another girl took her place at my cock to feast on my copious juices, the sensations became almost overwhelming. I closed my eyes, letting it all wash over me, the hands, the mouths, the surf, the drumming.

I opened my eyes, finally hearing the knocking at my apartment door. I opened it to find my girlfriend standing there, a bag of Chinese takeout in her hand.

"Hey, you look a bit flushed," she said, touching her hand to my forehead. "Are you feeling all right?"

I nodded in response, then took the bag out of her hand and embraced her, pressing her body against my erection. "Never better, honey. Never better."

—*Mr. R.W., Chicago, Illinois*   O⊢▪

Hot New Employee Has His Imagination Working Overtime

All right, so maybe Denise doesn't realize that she's my secret fantasy Valentine. I have been watching her, nevertheless, ever since she was hired about ten months back. To most of the younger guys in the office, she's just the no-nonsense woman brought in by senior management to shake things up, a first-class troublemaker. To me, however, she has been an unending source of highly erotic fascination.

To begin with, forty-something Denise has a body that most twenty-year-olds would envy; she is petite with smallish but well-formed breasts and a marvelous heart-shaped ass atop long, shapely legs. She has the face of a Botticelli Venus, with high cheekbones and large eyes. A cloud of wavy, streaked blonde curls completes the picture. She also has a fabulous sense of style, always dressing fashionably. And always completely buttoned up.

There's usually been a sense of cool distance between us, but this morning I caught Denise looking at me in a way that was frankly appraising, almost predatory. I'm sorry to say that it passed as soon as she saw I'd noticed. Too bad, because my mind has been in overdrive fantasizing about her, and I've been half-hard ever since seeing her at the coffee station this morning.

I keep picturing myself making passionate love to her and leaving her begging for more. Here's my favorite version:

I notice Denise's office light burning late into the night, so I stay late myself, finally working up the balls to knock softly on her door. It is unlocked, so I enter. I'm greeted by the sight of demure Denise facing her computer screen, but she isn't working. Her silk blouse is unbuttoned and her left hand is cupping a perfect breast through a very expensive-looking lace bra. Her right hand is busy somewhere between her legs, one of which is propped on the desktop, knee askew. Her head is back, mouth open, eyes shut. Tiny gasps are coming from her throat.

My footsteps are muffled as I cross the thick carpet to stand behind her chair. I bend over her, tracing the outline of her left breast with my forefinger. This brings a louder moan. Evidently she is too far gone to realize what the appearance of extra fingers means. Or maybe she doesn't care.

Or perhaps this is what she has been expecting all along. So I whisper in her ear, very softly, "Are we having fun yet?"

At that, her eyes fly open and her hands dart about, trying to bring her blouse together and pull her skirt down. Her face turns beet red, her eyes staring up at me and her mouth open in surprise.

"I . . . I was . . . just—" she stammers to explain.

"I know," I reply. "And I don't mind one bit." And before she has time to react, I have spun her chair around to face me. She rises, and when she is on her feet, she finds my hand in her hair, pulling her head back as my other arm slips around her waist, pulling her close. "Oh!" is all she can utter before I cover her mouth with a lingering kiss. As I pull away to trail kisses down her throat, her hands are in my hair, on my back, and she is heaving against me.

I ease her down onto her desk, scattering papers in all directions. I continue kissing her throat, and then go lower, first skimming the top of her lovely bra, then licking and sucking her nipples through the thin fabric. Since it is a front-closure type, the bra opens in an instant, and Denise's left nipple, as hard as a tiny marble, is between my lips.

I think she is going to come immediately when I caress the tender nub with my tongue tip, but although her moans become louder, she has the presence of mind to guide my head to her other breast. I take the nipple between my teeth this time, tugging gently upward, lashing the tip with my tongue. Immediately her body arches upward and her hands seize my hair, pulling my head down with force. She apparently has very sensitive breasts. She comes immediately, her entire body jerking spasmodically on the desk.

While Denise drifts gently back to earth, I remove her skirt and panties. Then, after removing my tie, I blindfold her with it. I ease her farther onto the desk, so her head hangs off the side.

Denise now lies quietly on the desk, blouse and bra open, taut stomach heaving, her neatly trimmed bush framing a very wet pussy. The eighteen-inch ruler I have discovered nearby isn't ideal, but it will have to do. When she starts to raise her hands to remove the tie, I tap the ruler on the side of her breast.

"Leave your hands at your sides," I say to her sternly.

Her breath hisses between her teeth. "Ow!" she squeals. Tap! Her other breast this time. She moves her hands to cover herself. Tap! A little harder, a little closer to the nipple, which I notice is stiffening.

I repeat, "Leave your hands at your sides." Tap! Tap! "Or I'll leave. Is that what you want?" Tap! "Is it?"

And finally her answer. "N-no. Don't . . . don't go. Please."

"You were very naughty to come like that. I didn't say you could." Tap! On the inside of the thigh. Tap! Tap! "Open your legs. I want to see you. Are you wet?" Tap! With a little whimper, she spreads her legs, her bottom grazing the very edge of the desk.

"What do you want, Denise? What do you want me to do?" Tap! Gently, on the outer lips. She seems to shrink from the blow, but does not move to cover herself. Tap! Tap! A bit harder, causing her to squirm. Her nipples are outrageously stiff, and a flush is spreading across her breasts. Tap!

"Answer me."

"I want you to fuck me! Now!" she howls, writhing.

"And so I shall, my sweet," I reply. Standing between Denise's legs, I began to rub my cock along her pussy lips and over her clit. Her hips are bucking upward and her hands are clenching rhythmically. As she pushes against me and raises her hips, I bend my legs and lodge the head of my dick in her cunt.

Then I begin to move slowly in and out, never more than a few inches. In no time, she is thrusting upward to meet me, and the edge of the desk is slick with her moisture.

I wrap my arms around her open legs and her back, picking her right up. With her legs over my shoulders, I hold her close to me as I let her slowly slide down the length of my cock. When her clit is nestled in my pubic hair, she is beside herself, moaning, howling, and trying to hump against me. I lift her again and drop her gently, this time angling my massive erection to slide along her clit. By the time she reaches the end of this trip she is wailing.

When I raise her again, I reach around and jam a finger against the puckered ring of her asshole. This seems to bring her back to her senses, and she begins to squirm. Her cries gradually mix with moans of pleasure. Slowly, inexorably, she sinks onto my fat finger, which is well lubricated with her honey. She comes at least once for every inch of finger that disappears into her ass.

Finally, the sensations became too much and she begins to heave against me. I wind my hand in her hair again and pull her head back so I can kiss and lick her. I feel the throes of her orgasm as her cunt grips my cock and her asshole clutches my finger tightly. She squeals as I erupt into her, completely filling her.

I could be wrong about Denise, of course. She may in fact be exactly as she appears: one tough-as-nails cookie without a sensual bone in her body. But in my fantasy, she is a perfect submissive, putty in my hands as I make her come time and again.

—*Mr. C.W., Via Email*

Painting a Picture of Total Submission to a Royal Lady

After a long and crazy morning at the office, I decided to take the afternoon off. I didn't know where I was going but I walked quickly, and somehow my body found its way up the cement steps of a museum. It had been years since I stepped foot in one of those places.

I paid the admission fee and walked through the quiet rooms, staring up at the tall ceilings as I listened to the sound of my shoes clicking on the floor. I stopped in front of various paintings on the walls and tilted my head in confusion and amusement at many of the modern pieces. I looked at a painting with splashes of color and stripes across the canvas and thought: *I can do that*. All of the bright colors and sharp lines made me tense up a bit more and I moved on, still unsure of what I was searching for.

As I entered another room, my muscles immediately relaxed. The colors around me were subtle and soothing. I stood in front of a painting and was taken in by its warm and real image. The woman pictured stood tall and voluptuous, yet she still seemed frail. Her hair was long and curly and so red I almost had to squint to look directly at it. Her eyes were wild and mysterious, although she stood composed and graceful. She wore a long white dress with gold trim and stood in front of a throne with a sword, long and powerful, in her extended hand. I was hypnotized by her wistful beauty.

In front of this woman, under the blade of the sword, knelt a man who looked to be of great strength. His shoulders were wide, and he was covered in the armor of a knight, except for his helmet, which lay neatly beside him as he bowed before the woman. I felt my cock stir in my pants and was shocked at my arousal.

After staring at the painting for a while, I walked around the wing and noticed that many of the other works featured women and situations like the one I'd fallen in love with. Clearly the paintings were of women who lived in a time when they were supposed to obey and serve their men, but you could tell that they were always in control and were able to seduce and tempt their male victims as they pleased.

After stopping at the gift shop to buy a book of the

paintings that had made me so hot, I headed home. I was going to explode if I didn't release my sexual tension soon.

Once home, I leafed through the pages of the book and found myself imagining what it would be like to be one of the men in the paintings. My job as a knight would be to protect the woman I served. I couldn't think of anything more stimulating.

In my fantasy, I am clad in my armor as I walk toward her. She is sitting on her throne, her hair pulled back all the way except for a couple of pieces that have fought to be free and curl wildly around her temples. She does not speak, only motions me forward. I kneel before her with my head lowered, raising my eyes slightly to see the tips of her toes peeking out of the bottom of her gown. If she knew how excited she made me she would have my head!

I say a silent prayer that she will not notice how heavily I'm breathing or the sweat dripping from my brow. She looks at me and then suddenly demands that the room be cleared. I try to rise, but she commands me not to move as all of her servants scurry about, racing for the exit.

"Are you not well, sir?" she asks. All the armor in the kingdom could not protect me from her. I freeze, unable to reply. "Have you lost your tongue?" Just as I am about to get my explanation out, she commands me to remove my armor and all that I am wearing underneath and kneel again. I look at her, puzzled, when she explains, "Deal with me or deal with my guards. It is your choice, sir."

Removing the clumsy metallic covering as quickly as I can, I kneel in front of her wearing nothing but my bare skin. I keep my head lowered and try to get my obvious erection to subside, but it is completely useless. She walks around me slowly.

Grabbing my hair, she pulls my head back and leans in close enough that I feel her warm breath on my lips as she checks the whites of my eyes and tells me to stick out my tongue as far as I can. "Uh-huh," she says, as if she approves. She releases her grip to check behind my ears and then resumes walking around me.

As she inspects me, she runs a finger lightly along my flesh. She starts at my neck and spirals around me like a slow tornado until she reaches my biceps and digs her nails into my skin so hard they leave marks.

"Stand up," she orders. She continues circling me until I feel dizzy from all the blood rushing to my cock. Stopping suddenly, she pretends to notice my erection for the first time. She grabs it firmly in her hand and pulls me toward her. "What do we have here, sir? Have you any idea what the penalty is for your impure thoughts? You are supposed to be a noble knight, yet I must treat you like a disobedient servant." Placing her tiny hand on my shoulder and pushing me back down on my knees, she orders me to follow her.

I crawl behind her, watching her heels lift off the floor as she walks before me. So absorbed am I that when she stops dead in her tracks I bump right into her, my face pushing the free-flowing material of her gown between her thighs. "You've just added five more lashes to your punishment," she says matter-of-factly, tapping a riding crop against her palm.

With me still on all fours, she gets behind me and places her free hand on my ass. She rubs my skin gently and a low moan escapes my mouth. "Don't make a sound," I hear her say. Then, without warning, I feel the sting of the crop on one ass cheek. In shock, I lose my balance and fall face-first to the cold stone floor with my ass still sticking straight up in the air.

My lady straddles my back and orders me back up on all fours. Twisting at the waist, she delivers the next few blows to my ass while she sits on top of me as if I were a horse. I know that she is not wearing anything under her dress because I can feel her pubic hair on my skin as she smears her juices all over me. She rides me, stimulating herself almost to the point of climax, then rises and administers the rest of my punishment from behind. Each blow makes it a little harder to contain the orgasm building inside.

My ass cheeks are red and throbbing as I follow her back to her throne, where she positions herself with spread legs. She lifts her dress, and then has me— her naked knight—kneel before her. "You are a brave man, sir. Your tolerance for pain is great. I admire that. I shall allow you to taste me." I close my eyes and lean forward to smell her arousal. My tongue reaches the folds of her pussy, and I lap up her juices.

The royal lady purrs in approval, and I dive in deep between her thighs, flicking my tongue furiously against her clit, sucking her pussy lips. Knowing that she is losing control, she tries to push me away, but I grab hold of her hips and pull her to the edge of her seat. Shuddering and thrashing about, she comes, glossing my face with her juices. I ravish her sex with my tongue until her body jerks for the last time, and she falls against the back of her throne in a blissful state of exhaustion.

"You're a healthy and noble knight," she says. "I shall allow you to penetrate me." Not wasting a moment, I impale her with my manhood just the same way I slide my sword into its sheath, with one clean, smooth stroke. She arches her back in my arms and her hair sways behind her as I move in and out. With her gown pulled up around her waist, my hands caress her milky-white thighs as her fingers run through my hair. I thrust into her until all of the sexual tension I have been building erupts inside her, triggering her paroxysms of pleasure.

My depleted cock slips out of her warmth, and I kneel before her once again as she holds her gown up high. I kiss the tops of her feet and her ankles, slowly sliding my tongue up her legs and thighs, licking up the semen now oozing out of her pussy. "You may go now, sir," she says softly.

My fantasy ended with me bringing myself to orgasm as I stared at the picture of the painting I had seen in the museum. I knew I would be servicing my lady in many of my future fantasies.

—*Mr. S.P., St. Louis, Missouri*

Breathtaking Thrills for a Dashing Zorro and a Wild Harem Girl

I met my husband, Gregg, at a costume party where he was dressed as Zorro, and I was having a fantasy night decked out as Barbara Eden's character in *I Dream of Jeannie*. He looked breathtaking. While we were chatting over sangria, I noticed him looking me up and down, checking me out. I knew he was interested and later, when I came out of the bathroom, he cornered me in the hallway.

"It's unwise to keep Zorro waiting like that."

He stepped forward and put one hand on the door on either side of me, so close that I couldn't move. Excited by his strong, masculine essence, I squirmed against his chest.

"Want to be my genie in a bottle?" he whispered into my ear in an earthy voice filled with sex. I mumbled something shy and stupid, but my trembling body gave me away.

"Come on. Let Zorro sweep you off your feet and ravish you," he said, moving his hands to my shoulders. As he began to gently massage them, I stayed frozen, my heart beating in my ears. "Let me show you something you've never experienced before. Trust me that this will be a night you will never forget."

I still can't tell you what made me open that guest room door. Whether it was the feeling of his powerful hands on my shoulders, the sexy sound of his voice in my ear, or my own hormones going berserk, I'll never know for certain. Once we were inside, he closed the door and locked it.

"For tonight, my lovely harem girl, you are my captive, and you'll get away only when I let you go. Understand?"

I nodded, and he told me to undress. In a few minutes I was standing naked in the middle of the room. Then I was ordered to undress him, and I did, starting with his boots. In fact, he made me get on my knees in front of him to remove them. Then, with his consent, I rose and took off his shirt and leather pants, releasing the bulge forming at the apex of his sturdy thighs. It was so thrilling to touch this muscular man with caramel skin and very little body hair.

Pushing me back to my knees, he said, "Pleasure me. Make me ready for you."

Oral sex was not my specialty, but he sure seemed like a great man to practice on. With one hand, he grabbed hold of my dark brown hair and held my head in place while he used the other hand to position his cock at the entrance to my mouth. He was so big, but I gently flicked my tongue on him and he moaned with pleasure. He started to shove more of himself in my mouth, and I wrapped both of my hands around his cock, so that when he thrust, only so much of his hard shaft went past my lips. There was no way I could take it all.

After a couple of strokes, he pulled my hands away before continuing to work his organ in and out of my mouth. I almost gagged and put my hands back on him. He grunted, and in a few moments I removed my hands again. He gave me a few more strokes, each one deeper than the last, and my instincts again found me wrapping my hands around the base of his cock to control its action.

"That's it," Zorro groaned, and pulled out completely. Walking over to the floor where his pants had been discarded, he picked them up and pulled his belt free. I trembled as he headed back toward me, lifting me up and putting me down on the floor at the end of the bed. With me on my knees again, he used the belt to tie my hands above my head to the bedpost. "Trust me," he said in a deep Zorro voice. "I know how much of my cock you can take. Now relax and enjoy it—okay?"

I nodded as my lower lip trembled. He inserted the tip of his cock into my mouth and used both hands to hold my head in place as he started to fuck my face.

"Oh, yeah!" he said, pumping in and out, deeper and deeper. When I gagged, he slowed down and gently caressed my cheek. The softness of his touch helped me to relax the muscles of my throat so his next thrust could go deeper.

I didn't take him all in, but I got a good bit, a lot more than I thought I could. And it felt good. I loved having his cock in my mouth, fucking my face until he spilled his come onto my tongue. I loved the taste of it, powerful and sexy.

"That was good, baby," he said. "You are a better cocksucker than you thought you were, huh?" He smiled and untied me.

Helping me up, he wrapped his arm possessively

around my hip and then pushed me back onto a pile of guests' coats on the bed. He got on his knees between my legs and buried his face in my pussy. He started eating me as if he were starving and I was an all-you-can-eat buffet. He ran his tongue up and down my slit, then sucked my clitoris into his mouth. His sucking motions were hard and frenzied, and I came fast, literally convulsing with pleasure.

Zorro kept going, stopping only to penetrate me with his tongue, and then went back to my clit. I came again, and this time I actually saw stars. I tried to push him away to regain my breath, but he wouldn't budge. The only response I got was a grunt as he kept licking and sucking me. As the next orgasm hit, I felt a little faint. His mouth released me, and he stood up to shift me into a more comfortable position on the bed.

"For a minute there I thought you had wimped out on me." His words were rough, but the look in his eyes showed real concern. I was touched by his gentleness.

"I'm fine," I said, and offered my lips up for a very soft kiss.

He grinned mischievously and said, "Let's continue then." He got down on top of me, his weight pinning me to the mattress as he nursed at my nipples and stroked himself to hardness again. Pulling my legs apart, he positioned his cock at my wet opening and began to push himself inside. I felt his magnificent cock stretching the walls of my love tunnel, filling me completely. Burying himself to the hilt, he pulled out teasingly and then slammed back into me.

We fucked hard and fast, my hips thrusting up to meet his plunging cock. I felt myself beginning to come yet again, and a scream of ecstasy escaped my throat. My dashing lover swallowed the scream with a kiss.

"Yes, baby," he growled. "Take my cock. Take me deep inside you." His body began to tense with orgasm. "That's it, little harem girl. You love it when I'm fucking you. I know you do."

Then he commanded that I come for him. My body, hot and sweaty, quivered beneath him. I was sated and absolutely exhausted. Zorro's come shot in hot spurts deep inside me.

We quickly pulled ourselves back together and returned to the party. Soon after, Gregg took me home and spent the night in my bed, taking me doggie-style in the early-morning hours. I dozed off, and when I awoke I found a note on the pillow where he had slept, saying, "Thank you for last night. I'll never forget it. Women like you make me thankful to be a man."

Even though I dated other guys after that, I ended up with Gregg. I was attracted to his sexy confidence; he knows what he wants and how to get it, at the same time bringing me almost more pleasure than I can endure.

Ironically, I met the strong, demanding lover of my dreams at a costume party, where we were both enjoying a night of fantasy.

—Ms. A.P., Tulsa, Oklahoma

Invasion of the Perfect People—Sci-Fi Fans Dazzled by Amorous Aliens

My wife and I are big sci-fi fans. As a matter of fact, we met at a convention of science-fiction enthusiasts ten years ago. Between the two of us, I think we've read just about every book about extraterrestrials and seen almost every movie. From *Invasion of the Body Snatchers*, a classic of the genre and one of our all-time favorites, to *Men in Black*, we've spent countless hours enthralled by a variety of stories about visitors from outer space.

Jenny and I are also very sexual people, so I suppose it's not all that surprising, given our fascination with things extraterrestrial, that our favorite erotic fantasy revolves around aliens. But our dream aliens are altogether different from those so often encountered in books and films; they're not misshapen creatures hell-bent on taking over or destroying earth. No, our aliens are peaceful, exceedingly sensuous, and pleasure-loving. They are humanoid, but of such grace and beauty as to define the word "perfection." The men all resemble Greek gods, with magnificently sculpted bodies and large penises. All the women are ravishing, statuesque goddesses, flawless in every aspect.

My wife's version of our erotic sci-fi fantasy differs from mine only in that her focus is, quite naturally, on the male aliens, their large cocks and their extraordinary stamina. I dwell on the unparalleled beauty and natural passion of the female aliens.

Jenny and I envision ourselves living in a farm-house surrounded by acres of land. Very late one night we are awakened by what sounds like an explosion in the sky. The bedroom is bathed in a white light. Together, Jenny and I go to the window and peer out. In the distance we see it, a saucer-shaped craft ringed with flashing yellow lights sitting in the meadow. The roar of its engine gradually subsides until all is quiet. My wife and I turn to each other and smile; our steadfast belief in life on another planet has been rewarded. We will be the first people on earth to greet the visitors.

Still in our pajamas, we make our way through the house and then out the front door. Hand in hand we start toward the spaceship, which is now a rainbow of color, the soft, inviting hues soothing our anxiety and drawing us ever closer. Jenny grips my hand tighter, but her gaze, like mine, remains on the spacecraft. Suddenly, a large door on the ship opens and a ramp descends to the ground. And then, in the doorway, we see a naked man and woman beckoning us to walk up the ramp and enter the craft.

Jenny and I feel we have no other choice; there seems to be some kind of magnetic force pulling us into the ship. No sooner do we enter than a feeling of calm washes over us. The man and woman smile, put-ting us even more at ease. They are incredibly perfect specimens of male and female, spectacular to behold. My wife seems mesmerized by the man and watches breathlessly as his impressive cock grows fully erect before her eyes. It's as if he is able to simply will his member to become completely hard. All the while he is smiling at her.

My attention is riveted to the woman, whose pretty face and figure are nothing less than breathtaking. She is tall, my height actually, with a body seemingly molded by a master craftsman. Her eyes are a sea blue and her golden tresses fall to her perfectly rounded buttocks. Like her companion (husband? lover?), she has a smile that is at once loving and wickedly seductive.

The man, now fully erect, his cock jutting proudly from his loins, holds out his arms in welcome to my wife. As if in a daze, she steps toward him and he takes both her hands in his. The woman, meanwhile, steps to me and takes me by the hand. Moments later, Jenny and I are being guided through the spacecraft to a comfortably cool, softly lit room containing but a single piece of furniture: a large bed with pillows. My wife and I are helped out of our pajamas and steered onto the bed.

Here, Jenny's fantasy veers off in a slightly different direction as she concentrates on the pleasure derived from her magnificent alien partner. I, in turn, focus on my gorgeous female from outer space.

I am truly in another world as the ravishing, statuesque blonde bathes my naked body with kisses. She is as strong as she is beautiful, arranging me this way and that as her talented tongue seeks out every nook and cranny of my body. She is careful, though, not to touch my cock, which at this point is as hard as it has ever been and aching for attention. Finally, with her long hair tickling my flesh, she licks her way down my chest and takes my erection into her mouth. I moan in gratitude, then continue to savor the sensations as she proceeds to give me an out-of-this-world blowjob, alternately licking and sucking my cock and balls until I'm about to burst with pleasure.

I look over at my wife and see that she, too, is in another world, her pretty face flushed with desire as she thrills to the cunnilingual expertise of her alien partner. From the way she is squirming around and whimpering with delight, it is obvious that his technique is nothing less than spectacular. With his face plastered to her pussy and his hands kneading her breasts, he is delighting her to no end.

I am ready to beg my luscious partner to make me come when she suddenly pulls my cock, dripping with her saliva, from her mouth and quickly straddles me. Moments later, she is posting on my manhood, riding it smoothly—up, down, up, down—her fingers tweaking my sensitive nipples as she smiles at me. (She, like her male counterpart, never speaks.)

A guttural moan from the other side of the bed makes me look over at my wife, who is now being soundly screwed by her alien lover. He lifts her legs and drapes them over his mighty shoulders, then drives into her again, pushing her knees back into her breasts as his cock goes balls-deep into her happy pussy. She looks my way, but I doubt that she really sees me in the haze of her lust.

The fantastic woman riding my cock now slides up my body to position her golden-haired pussy on my face. She smells and tastes like no other woman I have ever known, and I drive my tongue as deep into her heavenly cunt as possible as I slurp up her juices. When I take her very aroused clitoris between my lips, she moans appreciatively.

It goes on like this for some time. My wife and I are treated to the glorious lovemaking talents of our respective alien partners, both of whom seem capable of sucking and fucking for hours on end. The man, for example, comes five times during his session with Jenny, amazing her, and me, with the amount of creamy semen his wildly throbbing cock shoots out at each ejaculation. His female counterpart, meanwhile, gives new meaning to the term "multiple orgasms."

Jenny comes many times herself, experiencing her most intense orgasm with her partner's amazing cock rooting in her rear passage. Watching my lovely wife being vigorously ass-fucked is more arousing than I ever thought possible, and with my fabulous partner sucking hungrily on my balls and finger-fucking my ass, I come so hard I almost pass out.

In a happy daze, my wife and I are escorted off the spaceship by our new friends, who stand in the doorway and wave good-bye as we start back to our house. It isn't until the next morning, when we wake up stark naked, that we remember we went to bed wearing pajamas. We laugh at the idea of our pajamas in outer space, then turn serious as we realize the magnitude of what has transpired and how envious our sci-fi friends will be when we tell them we got it on with aliens.

—*Mr. N. F., Miami, Florida*

Comic Book Character Leaps Off
the Pages to Thrill Her Creator

I'm an accountant, but I've always enjoyed drawing and have a collection of comic book scenes that I have copied hanging on my walls.

When I was younger I used to draw country scenes with plenty of fall foliage and the sun glistening on a nondescript lake. I didn't start to draw people until I met Melinda. She was so beautiful, I found myself sketching her face on the edges of the newspaper or on the phone message pad in my friends' homes. But when our relationship ended, I erased all traces of her.

That was when I started to copy comic strips. I found the women in many comic books to be attractive and busty, really fun to draw. And you never have to worry about them breaking your heart.

I took a special interest in Rogue from the X-Men. She is one hot little comic book character. She is tall and has auburn hair with a white streak running through the front. And what a rack!

I began thinking about my own Rogue-type fantasy woman while driving home in my car at night. And then at home I would sketch what I had imagined.

Six months' worth of daydreaming and nighttime jerking off turned into a comic book adventure called *Pleasure Quest*, where a super-beauty named Thalia sets out on a quest to please my every desire. Neat, huh?

Like Rogue, Thalia had auburn hair and a fantastic body, only Thalia's résumé of superpowers did not include the ability to punch through walls or fly. Rather, Thalia had the ability to make a man come by barely touching him and an unearthly knack for giving head.

In one of my favorite fantasies, Thalia walked into a club where I was seated by myself drinking a gin and tonic. She was hard to miss with her sports bra, daisy dukes, and knee-high boots (typical superhero garb), and I spotted her right away. I pretended not to see her, though, and went right on drinking my gin.

It wasn't until I felt her ice-blue eyes on the back of my neck that I turned my head to meet her stare. Her cheeks beat with a deep flush, and I lost my breath from the sight of her. The air began to feel thick, almost suffocating, as we looked at each other. My cock had instantly hardened and an orgasmic-type shiver shot straight through my core, awakening my body and filling me with an absolutely voracious need that I knew she felt as well.

Thalia came toward me, the rope she carries fastened to her belt swiping her exposed leg as she walked. Just eyeing her milky flesh made me yearn to touch her, to kiss her. But I fought the desire, wanting her to work for my affection.

At that very moment, Thalia tied her rope into a noose big enough for a bull and lassoed me out of the bar, off to someplace dark and quiet.

I couldn't see her at first; my eyes hadn't adjusted to the dark. But I could feel her breath on my face, and I could smell her musky scent. She lightly grazed my throat with her fingertips, and that electric shock came again, wracking my form and claiming me.

She began to unbutton my shirt, each finger dancing over my flesh, sending me into an orgasmic high. I could no longer play hard to get. I had to have her, to touch her. I nudged my lips at her mouth, opening it so that I could slip my tongue inside. Thalia sucked it in eagerly and began winding her tongue around mine as she continued to disrobe me—her long, slender fingers now working on the buttons of my jeans. My mouth locked on hers, and I kissed her like I wanted to swallow her.

Finally naked, my cock poked at her bare stomach and my hands tore at her clothes. Her breasts brushed against my chest, and I swore that I was going to lose it.

I began smothering Thalia with kisses, sucking her neck hard enough to leave a mark, biting her nipples just enough to cause a delicious sting, and she tongued my neck lusciously, sweeping me away with her sweet kisses.

As it was Thalia's goal to please me, she took over then, gathering up my balls in her right hand, massaging them gently—ever so gently. Her lips sucked on my neck, and I thought I'd go mad. She made her way down my chest, biting into my flesh, licking at it, pulling on my chest hairs with her teeth. My skin had come alive all over, and my cock was now jabbing at her pussy, pushing to enter her. The feel of her was too exquisite; I wanted inside.

My body went rigid, and my cock pulsed. Thalia's fingers let go of my balls and closed around the shaft of my penis, stroking it upward. I continued to kiss her all over her face, sucking at her cheeks and lips.

My cock was pumping, hardening with each stroke

of her palm, and I started to moan and mumble, telling her I was going to come, telling her not to stop, that it felt so good.

Thalia pushed me back on a couch and straddled me. Then came the exquisite feeling of her cunt opening as I penetrated her and her pussy lips wrapping around my cock, hugging it tightly as she took me in. A thumping sensation coursed through me as she began to ride my dick, intensifying with each thrust of her curvy hips.

Thalia's whole body moved in a graceful undulation to receive my shaft. I watched her delicate form rising and falling as she took me inside her. Her arms were wrapped around my shoulders, her fingers digging into my flesh, driving me on faster, harder. She pushed up, her hips thrusting into mine, our bodies slapping slightly. I squeezed one of her nipples with my left hand, trying to match the delicious pinch of her nails on my back.

Her cunt was so tight and wet, and with the sexy curve of her naked belly and the slight brush of her beautiful breasts against my chest, I was pushed to a state of delirium.

I brought my hands down to rub her ass cheeks and push her down deeper on my cock. She was moaning my name, crying out occasionally, and my body coursed with a wave of small orgasmic-type quivers—orgasms caused by her fingers, her kissing, her breath on my ears. And then finally I came, spurting my come deep inside her hot, wet cunt.

But Thalia wasn't through. She slid down on the

couch, positioning herself between my legs, and then took my flaccid cock in her warm little mouth. More orgasmic jitters traveled over my flesh as she slid her lips over the head, the fingers of her right hand wrapped around my shaft and her left hand grabbing my balls.

She took my cock and my balls all the way down her throat (after all, she is a superhero) and feasted on them, sucking me, licking me, slathering me with her saliva. It was heaven and hell combined as I neared another preternatural explosion, my body craving an orgasm and wanting to postpone it at the same time.

My body could handle only so much of Thalia's unworldly power, and in seconds I was shooting my load down her throat. She swallowed it all, and then licked her lips as if she were hungry for more.

Thalia climbed on top of me and began to kiss me . . . But that is another frame altogether.

      —*Mr. L.T., Brockton, Massachusetts*

Rebellious Rocker Takes Starstruck Fan to His Hotel for Some Burning Love

After the first few chords of music, I ran out onstage, my guitar slung around my neck. The audience started to scream even louder, and as I looked out over the seemingly endless rows of excited fans, I saw only one thing: girls. Hundreds, maybe thousands of them, their lipsticked mouths just waiting to be kissed, their perky breasts encased in tight cashmere sweaters. My imagination took me lower, to straight wool skirts hugging curvy hips and smooth, slender calves ending at cotton socks and penny loafers.

It was a good thing I was wearing my tight sharkskin pants, because my cock hardened instantly at the thought of all those girls lusting for me. I grabbed the mic and began to sing, shaking my hips and grinding my pelvis. The crowd went wild, and for the rest of the concert the music could barely be heard over their screams.

Afterward, I ran backstage, brushing off my manager and members of the press to make my way to my car. I wanted some action and knew there would be girls waiting for me by the stage door. When I stepped outside, they went frantic, screaming my name and shoving paper and pens at me. I signed a few autographs and then picked out a cute redhead, nodding in her direction. Stan, my bodyguard, went over and had a few words with her.

He returned with the girl, and then knew enough to disappear back inside the concert hall. I ushered her into my limousine, and we were driven to my hotel. She told me her name was Cathy and that she worked as a teller at the bank. I didn't need to know much more than that.

We got to my room and I locked the door behind us, hung up my jacket, and turned on the radio. One of my songs was playing, and I hummed along. Cathy waited quietly on the bed. Sitting down beside her, I took her face in my hands. She closed her eyes and tilted her head back for a kiss, so I placed my mouth on hers. Her lips parted and I slipped my tongue between them, placing my hand on the soft wool covering her breast to rub her nipple, which hardened under my thumb. Cathy's back arched, pressing her breast into my palm, and I thought I heard her release a faint sigh.

Sliding my hand up Cathy's skirt, I fingered the tops of her stockings as she slipped off her pumps. I crept higher up her thigh and felt the elastic leg of her panties and a few stray curls of hair. She melted at my touch, so I found my way into her panties and she shifted her body to meet my exploring fingers.

Cathy's thighs parted when I found her slit and skimmed my finger up and down. She was already wet, although I'm sure many girls at the concert were. Most of them went home to get themselves off to my records—only Cathy was lucky enough to spend some time with the real thing. I fingered her pussy, rubbing circles over her hard little clit as she squirmed in my arms. And all the while I fondled her breasts, although my hand had since slipped into her sweater. I had pushed up her bra so that my guitar-callused fingers made direct contact with soft flesh.

It seemed like Cathy wanted more, so I thrust a finger into her tight cunt and fucked her with it. She liked that so much I added two more, causing quite a stir. Breaking our kiss, Cathy threw back her head, biting her lip and making little mewling sounds. I finger-fucked her faster and harder, smearing her honey all over her sex and sometimes moving up to tickle her slippery button. As she came, I nibbled and sucked on her neck, leaving a big red mark she could show off to her friends.

Stroking her long, silky hair, I held Cathy tightly as she shivered and shook in my arms. She seemed so pleased by that one little orgasm, I wondered if it was her first—at least at the hands of a man. Then she surprised me by tentatively pawing at my prodigious erection, which rested against my thigh. Her other hand was still at my neck, so I took it and moved it to my waistband, and she immediately got the picture. She fumbled at my belt and fly, but soon enough, my cock was free and demanding attention.

With a light, uncertain touch, Cathy stroked my dick from head to base, even dipping down to my balls. I nuzzled her neck and murmured encouragement, moving my hips up and down to prompt the rhythm that I prefer. Cathy grew bold and started pumping harder, which felt good, but it wasn't enough.

I broke away from her grasp and quickly stepped out of my slacks. My shirt and tie followed, and then I undressed Cathy. She was shy at first, but I told her how beautiful her body was as each garment fell to the floor. By the time she was completely naked, Cathy was more at ease with herself. I wasn't lying; her rounded tummy was irresistible, and I kissed her belly button as I pulled off her sweater. Her bra came with it, exposing full, firm breasts capped by pink nipples. Her hips and ass were also round and feminine, and her pussy was covered with a soft down that matched the red hair on her head.

I sat on the bed facing Cathy again, my cock pointing out from my belly. We resumed necking, and I tangled my hand in the back of her long hair. Then I gently urged her down lower, so she kissed down my chest and stomach until she was right above my pubic hair. She stopped and looked up at me questioningly, and I nodded.

Parting her lips, Cathy touched her tongue to the tip of my cock and then licked around the rim. I thrust my hips slightly so that the entire head was in her mouth, and she closed her lips around it. Little by little she moved over my length until she reached the middle of my shaft. It was quite a sight—the red "O" of her lips encircling the circumference of my dick. I was throbbing even before her mouth came back up, her tongue dragging along the underside of my shaft, and then slid back down again.

My hand was still in her hair, so I used it to guide her some more. When she developed the rhythm that I like, I moved my hand down to her pussy. As I stroked her with my fingertips, I kneaded my balls with the other hand until Cathy pushed me away, understanding that was something I wanted her to do. She rolled them around in her palm, liking the way they felt and also liking the way my fingers in her cunt made her feel. She was moaning from deep in her throat, and I could feel the vibrations on my shaft. That got me so hot I could hardly stand it.

My hand was coated with Cathy's juices, and we were both so far along that I wasn't sure either of us could hold out much longer. But before I sent her home, I had to fuck her. So, even though it killed me to do it, I lifted her mouth off my cock and pushed her onto her back.

Cathy's face and body told me everything I needed to know. Her eyes were glazed, a small smile was playing at her lips, and her legs were spread wide, her labia peeled back so that her cunt hole was open and inviting. Getting between her thighs on my knees, I positioned my cockhead at her center. When I shoved inside her, she gasped sharply as her body tensed and her pussy tightened considerably around me. But she relaxed a bit as I began moving gently in and out of her hot cunt.

Initially, Cathy had been really tight, but soon my thrusts slid home smooth and easy. As we fucked, she clawed at my back and her legs flew up in the air to wrap around my waist. It was as though she instantly went from virgin to vixen, and I pounded into her forcefully as she got more and more into it.

Then I went crazy. All I could feel was her satiny vagina pulsating around my cock, her heels digging into my ass cheeks, and the wads of bedding in my hands. My balls bounced against her ass and my shaft became slick with our fluids. The sounds of slurping, gasping, and moaning drowned out the radio, which was playing some girl group of the moment.

I stuck my tongue back into Cathy's mouth, which still tasted minty from the gum she'd been chewing. But her breasts were beckoning to me, so I lowered my head and lapped at her sweat-salty flesh. I kept driving into her cunt, my hips moving rapidly, my cock rubbing against her clit with each in-and-out. Cathy bucked wildly, crying out her pleasure and arching her back so that her hips met mine.

Cathy was close to climax again, and I was determined to come with her. Steeling myself for the impact of orgasm, I thrust hard once more and felt my balls unload as her eyes grew wide and her body stiffened. Her pussy continued fluttering as I flooded her with a huge load of come, releasing two long bursts followed by a few more quick shots. Finally, she went slack as I collapsed on top of her.

Now that we were done, I pulled out, kissed her lightly on the nose, and then led her to the bathroom so she could freshen up. Then, with just a towel around my waist, I helped her get dressed and handed her an autographed eight-by-ten photo. Kissing Cathy goodbye, I told her that she would find my driver outside the hotel, and he would bring her wherever she wanted. Once she was gone, I settled in for a restful night of sleep, for I knew that tomorrow meant another town, another show, and possibly another girl.

—*Mr. R.S., Macon, Georgia*

Though Men Would Die for Her, Only One Was Worthy of Her Attention

The following letter was sent to me by a business associate who lives in another city. We have never dated because of our professional relationship, and we've never engaged in any sexual activity for the same reason. But that doesn't mean we can't fantasize! The following is Troy's fantasy about me, and I'm sure he'll be thrilled to see it in print:

My desert queen. I came upon your beauty two years ago and have been a prisoner of it ever since. No other woman can compare to the beauty that is you. Many men have fought and died for one moment in your presence but few have succeeded. They have tried to conquer you, my queen, but were squashed in their feeble attempts. No man can possess you—your beauty humbles us. As one of your devoted soldiers, I would fight and die for you.

And then it happened. I stood upon the hot desert sand, in formation with my fellow soldiers. But it was me you motioned to come forward, and I could only hope that I was not dreaming. I drew closer and was even more awestruck by the picture you presented. Your skin is the color of mahogany, smooth and aged to perfection. Your eyes are like fires dancing before me. Your lips are full and red, and for a moment I let my mind drift and imagined kissing them. You smiled at me, and all of my strength melted.

You motioned me to your tent, and I was happy to obey your command. Nervously, I awaited your arrival, and a quick glance around told me that your tent reflected your high birth and rank. Adorned with silk and gold, it truly befitted a woman such as you.

Then you entered the tent, and that was the moment my world truly came to life. The sensuousness of your walk as you approached me stirred up feelings that I knew were forbidden. But I could not help myself;

my cock responded of its own accord. Once you were standing before me, your eyes captured my soul as well as my body. I was yours, totally.

You whispered to me that it was my duty to please you. A duty, I should add, that was really much more a pleasure. I could smell the scent of sweet jasmine and musk from your skin and hair and was captivated by it. Then you leaned forward and kissed me. Our lips brushed lightly together and then parted, and we tasted each other with our tongues. My tongue slowly traced the contour of your lips, leaving a trace of warm saliva with each pass. Your moans of ecstasy let me know that so far you approved, and I could feel my cock begin to throb.

Then we embraced, and for the first time I knew why men die for you. Your hands searched my body and found my erection, and they were smooth and experienced as they caressed my shaft. Then you moaned for me to touch you. My fingers searched beneath your garments to find your wet cunt. As I slowly stroked it, I noticed it was hairless, and I reveled in the silky sensations. The touch of my fingers on your soft, bare skin set my whole body aflame.

I inserted one of my fingers into your warm canal and was accepted by its snug embrace. An encouraging moan escaped from your lips as I began thrusting in and out of your cunt. As my pace quickened, your tongue searched for mine, its wet heat asserting itself between my lips. Oh, my desert queen! I had to taste your treasure.

I placed you carefully and gently down on the fur rug, my heart almost exploding with ecstasy. "You have such a pretty pussy, my queen," I said, and then boldly asked if I could kiss it. You immediately granted me permission, so I got down on my knees and began by kissing your thighs. I was in no hurry, and I placed warm kisses over your flesh as I moved slowly upward.

When I encountered your sex, I saw your moist, puffy lips, which seemed to beg for my attention. I began licking them slowly and sensuously, hoping that my performance would allow me further entrance. Your legs parted slightly, and I knew that I had succeeded in my quest. I parted your nether lips with my fingers, and my mouth quickly found its mark. I drew broad strokes over your pink center with my tongue. Your pussy tasted so good, each drop of moisture like a sip of pure nectar. My tongue raced up and down your inner lips until I could see your little button quivering with anticipation. Then I sucked on your entire cunt, slowly at times, fast at others. But above all, I centered on your clit, inserting a finger into your hot, wet pussy to intensify the pleasure.

I wondered if I was pleasing you, my queen, and a look at your face was all I needed to know. The ecstasy was evident in your closed eyes, the half smile, the flush across your cheeks. But I wanted to hear it from you, for you to tell me how much you liked it. I didn't have to ask. Just then you moaned and demanded more, and it was my pleasure to give it to you.

After I had sucked your pussy for a while, you pushed me away and got up on all fours, your desire immediately apparent. First I poured scented oil on your beautiful body and massaged it in until your skin glistened like the moon above. Then I began to kiss and tongue your body, purposely leaving wet traces behind so that I wouldn't traverse an area more than once. I wanted to be sure that I covered every inch of your flesh.

When I reached your beautiful behind, I covered your cheeks with kisses and a thorough tongue bath. Then I asked you to hunch up so I could see your pussy from behind. I dove for it immediately, my tongue performing its dance like never before. Then I returned to the fleshy globes of your ass, kissing and licking while I fucked your pussy with my fingers. I slid two digits, held together so that they resembled a tiny cock, in and out until you came. Your muscles squeezed around me, and your sighs filled the tent and drifted off on a warm breeze. I was elated that I could bring you such pleasure.

Still on your hands and knees, you ordered me to fuck you from behind. I hesitated, knowing I wouldn't last long in that position, and it was your command that I last all night. You then faced me and grasped my cock. It twitched in your hands as you kissed the crown and the shaft, and then with one quick swoop, you swallowed my entire manhood. Then, inch by inch, my cock slowly reappeared from between your lips, and you teased the head with your tongue. Never the one to miss a chance of sucking some royal pussy, I suggested we engage in a lusty sixty-nine.

You accepted my invitation, and I got down on my back. You hovered over my face, and I awaited the arrival of your cunt on my lips. Your mouth felt like pure volcanic heat as it engulfed my cock. "Fuck my face!" I commanded you, and then fell silent, realizing my impertinence in thus addressing my queen. But you loved it and ordered me to say it again. "Fuck my face! Grind your sweet pussy on my mouth." Your hips and pussy ground against my lips as you fucked my face with complete abandon.

I loved the taste of you and never wanted to stop dining on your cunt. But after some more oral pleasure, we began some serious fucking. You were truly wild. You loved it from behind, you loved it from the side, and you loved it from the front. I realized that I had no control, whether it was me on top or you. Your body controlled every one of my actions.

We settled on a position in which you were on your back and I was above you, your legs draped over my shoulders. I made sure a silken pillow was under your ass for maximum penetration; your pleasure was my only thought. Then I lowered my cock so that it rested against your pussy. Impatient, you grabbed my staff and pulled me the rest of the way in. I knew then that you would be difficult to satisfy.

But I tried my best, thrusting hard and deep into your center. As my stroking rhythm increased, your bucking motion quickened as well. I lowered my head to kiss the rosy tips of your perfect breasts, sucking each sensitive nipple in turn. You moaned and urged me on, obviously loving this new twist in our lovemaking. I bit lightly and waited for your response. It came immediately as your pussy spasmed around my cock and your cries announced your orgasm.

I continued to fuck you through yet another climax,

until I could hold back no longer. "Give it to me," you cried. "Fill me with your come!" How could anyone not obey such a command? I pumped my cock into you for a few moments more until I could hold back the gates no longer and deposited my seed deep into your pussy. I spent the next few hours just lying in your arms, stroking your silky skin and murmuring words of my love for you. Then I jumped up, realizing that I must go to battle once again.

And off to battle I went, for you, my desert queen, now armed with the knowledge of why men fight and die for you. My only hope as I marched off was that I would soon return.

—*Ms. C.S., Thousand Oaks, California* O—■

Prim and Proper Wife Sparkles as a Sassy, Elegantly Decadent Lady of the Evening

I suspect that most women, even seemingly prim and proper ones like me, occasionally find themselves fantasizing about living, if only for one night, the life of a high-priced call girl. And I have an idea that all men, even happily married pillars of the community like my husband, Clay, daydream about hiring an elegantly decadent lady of the evening for an anything-goes sexual adventure. Mostly it never goes beyond fantasy, but Clay and I turned it into an incredible reality one night not long ago.

Clay had gone to a business convention. After a few days apart we were both tuned to a fever pitch, and our nightly phone calls turned very sexy—which was fun but frustrating. Long-distance sex is no substitute for the real thing. I joked that this was the perfect time for Clay to fulfill his dream of hiring a call girl, and he teased back that I should dress up in my sexy best and go solicit some illicit business of my own. It was all in fun, of course, but suddenly we both flashed on the same idea—why didn't I fly there and meet him? Perfect!

Everyone in the cocktail lounge turned to stare as I walked in, my pencil-thin heels sounding an erotic tattoo on the hardwood floor. I could not have felt more exposed if I had been naked. My braless breasts jiggled with every step. My hard, swollen nipples pressed conspicuously against my low-cut second-skin minidress. I was not wearing any panties, and tiny, warm droplets of arousal oozed from between my puffy lower lips, dampening my thighs down to the tops of my gartered nylons. The sexual rush was really fantastic, and the game had barely begun.

I spotted my husband at a table with two colleagues, Florida partners he'd been negotiating with all week. Clay saw me and did a double take. He was expecting me, but not dressed quite so provocatively. I mouthed the words "You don't know me." His tablemates turned to see what had captured his attention, gawking in happy disbelief.

Approaching their table, I looked at my husband, struggling to keep a straight face, and said, "Gray suit, polka-dot tie—you must be Clay. I'm Honey, from the escort service. You called and asked for a blonde?" He nodded, speechless. His friends leaned closer, their intense interest visibly heightened. "Will I do?"

Clay came out of his stupor and grinned, saying, "Yes, you'll do just fine."

I leaned closer, aware of my breasts spilling out of my dress and how intently his friends were watching. "I didn't know you'd have friends along," I whispered, loud enough for the other two men to hear. "You do know it's five hundred each, don't you? Plus the room, of course."

Clay hesitated for a split second, and I held my breath, knowing he'd also fantasized about sharing me with other men. He finally said it was just him and gave me his room number. I don't know whether I was more relieved or disappointed. I turned to leave, feeling his friends' eyes burning holes in my dress. Knowing they really thought I was a high-priced hooker made me so giddy with excitement, I could feel the first tiny ripples of my impending orgasm.

I was barely at the door when Clay arrived. Once in his room, he took me in his arms, his erection pushing against me as he tugged my dress to my waist, sliding his hands over my unpantied bottom, his fingers dipping into the furnace between my legs. He laughed about how turned-on the other two guys were, and I said he should have brought them along. As he slid his thick finger up between my wet and swollen pussy lips, nudging my inflamed clitoris, I told him I was excited enough to take on all three of them.

That aroused my husband beyond words. He took hold of the low neckline of my dress and pulled. It ripped open and my breasts spilled free. He buried his face between them, sucking and licking and biting my tender nipples. We tumbled back on the bed. Pushing my legs apart, he knelt between them, unzipping his pants and freeing his excited cock. I had never seen him so huge or so hard. But when he started to guide its mushroom-shaped head into my dripping pussy, I scooted out from beneath him. "Not so fast," I said. "Where's my money?"

He stared at me in disbelief, reached for his wallet, and spilled the contents onto the bed. It was only about a hundred and fifty dollars. "That should cover the room," I said, "but there's the small matter of my fee. No pay, no play." Suddenly realizing I was serious, he pulled up his pants and told me to wait right there while he went to the ATM downstairs.

When Clay returned I took the twenty-five crisp twenties from his hand. "For this kind of money I should get anything I want." The steely edge in his usually gentle voice sent a shiver of excitement down my spine. I shrugged and agreed, and he told me to strip and suck him right there in front of the window. Trembling with arousal, I shed my torn dress, but when I started to kick off my pumps he stopped me, telling me to leave on the garter belt and stockings as well.

Doing as he said, I sank to my knees in front of him. Loosening his belt and lowering his pants and shorts, I took his engorged cock into my hand, my fingers barely able to span its girth. Licking a gleaming droplet of anticipation from its rosy tip, I swirled my tongue over and around the end.

His legs went wobbly. He closed his eyes and gasped, grabbing my shoulders for support as I pushed my glossy lips over him. Knowing that someone might see what I was doing through the window only made me more excited. I grabbed his ass and pulled him to me, slowly sucking him deep into my mouth.

When his spongy cockhead touched the back of my throat, I pulled back on his hard flesh, still sucking, none too gently scraping my teeth over the tender ridge of his cockhead, delighting in his moans of excited anguish. Breathless, I gulped for air and went down on him again, moving faster, feeling the thick vein traversing the bottom of his manhood pulse incessantly against my tongue, not stopping until his wiry pubic hairs tickled my nose.

Halfway through my next upward journey, I teased my fingertip into the deep crease of his ass and touched his tight rectum. He gasped and tensed, gripping my shoulders and emitting an animal-like moan. His testicles contracting, he exploded down my throat, his hot come filling my cheeks to overflowing and dribbling from the corners of my mouth as I struggled in vain to drink every bittersweet drop.

When his cock had at last stopped jerking and fell limp from between my lips, I looked up at him and smiled sweetly, dabbing a droplet of pearly semen from my lower lip and daintily sucking my fingertip. It had been ages since I had attacked his cock with such ferocity and it showed. He was sweating and his face was pale with exhaustion, but he was grinning from ear to ear. "Where the hell did you learn that trick?"

he asked. "I love you, but you'll have to wait awhile before I can return the favor."

"Professional secret," I replied. "Save the sweet talk for your wife, mister. Time is money. All-night gigs cost more."

"Okay by me," he replied groggily, reaching for his wallet. I tucked the wad of cash into my shoe and lay down beside him as he fell asleep in my arms. This was the best part of all, in a way, no matter how exciting the call-girl impersonation had been. Clay is my husband, and I love him dearly.

—*Ms. J.R., Topeka, Kansas*　⚲

Sporting Couples: The National Amatory Mixed Wrestling Competition!

Every time my boyfriend takes me to one of the professional wrestling matches in the city, I'm always fantasizing about another kind of wrestling altogether. It makes no sense to me that the entire point of the sport is pushing your opponent's shoulder to the ground. Wouldn't getting fucked be a better goal all the way around? And let's get some beautiful, sex-hungry girls into the sport, and let's make sure they win sometimes.

So here I was in the semifinals of the National Amatory Mixed Wrestling Eliminations, held in an outdoor amphitheater on an early-summer evening. I was sitting in a corner of the wrestling ring, enjoying the feel of the warm breeze in my little stretchy Lycra shorts and athletic bra, sans underwear. I felt a tremor of sexual anticipation, knowing that very soon I'd be naked; very soon I'd be fucked right here outdoors, in the warm evening breeze, with hundreds of people watching. Whatever the place I earned in the competition, I couldn't imagine a better way to spend my time.

I looked across the ring at Collin, the man who would, in a few moments, be attempting to rip off my clothes to fuck me. This was his first time competing in the Eliminations. One of his two female helpers had just finished undressing him, and I studied his beautiful muscled body as she fondled his penis.

In the preliminary round, Collin had ravished the strong and lovely redhead he'd been paired with in under three minutes. He was standing as he entered her from behind, holding her off the ground. Then he gently laid her down and fucked her for ten minutes, giving her multiple orgasms without ever ejaculating himself. It had been an amazing demonstration of sexual passion.

The referee finally walked out to the center of the ring, blew his whistle, and motioned for Collin and me to walk toward him. When we approached, he gave a summary of the rules for the upcoming bout.

"Collin, you have nine minutes, apart from any time-outs, to attempt sexual penetration of Lana. The clock will stop when Lana is both completely naked and you have penetrated her vagina with a fully erect penis. I will determine when and if this has happened. Lana, you may resist Collin's efforts in any way you like, except that neither of you is to do anything to hurt the other. If, in my judgment, either of you causes pain to the other, the match will end and the one causing the pain will forfeit all prizes and any further participation in the Eliminations.

"There will be up to three rounds of three minutes each, with a one-minute break between rounds. During the first round, Collin, your helpers may not touch Lana. But if the match continues into the second round one of your helpers may assist you. During the final three minutes, both of your helpers are permitted to aid you in your conquest. When and if I declare penetration, feel free to embrace and enjoy each other for up to ten minutes."

Having competed in several of these amatory wrestling meets over the years, I decided not to play this event in the usual way. I wanted to tease Collin a little bit, so as he came toward me, I didn't try to escape him. Instead, I aped his motions and approached him at equal speed. When he grabbed the front of my bra, intending to rip it off me, I went completely limp, forcing him to hold me up rather than let me fall to the ground and be hurt. As Collin supported me with a hand behind my back, I recovered my balance, wrapped my arms around his neck, and kissed him on the lips, driving my tongue into his mouth. I felt his member come to life against my stomach, and I began rubbing myself back and forth on it.

Still trying to remove my clothes, Collin gripped the back of my shorts with both hands and pulled them apart, creating a tear right down the middle. I allowed him to continue to disrobe me, all the while concentrating my attentions on his penis. I held myself close to him, with an arm around his waist, and used the other hand to stroke his organ. Then I dropped to my knees, gripped his waist, and sucked his swollen member into my mouth. I heard Collin moan slightly as I slid my mouth down his shaft, stuffing it with as much cock as possible. Collin started to step back as if he were trying to get away, so I grabbed his thighs and began sucking ferociously on his shaft. I clutched his balls and rolled them in the palm of one hand, the other hand grasping his butt cheeks, pulling him in closer to my face.

Collin had not expected this. The usual technique in amatory mixed wrestling was for the woman to resist her opponent's efforts of vaginal penetration as long as possible. The man's usual strategy was to weaken his opponent's resistance and then impale her on his cock. Instead, I had already managed to stimulate Collin to uncontrollable horniness.

Enjoying himself too much to stop me, Collin submitted to my oral ministrations, and in no time he was pumping semen into my eager mouth. I sucked hungrily, hardly believing my good fortune, until Collin gently took my head in his hands and pushed me away from him. Some of his semen spurted on my face and breasts. When he was done, I smiled up at him, swallowed, and licked my lips like a cat.

Collin pulled me to my feet and turned me away from him, wrapping his arms around my midsection. He slid his hand up to my breast and glided his index finger across my erect nipple, then squeezed it between two fingers. Placing his free hand between my legs, he slid a finger across my moist cunt, feeling for the button of my clitoris. He began applying pressure until I was squirming in ecstasy.

Although Collin did not need long to recover his erection, the first round was almost over. He began stroking me lovingly, giving the spectators quite a view. I could feel his breath on my neck as he leaned back to hoist me off the ground and then rotated us slowly around to expose my arched and writhing body to the audience. I laid my head back, turned my mouth toward Collin's face, and kissed him. Spreading my limbs, I stretched my right arm over my head and parted my legs, making more room for Collin's hand at my crotch. At that point the referee blew his whistle to signal the end of the round.

When the second round began, I got on my hands and knees and moved slowly toward Collin and his helper, meowing like a cat and happily wagging my behind. The helper came toward me first, a very strong blonde woman with a beautiful figure. I recognized her from the preliminary round. Her name was Sandra. She reached for me, and I quickly tucked myself into a ball and rolled off to the side. As I opened up again, I found myself in Collin's firm but gentle embrace. He knelt on the ground and worked to separate my legs, hoping to insert his cock between them. I wriggled free and rolled off to the side again.

This went on for a time, but soon Collin and Sandra had me cornered, with Sandra in position to hold my legs apart. Collin restrained my arms and maneuvered my body into position to enter my cunt. I squirmed and writhed, moving my pelvis from side to side, temporarily avoiding Collin's now fully restored member. However, in one quick motion he was suddenly inside me. I cried out in pleasure as I felt the sudden but welcome intrusion of his delicious cock.

The referee blew his whistle to signal the penetration and announce the time, but I did not hear any of his words. Collin was fucking me with abandon while his two helpers lightly stroked our entwined bodies. All those hands touching me, aiming to please me, were wonderful. But it was Collin's hands on my hips and his cock inside my pussy that really sent me reeling.

Collin kissed me hard on the lips as he continued to impale me with his cock. I thrust my hips up to accept him again and again. He grabbed at my breasts and ran his hands down my belly and hips. Our sweaty bodies suctioned together from the summer heat, and Collin's balls smacked hard against my pussy as he thrust into me.

Never had I come so hard as when Collin shot his load deep inside my pussy. I wailed and shook in orgasmic ecstasy, then kissed my lover sweetly on the lips—seconds before I was brought back to reality by the sound of my guy, seated next to me, screaming insults at the hairy bruiser in the ring as he pummeled the crowd favorite. I smiled inwardly. As much as Tony enjoyed this match, I knew he would find my wrestling fantasy more exciting.

—*Ms. L.K., Chicago, Illinois*

Of Eighteen-Wheelers, Saucy Waitresses, and Fun-Loving Gals Looking for a Ride

When I've had it with life in the big city, the noise, the pollution, the rude people, the corporate buffoonery, I like to picture myself on the open road in one of those majestic chrome-and-steel eighteen-wheelers, country music on the radio as I barrel down a major highway with my belly growling for food and my cock hungry for pussy. You see, this fantasy of mine not only liberates me from the constraints of city life, allowing me in my imagination to escape the harsh realities of the real world, it also provides delightful opportunities for sexual adventure.

For example, here I am pulling into one of my favorite truck stops, skillfully maneuvering the gleaming rig between two other less-impressive eighteen-wheelers in the crowded parking lot. It's late at night, and I'm starving. I'm hungry for company as well, having been on the road for a solid six hours with only my country music to keep me sane. I need a bowl of Red's special chili, a few cold brews, and most of all, some lovin' from Rosie, one of my favorite waitresses. Hitching up my worn jeans, I enter the noisy roadside diner and make my way to the small, unoccupied booth in back, spotting Rosie along the way. She acknowledges my presence with a smile, and then goes about her business, leaving me to recall the last time we fucked in her neat white clapboard cottage down the road a piece.

Rosie is one fine-looking gal, a free-spirited, green-eyed redhead curved in all the right places who knows exactly how to put life back into a road-weary trucker. Not that Rosie's promiscuous, mind you. She's very discriminating, and I consider myself very fortunate to be one of the select few she welcomes into her bed on a more or less steady basis. Playing it safe, I had called ahead to let her know I was coming and to be sure she didn't have other plans. Rosie had said she'd be looking for me.

She comes over now to take my order and we make small talk, playing it cool. No need for the truckers nearby to know that we'll soon be fucking like bunnies. Sometime later, having enjoyed a large bowl of Red's chili and several bottles of my favorite brew, Rosie returns with my check, whispering that her car's parked in back of the diner and to meet her there in five minutes when her shift ends. I do, and off we go to her house about a half mile down the road. Once there, we waste no time getting reacquainted.

Naked, I refamiliarize myself with Rosie's comfortable armchair in the corner of the small bedroom. Having stripped down to her lavender panties, Rosie kneels between my legs and takes my cock into her mouth, sucking it with the kind of enthusiasm I had displayed when downing Red's chili. Rosie is not only skilled at sucking cock, she genuinely enjoys it, which makes for a dynamite combination. When she suddenly takes me deep, my whole dick disappearing in her hot mouth, I throw my head back and moan in delight. I try to think of a woman I know who sucks cock better than my Rosie and come up empty.

With her mouth full, Rosie looks up at me and winks, then commences a deliciously lewd licking of my cock and balls, slurping the latter into her mouth and sucking hard. Then it's back to the shaft, her teasing tongue trailing over the very sensitive underside and up to the bulbous head, which she nibbles playfully. Several minutes more of this and I'm close to blasting off, so I ease Rosie away from my throbbing erection and help her out of her pretty panties.

Moments after she tumbles into her bed, I'm sprawled between her spread legs with my face plastered to her aromatic, copper-colored pussy. As always, she tastes wonderful and, as always, her cunt is sopping wet. I know it won't be long before she's urging me to plant my meaty member balls-deep inside her.

To hasten that moment, I zero in on her excited clit, tonguing it passionately and then taking it between my lips and tugging gently. On cue, Rosie lets out a moan of approval and, seconds later, is pulling me up by the hair so I can plant my cock in her dripping cunt. When I do she cries out with joy, quickly wrapping her arms and legs around me as I begin pumping in and out of her hot wetness.

My Rosie's got quite a mouth on her, and nowhere is that more evident than when we're in bed and I'm drilling her good. In very unladylike terms, using language more suited to badass truckers, Rosie lets me know what she wants and how she wants it. I follow instructions, pounding into her pussy again and again, until finally we both let out groans of ecstasy and come.

I conk out for a few hours, get up, shower, and then

hoof it back to the diner and my rig. Before leaving, I scribble a short note telling Rosie how much I had enjoyed seeing her again and place it on the pillow next to her head. I blow her a kiss as I quietly let myself out.

Climbing back up into my rig, I turn the key in the ignition and for a few moments savor the rumble of the powerful engine before steering out of the diner parking lot and onto the highway. Further wonderful adventures await me out on the road, of that I'm certain.

And sure enough, the very next day, as I'm taking in the beautiful scenery, who do I see up ahead but a gal in fanny-hugging white shorts and red halter top trying to thumb a ride. The closer I get to her the more appealing she becomes. Slowing down, I come to a complete stop in front of her. "Hop in, honey," I say cheerfully. She climbs up into the cab and settles into the passenger seat, introducing herself as Joanne. Already my cock is looking to escape the confines of my jeans. Joanne is one honey of a hitchhiker, a blue-eyed blonde with the toned body of one active in sports.

We start talking, and I learn that Joanne, a graduate student on summer vacation, is hitchhiking her way to California and her surfer boyfriend. Every so often I catch her glancing down at the obvious bulge in my jeans and wonder what she's thinking. When we're about a mile from where I'll have to drop her off, she asks me if there's a rest stop coming up soon. I tell her there's one right up ahead, and she smiles sexily and suggests I pull into the rest stop for a while. When I ask why, Joanne answers, "So I can thank you properly for giving me a lift."

Minutes later, after I've parked in the area reserved for trucks, Joanne is fishing my swollen cock out of my jeans and wrapping her luscious lips around it. She pauses long enough in her sucking to inform me that she loves "nice, big ones," then resumes blowing me with a skill and passion that reminds me of Rosie. When I'm so hard it almost hurts, Joanne pulls my saliva-coated cock from her mouth, looks out the windshield, and says, "Over there. No one will see us."

Jumping out of the cab, she takes my hand and leads me into the woods. The next thing I know I'm stretched out on a bed of tall grass with my cock sticking out of my jeans and watching my hitchhiking honey shimmy and shake her way out of her tight shorts and panties. And then she's on top of me, impaling her pretty blonde cunt on my cock with a sigh of pleasure.

Up and down she goes, her hips bobbing and weaving as she rides me, fucking herself on my hard cock. Reaching up, I work her breasts out of her halter and squeeze them lustily as she continues bouncing on my manhood. She comes soon after starting to rub her clit, slumping onto my chest as the pleasure of her orgasm tears through her.

That's when I let go, shooting my load up into her still-contracting pussy. It's beautiful.

Not much later, we're back in the truck and humming along the highway. As we approach the spot where I'll be dropping her off, Joanne leans over and plants a big kiss on my cheek. "Thanks," she says. "You're one cool dude." I slow to a stop, and she hops out. I wish her luck and drive off, watching her wave to me in the driver's side mirror.

In minutes I'm back on the road again, chatting with my buddies on the CB and smiling inwardly as I wonder what further sexy adventures await this truck drivin' man.

—*Mr. G.C., Minneapolis, Minnesota*